SAINT-GERMAIN:
MEMOIRS

Saint-Germain: Memoirs is published by Elder Signs Press, Inc.

This book is © 2007 Elder Signs Press, Inc.
All material © 2007 by Elder Signs Press and Chelsea Quinn Yarbro.

Design by Deborah Jones.

PUBLICATION HISTORY
"Harpy," *The Secret History of Vampires,* DAW Books, 2007
"Intercession," *The Repentant,* DAW Books 2003
"A Gentleman of the Old School," *Dark Delicacies,* Carrol & Graf, 2005

FIRST EDITION
10 9 8 7 6 5 4 3 2 1
Published in October 2007

ISBN: 1-934501-00-X (Hardcover)
           1-934501-01-8 (Trade Paperback)

Printed in the U.S.A.

Published by Elder Signs Press
P.O. Box 389
Lake Orion, MI 48361-0389
www.eldersignspress.com

SAINT-GERMAIN: MEMOIRS

BY CHELSEA QUINN YARBRO

2007

CONTENTS

INTRODUCTION

I OFTEN WONDER WHAT A reader thinks when picking
up a new book and the sense of anticipation it brings.
With *Saint-Germain: Memoirs* many of you are looking forward to spending more time with a favorite character
whose adventures you have followed through for years. But
there are also some among you who may have picked up this
book without knowing anything about this character. There
are many pleasures in store for both types of readers. For those
familiar with the work of Chelsea Quinn Yarbro there is the
opportunity to further your knowledge of her character, Saint-
Germain, to see him in new circumstances. For the first time
reader these short stories, novelettes, and novella provide an
excellent introduction to this enduring fictional persona and
his adventures. The range of the selections exemplifies the
historical time span of the entire series of stories and novels.
Everyone has the opportunity to both encounter eras that
are familiar and to learn about periods that might be more
obscure. The experienced reader will find moments in Saint-
Germain's past clarified. But some of you may even wonder
what is meant by a memoir in this context. Memoirs are associated with real-life memories either from the perspective of
the subject or that of others describing the subject. In this case

the selections provide the reader with many ways of viewing Saint-Germain from the brief episode of a short story to the more detailed exploration of a novella. Memoirs suggest the idea of biography and concentrate on the events in a specific person's life. In this sense *Saint-Germain: Memoirs* may differ from the other literature about this character that give a broader picture of an entire historical period.

The varying lengths of the selections allow you to have widely different experiences with Saint-Germain. The two short stories, "Harpy" and "A Gentleman of the Old School," that begin and end the collection present short intense encounters with this character. The structure of the short story also allows the author to explore just one aspect in greater detail over a shorter period of time and focus on a single plot. As there are fewer secondary characters Saint-Germain stands out in sharp focus, and the reader can see him from the perspective of another person rather than seeing the world from his point of view. Both stories are also set in historical periods that may have a certain familiarity for the reader. But short stories also limit the amount of information the author can provide and the complexity of the development of the plot. The novelettes, "Lost Epiphany" and "Intercession" and the novella, "Tales Out of School" give the author more room to develop interactions between characters. Not only Saint-Germain but also all of the people he encounters are more fully described. It is also easier to cover longer periods of time in these formats. Short stories are like snap shots. They capture a brief moment in time with a certain amount of clarity. The longer formats are like a series of photographs or a family album. They provide a context for the events and give us a greater understanding of their implications for the characters.

If you have never encountered Saint-Germain the first story will provide a brief introduction to this unique character. The two novelettes that come before and after the novella give more information about him. But the fullest presentation of his persona comes, of course, in the novella. "Harpy" actually raises more questions than answers about this strange man who comes to the aid of a desperate woman. Some of those questions are answered in "Lost Epiphany." We begin to receive clues that lead us to recognition of his true nature. If you have already encountered him before, you have the pleasure of anticipating the problems he will face once you see his current situation or, as is the case with the first story, confirm what you already know about his generosity and his need to rescue those who cannot take care of themselves. The first story introduces the positive elements of his personality, those that separate him from the traditional vampire. In the second story this unique character merges with some of the traits usually associated with the genre. He has difficulty with boats and water and he must find appropriate sustenance.

By the time you get to the novella you receive the full impact of Saint-Germain. In what is really a condensed version of the plot and character development of the longer novels a whole historical period is presented. The conjunction of time and place that is central to Saint-Germain's experiences in the longer works also allows for a fuller examination of those thematic elements that define the novels and set them apart from other works in the genre. The novelette that follows actually amplifies a period already presented in a novel, the Inquisition in Latin America that is also found in *Mansions of Darkness*, and is set immediately after the conclusion of the longer work. This story is also interesting because Saint-Germain, while central to the narrative, never actually appears with his own voice. It also provides information about a key moment in the life of another important character in the series, Olivia. The experienced reader will see another side of events that are already somewhat familiar, while the new reader will get a taste of what the novels cover. The final short story provides another brief encounter, this time in the present, which allows both old and new reader a chance to see how the character might operate in a familiar period and setting. We see how we might react if we met such an interesting person in our own lives. We may wonder if we would see him as " a gentleman of the old school," a phrase that has far reaching implications when applied to Saint-Germain. It brings up the ironically genteel traditional depictions of the vampire that are so much a part of our popular culture. A gentleman of the old school is both the character presented in the short story and that series of tuxedo-clad men associated with the genre that are so suave on the surface and so evil beneath. This story is, in a sense, the final clue to Saint-Germain and to the way he alters our traditional expectations of the vampire fiction.

There are ties to traditional vampire fiction throughout the collection. Yarbro has acknowledged this connection from the beginning of the Saint-Germain series. While there have been many literary vampires, the central influence for most modern examples of the genre is, of course, Bram Stoker's *Dracula*. In fact, the genre would not probably exist as it has through the twentieth and twenty-first centuries if it were not for that novel. Yarbro's Saint-Germain series makes both implicit and explicit references to this touchstone work. While not all of the shorter pieces contain the central phrase from the novel, "I do not drink wine," it does appear in all of the longer works. This direct acknowledgement of the importance of the source is also an indication of the way that *Dracula* relates to the series. Because we know the origin of the phrase it acquires an ironic or even humorous tone when spoken by Saint Germain. The humor is emphasized when the reference is recognized as in "A Gentleman of the Old School." The letters that are an integral part of the novella and open all of the novels demonstrate the way that Yarbro has adopted and adapted one of the structures of Stoker's work in her own. *Dracula* is an amalgam of letters, journals, and newspaper accounts that provide the various points of view that form the story. While Yarbro honors the tradition by using letters, hers establish period and location at the beginning of the story and are, among other things, a way to provide important pieces of information, introduce characters, and give insight into the history of the period. In "Intercession" she takes this form further by telling the entire story through a series of letters. At the same time that she recognizes the tradition she completely alters it as well.

Count Saint-Germain is the antithesis of Count Dracula who can be seen to represent a challenge to the existing values of his time. Dracula is the alien intruder who must be destroyed before order can be restored. Saint-Germain is the positive force in a troubled world. The humans he encounters run the gamut from good to evil. Saint-Germain feels compelled to use his powers to make life better for the good people who are so often the victims of either natural or human injustice. In "Harpy" he cannot abandon a poor woman who is destitute. But he does not support all humans. While he loyally strives to rescue his own men in "Lost Epiphany" he is happy to let the 'bad guys' work it out among themselves. Yarbro further confronts the tradition by making Saint-Germain a healer, someone who is well versed in ancient medicinal teachings. His role as an instructor in these arts is the basis of "Tales Out of School." Rather than destroying humanity he works to ease pain and prolong life. Dracula transforms the unwilling into his own kind, but this Count only offers his form of life to those he loves and those who willingly accept it. The vampire tradition is completely upended in "Intercession" as religion is the source of evil rather than the means of defeating it. The evil religious zealots of the Inquisition hold Saint-Germain captive. "A Gentleman of the Old School" presents another type of inversion of the genre. Saint-Germain may be 'old school' living as a gentleman in modern-day Canada, but he is definitely not the old school vampire. This irony is furthered by his aiding in the investigation of a serial killer, the kind of crime associated with vampires. *Saint-Germain: Memoirs* demonstrates the way that Yarbro honors *Dracula* and its genre by recognizing the past at the same time that she looks towards the future.

Yarbro's expansion of the scope of the vampire genre is further expressed in the themes she develops throughout the series. Stoker, who wrote at the end of the nineteenth century, dealt with conflicts between good and evil, past and present, the role of women, sacred and profane love, and the outsider, among many other ideas. His concerns are developed in much of the literature of the genre. Yarbro explores some of these themes in a uniquely modern way. Her concern with the position of women in society is expressed through Saint-Germain's interactions with the women he encounters. They are no longer the prey of Dracula, but have, instead, become, the center of this other Count's world. Only by making them happy can he be truly fulfilled. The sex-like attack of Dracula is transformed into the sexual fulfillment given by Saint-Germain. Women also become central characters in his world. Only "Lost Epiphany" does not deal directly with them. "Intercession" recounts the death of Olivia, another one of Yarbro's adaptations of the original novel. She is one of the positive female vampires created by Saint-Germain and is the subject of a trilogy of novels. Saint-Germain is a foreigner, an outsider, in the tradition of Dracula. But his feelings of alienation lead him have compassion for those people he meets who also live on the fringe of society like the central character in "Harpy" or the widow in "Tales Out of School." Societal conditions make women the outsiders because they are caught at moments in history when they have no rights. "A Gentleman of the Old School" still depicts Saint-Germain as an outsider, but this time the woman only needs information from him and companionship rather than protection. The knowledge that she gains relates to yet another concept developed by Yarbro that of Saint-Germain's wisdom garnered from the experiences of his long life. "Tales Out of School" foregrounds his mastery of the healing arts by making him a teacher. Once again Yarbro transforms a concept suggested by Stoker into a positive element in the construction of her own character's world.

The various tales in *Saint-Germain: Memoirs* provide a broad array of experiences for all readers. The short stories compress the action into intense encounters with Saint-Germain at a single moment in his history. The novelettes expand that moment a little further. The reader gains deeper insight into those concepts that are central to the series. Finally the novella allows the breath of character development and setting associated with the reading of one of the novels. All of the various formats have their unique pleasures and all give every reader new insight into the world of Saint-Germain.

—Sharon Russell
Terre Haute, Indiana
January, 2007

HARPY

THERE WAS NO DOUBT that the woman was poor: her brass-colored hair was touched with gray and her face was fretted with fine lines although she was no more than thirty; her clothing was made of rough, homespun linen and was far from new, its color faded from what might once have been blue to a foggy shade of gray; its skimpy folds did not conceal her advancing pregnancy. She toiled up the steep, crowded Athens street, a yoke over her shoulders balancing two large buckets filled with water that depended from either end, picking her way among vendors, slaves, goat- and shepherds, men of every age and description, and a smattering of women as hapless as she. The sun baked down on the city, making the colors on the buildings and the statues brilliant, and heating everything so that the scent of it all hung in the still air like dust-motes.

When the toe of her rawhide sandal caught on a loose paving-stone, the woman, light-headed from hunger, nearly went down; as she struggled with the yawing yoke to keep from falling, a stranger in black Egyptian garb but with thick-soled Persian boots on his small feet, stepped out of the throng and held her up as she regained her footing. "Thank you," she muttered, prepared to pass on.

"Let me take that for you. Please," the stranger offered in excellent Athenian Greek, but with an accent the woman had never heard before. As the crowd eddied around them, she studied him, frowning, trying to discern his intentions: to her surprise, she did not find what she saw objectionable, and she realized she needed help with her load. Again she contemplated his face, trying to agnize his motives: he had attractive, irregular features, an angular brow, dark hair close-cropped, and wore a silver sigil-ring on the first finger of his right hand; his manner was distinguished, with a degree of reserve that marked him as a foreigner as much as his accent and his dress.

She held tightly to the yoke on her shoulders. "No. I will manage."

The stranger gave a swift smile. "No doubt: I see you are more than capable—but why should you?"

Staring at him, she demanded "Why shouldn't I?"

"Because you are carrying a child," he said calmly. "That is burden enough."

This time she was more firm. "You need not bother." She made an attempt to wrench herself away, and was somewhat surprised when she was unable to do so, for he made no apparent effort, yet he kept her from going on. "I'm no weakling."

"Possibly not," he agreed affably. "But your unborn infant is, and it depends upon you for protection. Your pulse is strong, but it is also fast, and you are sweating, which is hard on your–"

She gave an impatient cough. "I will manage," she said again, watching him with suspicion, distrusting the attention he gave her.

The stranger turned his dark eyes on hers. "I ask you to permit me to do this for the sake of your baby."

"And why should that matter to you?" she countered sharply, making no apology for her abruptness.

"Does it not concern you?" he inquired, standing so that the busy traffic of the street would flow around them. "I would have thought, from the way you are walking, that you are apprehensive about carrying the child. If I am mistaken, or if my observation is impertinent, I ask your pardon."

She stared at him. "How can you know that?" If she were not so hungry, she thought, she would not feel the need to defend herself; she could walk away from this stranger. As it was, she wanted a little time to order herself, to muster her waning stamina before continuing upward.

"Because I am something of a physician, and while I do not think coddling helps a pregnancy, I know that strenuous toil is equally compromising, particularly to someone who has miscarried in the past, which I believe you have done?" He saw her nod as he took the yoke from her shoulders and rested it across his own. "Tell me where you would like me to take this."

She sighed. "If you must—follow me," she said, resuming her climb. "But don't expect me to give you anything more than my thanks for your efforts."

"I will not," he told her, easily keeping pace with her.

"I have no money to pay for your service, and I will not be whored," she stated flatly as she reached another confluence of streets and chose the one leading off to the oblique right; she shoved past a man on a donkey and continued upward past increasingly mean dwellings. "I will not bargain about the matter."

"To your credit," said the stranger.

Three young men, their hair fashionably clipped, their beards neatly trimmed and perfumed, dressed in handsome chitons of dyed-and-painted linen came along from the street above; they were laughing among themselves, paying little heed to their surroundings, knowing that the crowd would give way to them. One of them had an amphora in his hands, and he held it aloft as if it were a trophy.

As they went past the woman, she made a sign with her hand to ward off evil.

The black-clad stranger watched this with curiosity. "Do you dislike them so much?" he asked when the young men were safely past.

She glanced over her shoulder at him. "They're trouble. All

rich young men are trouble."

The stranger nodded, and continued to climb.

A short while later she slipped into an alley, motioning him to stop. "You don't need to come any farther. I can carry the yoke from here."

"I am aware that you are able to," he said with a kindness she had rarely known. "But, do you know, I think I will take it the rest of the way."

She shrugged. "If it suits you. I warn you, the house isn't much." The alley continued to turn to the right, growing narrower as it rose.

"That does not trouble me," he said.

"Please yourself," she said, and went on beyond the end of the alley where the street vanished into the scrubby grass where a house that was little more than a tumble-down shed stood, a rickety fence around a small portion of land inside which a scrawny nanny-goat grazed on the stubble of thistles. "This is my home," she stated with an air of defiance. As she spoke, three skinny youngsters came tumbling out—two boys and a girl; all three were in stained and threadbare clothes, and only the oldest—the girl, around nine or ten— wore sandals, and they were old and tattered. "And these are my children."

"Indeed," said the stranger, setting down the water-buckets and leaning the yoke on end against the fence.

She patted the younger boy—a small six-year-old with a distracted air about him—and murmured something to his tangled hair, then looked at the stranger. "He's not quite right, this one. He doesn't talk very much, and he— But the other two are fine." Her smile almost shattered as the younger boy hugged her leg.

"Has he been so from birth?" asked the stranger, no suggestion of condemnation in his manner.

"No; he took a fever when he was not quite two, and he hasn't been . . ." Her words trailed off as she swallowed hard. "Two others died of the fever—a boy and a girl. And, as you said, I have had miscarriages—three of them."

"That is unfortunate," said the stranger.

"It could have been much worse," said the woman. "They could have lived."

"I must suppose then, that you are a widow," said the stranger in the silence that followed.

"You would think so, wouldn't you? It certainly seems that way," she said with sudden heat as she squinted up toward the brassy sun. "But no, I am not. I have a husband."

"And he is away?" the stranger asked.

"No. He is here in Athens," she said. "For a while." His attentive silence prompted her to go on, "He is likely to be exiled. And we with him, or be sold into slavery."

"What has he done?" The stranger looked genuinely concerned.

"Why should you want to know—it is nothing to you," she said gruffly as she tried to smooth her hair off her face.

"I am curious," the stranger admitted.

"There is nothing to be curious about. He is determined to make an example of himself, and us along with him."

"Make an example of himself?" The stranger's repetition held her attention.

"So it would seem," she said evasively.

"For what crime?" he persisted. "Surely not treason, or murder—you would be in the hands of the authorities if that were the case, so there must be other charges. What has he done?"

"Corrupted youth," she said bluntly. "That's the charge: that he has corrupted youth. As if those young men who follow him could be corrupted more than they already are."

"How has he done that? What youth has he corrupted?"

"They accuse him of corrupting the sons of important men. My husband says he is their teacher, and it is true that a group of them follow him as if he were. It seems his teaching has corrupted them, or so many powerful men have sworn, and declared that their sons have been tainted by what my husband has taught." She reached down and picked up the younger boy, who began to tug loose the knot of hair at the back of her neck, which she endured patiently. "I know the fathers of the young men who follow my husband are opposed to him."

"What does he teach that is so intolerable—here in Athens—that he must be stopped?"

She looked at the stranger. "I don't know. He teaches them, not his family. His sons do not read or write." She was about to turn away, but abruptly continued. "Women are the beautiful evil, as we know, and when our beauty is gone, only the evil is left, or so my husband has told me on several occasions. He says I will betray him if he reveals anything to me, so he tells me little, but that I am worse than a shrew for urging him to abandon his companions and undertake to provide for his family."

"His students do not pay him?" The stranger sounded puzzled. "Teachers are usually paid for their knowledge."

"No; he will not permit them to pay him." She sighed.

"But how do they expect him to survive?" the stranger wondered aloud.

"Oh, they take him to their banquets and other entertainments, so he doesn't starve. A few of them fawn on him as if he were their older lover—and he may well be, for all I know. His ideas are exciting to them, and he . . . He is encouraged to talk, to impart his wisdom, as they call it, and he does it willingly enough. They see he is clothed, although he doesn't ask it, and prefers older garments to new ones; it is a matter of principle with him, or so he tells me. The young men attend him and strive to guard him against those who . . ." She could not go on.

"They provide nothing for you?"

She gently disengaged her son's hands from her hair. "I doubt they know much about us. My husband subscribes to the custom of saying little about his wife, although he does insist that I complain too much."

"Which you have every reason to do, if the case is as you say it is," the stranger told her.

"I do not dissemble," she said sharply. "And I do not lie."

"Judging by appearances, you have good cause to be distressed."

"I will be much more, when he is condemned, as will his

children," she said. "This may be hard, but what is ahead of us will be far worse, I fear."

"Will none of his students take these children into their households?" It was not an uncommon arrangement, and he was somewhat surprised she had made no mention of it.

"I doubt most of his students know much about us, or our situation." She put her boy down, tousling his hair as she did.

"Because he says nothing?" the stranger suggested.

She nodded. "And his silence contributes to his troubles, and ours."

"Then he is truly in some danger," said the stranger.

"Yes. Oh, yes. When he first became the object of suspicions, it sickened me. Now—" She pinched the bridge of her nose. "If our children weren't in want, I wouldn't object to what he does, not any longer. He is a man who has purpose and understanding. He has chosen his way, and I would not deny him anything that aided him if our children were well-fed and properly clothed. But you see how it is. My husband has forgotten us, and we are left to flounder. He does what he must, and I honor him for that, but I can't ignore the plight of these three."

"Doesn't he see what has become of you and your children when he visits you? He does visit you, does he not?"

The woman directed her gaze past the stranger's shoulder. "He visits occasionally, when he has no other obligations. When he is here, he cares only for a compliant bed-mate and I do not refuse him that. I do what a wife must, but I am no longer happy about it. He has made himself a figure of importance, not to say infamy, among the great ones of the city. He is well-fed, he has a soft bed to sleep in, his clothes are clean, and that suffices him. If he would only see that the house was repaired and I had cloth enough to make proper chitons for the boys, and a peplos for Thalia; she is getting to an age when she must be more attentive in her dress. If he would only think of finding a husband for her."

Thalia frowned at her mother. "I don't need anything

yet—not new clothes or a husband."

"But you do," said her mother. "If your father cares nothing for your welfare, so be it; but you deserve better than he has given you." Her bitterness startled her daughter, and she modified her tone, "but I can't be so lax, or so preoccupied as he is. What would become of you if I didn't look after you?" This was clearly an old dispute among them, and no one bothered to continue the ritual of argument. The woman turned to the stranger. "So you see how it is."

"Yes; I do," he said, and apparently changed the subject. "Have any of you eaten today?"

"There was a little cheese for the morning," said the woman evasively.

"Which it would seem you did not eat. I suppose you gave what you had to your children?" He held up his hand before she could summon up some sort of denial. "Is there anything more in the house?"

"A little flour, and we will have a bit of milk from our goat," she admitted, amazed that she should reveal so much to him. "With that and a handful of nuts, I can make flat-cakes for us all."

"Hardly sufficient nourishment, particularly for your unborn child," said the stranger. He studied the three children, then said to their mother, "Would some meat and a string of onions be useful to you?"

Her sarcastic laughter sounded unusually loud. "And oil, and melons, and garlic, and cabbages, and cheese."

"Certainly," said the stranger at once. "All of that, and more besides. But have you vessels in which to cook? Do you have wood for your fire?"

"What business is it of yours?" she demanded, then fell silent.

What business, indeed? he asked himself inwardly, and decided it was as much curiosity as compassion. "I am willing to make it my business," he said aloud, "if you will permit me to." He inclined his head. "You may call it a whim, if you need an explanation."

"Such whims can be costly." She pinched the bridge of her nose again. "I do not want to be beholden to you; I have no way to redeem my obligation but with the lives of my children."

"You have no reason to fear me," he told her as Thalia tugged at her mother's garments.

"Mama, I'm hungry," she said just above a whisper.

"We're all hungry, girl," said the woman.

"If you will not object, I will fetch foodstuffs for you, and a proper pot to cook them in, and new bread." The stranger could see the disbelief in the woman's face. "I am not mocking you: believe this."

"I do as best I can," she said.

"No doubt," he agreed. "But with a little help, you will do much better."

She glared at him. "If you seek to discredit my husband—"

"I should think he has done that all by himself," said the stranger in the black Egyptian clothes and Persian boots.

Now she bristled. "He is a fine teacher, my husband, for all he is unwilling to provide for us. He is an eminent man, a hero, trying for greatness, to teach so that his teaching will be remembered. He may not treat us any better than most poor men treat their wives, but he has much to offer, and would be held in high esteem if only he didn't insist on clashing with the authorities." She squared her shoulders. "He has knowledge and imparts it well, and it is to his credit that he will not be intimidated, little as I may like what that means to us. He may have been unwise in his choice of students, and he has become a thorn in the side of the State, but his teaching deserves to be heard."

"All you say may be true, and to the extent that he is a good teacher, he deserves praise, but he exacts too high a price from you and your children for his teaching if you are hungry and he is not," said the stranger, fully aware that he had not heard the husband's side of it, but keenly sensitive to the deprivations the man's wife and children were enduring on his account; he sensed her thoughts flickering like fish in shadowed water, and he wondered what they held.

She folded her arms. "I do not want to see him harmed, but I can do nothing about that, so I will do everything I can to see that our children suffer no more for his folly." She cocked her head. "My father was a rope-maker—he did quite well for himself, supplying ropes to quarrymen and the builders of temples. He arranged this marriage for me because he thought it would advance me, to be married to a man of learning. If he were still alive, he would be appalled at how I live."

The stranger nodded, and glanced toward the complex of temples on an adjacent hilltop. "Rope-makers have much to do in Athens."

"Yes, they do," she said, making no apology for the pride in her voice. "He kept us fed and we lived in a sturdy house. All my sisters had dowries—not large but enough for–" She stopped, as if fearing she had said too much. "My father helped us, before he died, and my husband thanked him for it."

"A pity that did not continue."

She shrugged. "Wives must share the lot of their husbands. At least I am not confined to the house as many women are."

"No, that fate has not befallen you," said the stranger, going on more crisply. "If you will ready your hearth, I will return shortly with food for you, and a pot, as I told you. If you can rest for a short while, it will do you good."

"Rest?" She laughed. "I will make ready for your return." She squinted at the goat. "I'll milk her; that will give the children something to drink more than water."

"I will be back," he reiterated, seeing the doubt in her eyes.

"Well and good," she said, dismissing him.

The stranger took a step back, watching the three children dejectedly follow their mother into the house; he considered what he had seen and heard, then he turned and made his way back down the hill to the agora, the central market-square where farmers offered their produce for sale and vendors of all sorts hawked their wares, while at the far end, livestock of all descriptions were bartered for. Taking stock of what was displayed, he bought a butchered lamb, a sackful of onions and peppers, a bundle of grape-leaves, a spray of mint and another of basil, two strings of onions and one of garlic, a bottle of oil, a large, pale-green melon, a round of cheese, three flat breads, an iron cleaver with a wooden handle, a skin of wine, a large iron pot, and a bundle of cut firewood. To this he added a bolt of green linen and one of soft Colchis wool. These he loaded onto a low sledge which he purchased from a vendor at the front of the market-square, and, after covering all with a sheet of rough linen and tying it all down with heavy twine, he set about returning to the woman's house, making his dragging of the sledge appear more difficult that it was so as not to draw attention to his remarkable strength. As he progressed up the slope, he was trying to decide how to approach her about more assistance. He was fairly sure she would reject anything so obvious as out-right gifts, or offers of patronage, but perhaps something could be done with her older boy. He was still mulling over the possibilities as he approached her house, where he noticed two soldiers were now flanking the flimsy gate, spears in hand. He slowed his approach, trying to discern what was happening.

One of the soldiers noticed him, and pointed at him with his spear. "You. Stop."

The stranger did as he was ordered. "There is trouble here?"

"And well you know it," said the soldier gruffly as he swung around to confront the foreigner in black Egyptian clothes.

"Why should I?" The stranger made sure his question had no element of challenge in it, only curiosity.

"You are bringing this woman—" the soldier began.

"I am bringing her food for her children," said the stranger, maintaining a respectful manner.

"For what reason?" The soldier put up his spear.

"They are hungry, and she is pregnant," said the stranger.

"There are many such women in Athens," said the soldier. "Why bring food to this one, whose husband is an enemy of the people?"

"I am not bringing food to her husband; I am bringing it

to her, and her children." He patted the covered sledge.

"For his sake, no doubt," said the soldier.

"No; I am unacquainted with the husband," the stranger said calmly. "I happened upon this woman by chance. I knew nothing whatsoever of her husband until she told me."

"It is only chance that her husband is condemned," said the soldier sarcastically, and nudged his comrade in the arm. "He is here by happenstance."

"I am," said the stranger.

"Very good," said the soldier, laughing. "A creditable liar."

"If I lie, then you may accuse me openly. You will find," the stranger went on, cutting off what the soldier was about to say, "that I am here from Egypt, although I am not an Egyptian; I lived there for some time." He did not mention that the time he had spent in Egypt was reckoned in centuries. "I arrived three days ago on the *Wings of Horus*, a merchant-ship bringing cloth and dates and papyrus to the markets of Athens. Erastos of Argos who dispatches ships for the Eclipse Traders at Piraeus will speak for me, if you require that I be identified by someone other than myself. My manservant, an Egyptian named Aumtehoutep, is at the house of Philetides Timonestheos, and will confirm what I tell you. I am trained as a physician and I am partner in a trading company."

"Why would a physician engage in trade?" asked the soldier.

"Because any good physician seeks to better his art. There are substances, herbs, and other healing items that are procured in distant lands," said the stranger politely but with an air of authority. "Being part of a trading company makes it easier to obtain those things that a physician may require."

"And you are?" the soldier asked, beginning to sound annoyed. "You must have a name."

"Djerman Ragosh-ski," he answered promptly, combining one of his Egyptian names with the patronymic of his very distant childhood. "I am a partner in the Eclipse Traders, as I told you."

"Not an Egyptian surname; and certainly not a Greek one,"

said the soldier, considering. "I will ask my officer if you might give this gift"—he made the word sarcastic—"to the woman for her children."

"Why is he here at all?" Ragosh-ski asked, making his inquiry one of curiosity, not challenge.

"Her husband's fate has been decided, and hers will be in the morning; it is likely that slavery will be her lot, and the lot of her children. There are plans she must make, and arrangements to accommodate the plans. She must hold herself in readiness." The soldier nudged his companion. "The girl should bring a good price: she's young but she's promising."

"True enough," said the second soldier, sounding bored. "They'll have to sell her even if they execute the others."

"The boys, too, I would guess," said the first. "Pity that younger one isn't . . .. right."

"There's bound to be a use for him somewhere." The second spat and leaned more heavily on his spear. "I don't like this kind of duty."

"The officer can't come alone," said the first soldier. "What if the woman and her children had friends with them."

"They have this friend," said Ragosh-ski.

"But you aren't here to fight, and you're foreign, so that wouldn't be prudent," said the first soldier. "Others might be ready and able to defend them."

"And two of us might not be enough to hold them off," said the second soldier with a shrug. He regarded Ragosh-ski for a long moment, then said, "You don't strike me as dangerous."

Ragosh-ski bowed slightly. "Not just at present," he said with a chuckle.

The soldiers joined him, and might have said something more, but their officer came surging out of the house, the woman behind him, shouting insults and imprecations at him; he paid no attention. He donned his horse-hair crested helmet and signaled his men to follow him, shouting over his shoulder, "We will return in two days, and you will have to be ready for face the consequences."

The woman screamed, "My husband will be newly dead

then. I must have time to mourn him with our children. There are offerings we must make."

"Mourn him in your servitude; the gods will accept your plight on his behalf. In any case, I suppose his students will probably buy you and your children," the officer yelled back at her, hardly breaking stride as he went away from her house, the two soldiers trailing behind him.

"You'd best not be here tomorrow, Ragosh-ski," advised the soldier who had questioned him. "It could work against your interests."

"It might," said Ragosh-ski, noticing the older boy staring out at him through a knot-hole in the wall of the shack.

"Well, I have warned you," the soldier declared as he reached the first turn in the street.

Ragosh-ski watched the three depart, his expression severe. He realized that a decision would have to be reached quickly. Once the soldiers were out of sight, he opened the ramshackle gate and went into the house, tugging the sledge with him. "I know this is not a good time, but you will want what I bring," he said as much to announce himself as to point out the fruits of his errand.

The woman looked up, staring at him. "I didn't realize you'd returned," she said, sounding dazed. She stared at him, as if not trusting her eyes. "You brought—"

The daughter lunged out of the alcove where she had re-treated. "Food! He brought food!" She slapped the covering on the sledge. "I can smell it!"

Her mother took her by the shoulder. "Calm down, Thalia."

The girl did her best to contain herself, stepping back from the sledge and saying only, "I'm hungry."

"We're all hungry," said the woman, sounding utterly weary. She glanced at Ragosh-ski. "So you brought what you said you would bring?"

"Have a look for yourself," Ragosh-ski offered, bending to untie the twine that held the load in place.

There was a long silence as the woman peeled back the

covering and stared at the food and the pot. "You have been . . . most kind." The words sounded harsh and unfamiliar as she spoke them. She bent down and touched the two bolts of cloth. "Most kind."

"If this suits your purposes, then I am content," said Ragosh-ski, stepping back so that the woman could begin to unload the sledge.

"This food will be useless by this time tomorrow, when the soldiers come again. They won't allow us to take food with us." She sighed. "But we will have an ample last meal together. Perhaps I can cut new garments for us, as well; we will look less like beggars."

"You need not be beggars," said Ragosh-ski.

"No; we can be slaves," said the woman without emotion.

"Not slave either," he said.

She rounded on him. "You saw the soldiers—it must be one or the other."

"Then I hope you will make the most of your evening to consider what I offer." Ragosh-ski paused, making sure he had her full attention. "The authorities may watch Piraeus to keep you from leaving, but they will not—they cannot—be at Megara, and I can arrange for you to travel with a merchants' train of ox-carts bound for there at dawn. From that place, I can arrange for you to go overland to the Gulf of Corinth, or by sea to one of the islands, as suits you. You can make your way in the world according to your desires. Depending on your skills, there will be work for you in any place."

"So you would expect me to work?" The woman did not quite laugh this time.

"No; *you* would expect to work. You have made it clear that you do not trust any aid too freely given." He looked at the children. "If you have work you would like to do, tell me so that I may find a situation for you. You would be together; your children would not be sold and you could deliver your baby in safety."

The woman looked toward her children. "I don't want to lose them."

Ragosh-ski smiled. "Yes: hard enough to lose your husband. Tomorrow the soldiers return. But they will not guard you through the night, will they?"

"Why should they?" The woman laid out the food on a narrow, plank table and pressed her lips together. "Where would they expect me to go? Where would I take these children?" She shook her head. "They know where they will find us tomorrow."

"The sea laps many shores," said Ragosh-ski.

The woman laughed harshly. "And what ship would take us? Megara is all very well, but what then? And for that matter, what merchant would carry us in an on-cart? Women are known to be unlucky on ships, and I haven't money to pay for passage, and women on the road are targets for mischief." She picked up the garlic and sniffed it. "I might as well try to walk to Thessalonika, or swim to Rhodes."

"Arrangements can be made," said Ragosh-ski.

"For what?" She raised her head and glared at him. "For removing us and then selling us to foreigners, far away, where the customs and news of Athens have no meaning?"

"No: for passage so that you may have the safety of distance from Athens, and some protection from those willing to provide it," said Ragosh-ski.

"And you would know such men?" The woman laughed bitterly.

"Yes," he responded simply. "I would."

The woman looked away. "You tempt me, foreigner."

"You may call me Ragosh-ski," he offered. "That way I will be a bit less foreign."

"With such a cumbersome name? It only serves to enhance your foreignness." She looked again toward her children huddled in the corner, then shrugged, making up her mind. "Come. Unload the rest of the sledge: put the cloth in the covered box in the corner. Thalia, use the wood to build up a proper fire so I can put this all to cooking." Taking up the new cleaver, she tested it against her thumb and nodded. "Well-honed."

"So the seller claimed," said Ragosh-ski.

She brought it down on the melon, watching the taut skin open and the soft interior with its load of seeds spill out. "Do you think there is a place it would be safe for me to go? A place where we could remain?"

"I do," said Ragosh-ski."At Chalcedon, widows are permitted to continue the work of their husbands, until the oldest son is of age to inherit."

The woman scoffed. "What manner of teacher would I be?"

"If your husband is unknown to the people of Chalcedon, then nothing constrains you, and you may select what suits you best," said Ragosh-ski. "You will have documents to show that this is your right. You may also have documents to say your place of business was destroyed and you could not afford to rebuild. So long as you have money enough, there will be no questions asked."

"And where am I to get money? If I had money, there would have been no call for you to purchase all this." She reached for the skin of wine, unstopped it and squeezed the blood-colored liquid into her mouth. Glaring at him defiantly, she said, "Would you want any of this?"

"No, but I thank you for your offer; I do not drink wine."

She stared at him. "Perhaps something else?"

"Perhaps," he agreed. "But later."

She took an old, wooden cup from the end of the table, tipped it over, then filled it with wine, then handed the cup to her daughter, "Share this with your brothers, mind."

Thalia smiled as she took a careful sip, smacking her lips before handing the cup to her nearest brother. She wiped her mouth with the back of her hand and stared longingly at the halved melon. "Mama?"

"Take it outside and get the seeds out for the goat, and then you may have some. Remember it must be shared." The woman stopped the wine-skin again and looked at Ragosh-ski. "Tell me why you are prepared to do so much for me? And never mind saying it is a whim."

Ragosh-ski answered her slowly, thoughtfully. "Most of

the people in Athens, as in all the rest of the world, are . . . as if they are sleepwalking. They live but they are not wholly alive, not vital, not immersed in living. Those who are are like beacons."

"You can't think I am one such," said the woman, shaking her head in disbelief. "How could I be?"

"It has nothing to do with situation," said Ragosh-ski, thinking back to his many decades at the Temple of Imhotep. "It has to do with the truth within."

"Now you sound like my husband," she said, and picked up the yellow and green peppers, sliced them in half, and pulled the seeds from within them, setting the seeds on a narrow shelf to dry out of habit.

"Then he must know your value," said Ragosh-ski.

"He calls me a shrew, and worse," she answered, vigorously chopping the peppers.

"In that, he is mistaken," said Ragosh-ski.

She stopped her work. "I thank you for saying so," she muttered, cautious of his praise.

"If you depart tomorrow, you will not have to answer for his actions any longer." He nodded to her.

"I would want him to know, if I decide to leave." She re-sumed hacking the peppers, making them into ever-smaller bits of vegetable.

"I will carry word to him, if you like," said Ragosh-ski.

She scraped the peppers into the large cooking pot, then set to work on the onions; their pungent odor quickly filled the little hut. "Better you than the soldiers, I suppose," she said thoughtfully. "At least you can tell him we are safe."

"Then you will go?" Ragosh-ski asked.

"I don't know. But tell him we are with friends, or anything you like, so long as it is not the truth." She used the edge of her hand to shove the onions into the pot.

"Not the truth?" He could not follow her intention.

"He has said he will accept whatever is meted out to him," she said, her eyes still fixed on the middle distance. "And I am certain he said it sincerely. But what if his followers persuade him to bargain? What might become of us then?" She bent to pick up the butchered lamb, slinging it onto the table and preparing to cut meat off it. "Tell him whatever story you think will most serve our purpose—the children's and mine."

Ragosh-ski ducked his head. "If that is your wish."

"It is what must be done, for all our sakes," she said, and stopped working long enough to stare at him. "No matter what I decide, I am grateful to you for this, Ragosh-ski."

For a long moment, Ragosh-ski said nothing. Then, "What is your husband's name? For whom shall I ask at the prison?"

"He is called Socrates. I am Xantippe." She slapped down a wedge of lamb and began to cut it into smaller chunks.

"I will attend to it," said Ragosh-ski.

"You will return before dawn?" Xantippe asked as her children came rushing back inside, each clutching a section of melon; the two boys were yelling.

"Certainly before dawn," said Ragosh-ski.

Xantippe reached to restrain her children. "I will have a decision by then," she promised. "I will hope that sleep brings wisdom."

Ragosh-ski nodded as he went to the door. "Then I will wish you sweet dreams."

LOST
EPIPHANY

T HE MAN CHAINED TO the other massive steering
oar beside his own was dead; the body was stiff, the
rigidity making him as great a weight as the long oar
was. His skin was cold and taking on the color of clay; he lay
bent almost double over the oar, his elbows poking out at awkward angles because of his manacles. Not that Sant-Germainus
cared, for he was consumed in the misery that only travel over
water could bring him. He had ceased to feel the hard blows
of the oar-master's lash two days ago, nor did he bother any
longer to look for distant land beyond the heaving sea as the
merchant ship plowed on through the advancing storm; rain-
clouds obscured the distance and heaving seas demanded his
full attention. The steering-oar shuddered as the ship climbed
the side of a wave. Below-decks all but a dozen oars were pulled
in; those that remained in the water were plied with steady
purpose to keep the boat from floundering.

"You there! Steersman!" The captain's first officer, known
as Ynay, struggled along the deck, clinging to the rope as the
ship pitched and wallowed. His language was a variation of
Byzantine Greek, but with an accent that indicated the man
came from Colchis.

Sant-Germainus lifted his head, his body aching with

fatigue, his clothes were soaked and clammily cold, his eyes almost swollen shut from the relentless waves washing over the deck. He stared at the first officer and forced himself to speak. "What is it, Ynay?" He knew his response could earn him a beating for insolence, but that hardly seemed to matter; being on running water without the protection of his native earth was more punishment than any whip could mete out. He found it ironic that this night or perhaps the next would be the anniversary of his birth.

"The other steersman!" shouted the first officer.

"He can't answer you," Sant-Germainus responded.

Ynay was almost up to the steering-oar; blinking into the wet; he reached to shake the second steersman, then hesitated. "Is he ill?"

"No longer," said Sant-Germainus. "He stopped breathing some time ago."

The first officer faltered. "Dead?"

"From a fever," said Sant-Germainus, who had recognized the disease as something that could not be treated on this boat at sea. "It settled in his gut. He complained of it last night: to you."

"But . . . he hasn't fallen," said Ynay, reaching for the amulet that hung around his neck.

"Because he is closely chained to me, and I can only hold the oar standing up. His oar is chained to mine," Sant-Germainus said as patiently as he could.

The first officer blinked, then nodded twice. "Yes. Yes. You shouldn't have to . . . I'll have the oar-master come and release you." He was hesitant to touch the corpse. He stood as straight as he could without letting go of the safety rope. "The captain is ordering the two of you to remain on deck until the skies clear. In such a storm as this, and with long nights, we must have the attention of every man."

"One of us cannot comply, Ynay," said Sant-Germainus. He looked over his shoulder at the frothing sea. "We should be nearing Paros or Naxos. You will need a guard in the bow as well as a second steersman."

"How can you be sure? We're probably off-course by leagues."

"Possibly. But there are more islands than those two in the Cyclades, and we should be wary of them. They are around us in the dark, and we may not see them until we are up against their shores." Sant-Germainus had to shift his stance as the dead body struck his legs. "We will all drown if we scrape a rock in this gale."

The first officer looked uncomfortable. "The captain doesn't want to risk any more lives. He's afraid anyone on deck could be washed away." As if to support this idea, the ship pitched toward its port side, and tried to turn abeam to the wave, which would bring a fatal shift in position: Sant-Germainus held the oar with all his strength, and gradually the prow came back to taking the waves straight on while the dead man slid as far down the other steering oar as his manacles permitted. Ynay dropped to his knee in an effort to keep hold of the safety rope.

"If you lose your steersmen, you will sink. That is certain," said Sant-Germainus.

"The storm could lessen," the first officer growled.

"If it does, we may run aground on one of the islands—if we are lucky," Sant-Germainus warned. "If we're not dashed apart on rocks or cliffs."

"I suppose," said Ynay, regarding the corpse of the second steersman with increasing distress. "He's got to go over the side."

Sant-Germainus nodded, trying to keep the steering-oar steady. "If there is no lookout, we may lose the bottom of the ships to unseen shoals." As much as he longed for solid earth under his feet, he dreaded the shoals, no matter how solid they were, that would rip the bottom out of the ship; he, unlike the others aboard, could not drown, and the thought of lying, chained in a wreck, alert and aware until his flesh was eaten away by sea-creatures appalled him. "Then more than cargo would be forfeit."

"I know," muttered the first officer; his voice did not carry over the roar of the waves and the wind's moan.

"The winds are rising," Sant-Germainus pointed out. "They have changed direction three or four times."

"We've furled the sail and pulled in half the oars. I don't know what else we can do." Ynay was clearly worried but unwilling to admit as much to this captured foreigner. "The captain won't permit us to lighten our load."

"You can put a watchman in the bow," said Sant-Germainus. "And bring that Egyptian oarsman to steer with me. He knows these waters and he has come through his share of storms."

"The Egyptian from your ship?" The first officer shook his head. "The captain would never agree."

"He must have someone else on the other oar, and all of you know it," said Sant-Germainus. "No one man can hold the ship on a single steering oar alone. If the other steering oar breaks, you will have no control on the starboard side, and the ship will roll more heavily than it does now."

"But you and . . . he . . . are chained together. Your oar and the other one are linked by the chain," said Ynay in a desperate attempt at reason.

"Think of the risk of my falling, or worse." Sant-Germainus regarded him steadily as the seas pitched around them.

"I suppose that's what you would have done on the *Morning Star*," said Ynay.

"At the very least, had I been caught in such a storm," said Sant-Germainus with more emotion; the loss of his merchant-ship five days ago to these Greeks still rankled; bales of silk lashed to the deck bore the eclipse symbol of his trading company, serving as a constant reminder of his capture, the capture of his men, and his cargo's theft. "You would do the same, Ynay; you know the sea."

"Our captain is not so willing to put lives—"

"He may risk one or two, or he may risk all," said Sant-Germainus over a new wash of wave.

"It is dangerous, to chain a man on deck in such a storm," said Ynay, then realized what he had said, and to whom; he added, "Your crew could drown if they are brought to help you. Let them be safe at their oars."

"Then the captain is risking all," said Sant-Germainus, relieved that he had taken no nourishment for more than six days, for had he received sustenance since then, he would now be enduring crippling nausea as well as severe pain in his muscles and joints from his exposure to water and light. His hunger was growing as he tired and with it his formidable strength was waning—another day or two like this and he would be utterly exhausted and disoriented by the enervation the water gave. He clutched the oar to his chest and hung on as the waves pounded over the bow of the ship, washing back to where he stood on the after-deck. "We will all pay the price for his greed and cowardice."

Ynay winced as he nodded. "So I fear."

"Then, for your own sake, convince him of what he stands to lose."

The first officer clung to the safety-rope, his face distressed. "I will ask the captain if he will accept volunteers to man the oar, and the watch. And I'll send the oar-master to–" He motioned to the corpse.

Sant-Germainus watched Ynay lurch back toward the middle of the ship and the hatches that led below. He frowned at the man's struggle to keep his footing. The ship rolled ponderously and threatened to capsize, but Sant-Germainus held the oar, his whole body leaning into it; the wood moaned in his hands, and for a long moment he feared the oar would break, leaving the ship at the mercy of the storm. The ship topped the swell and righted itself, sliding down the wall of water into another trough, and he used this short time to align the bow more safely.

How he hated crossing running water! At least it was the dark of the year, so that sunlight did not join with the sea in wearing him out. Even the hard months crossing the Takla Makan in the Year of Yellow Snow, thirty years ago, was less arduous than this passage through the Aegean Sea—then there had only been cold and hunger to exhaust him, not the vitiation of running water and unrelenting labor. He wondered briefly how Rutgeros was doing below-decks, and hoped that his bondsman was faring better than he was. Looking over at the dead man, he said, "May you rest quietly."

Some while later, the oar-master—a massive fellow from Odessus called Dvlinoh—came wallowing along the safety-rope and unlocked the manacles holding the corpse to the oar. "I'll bring someone up to help you," he said bluntly. "No one can hold these oars alone, not in a storm. The captain's a fool."

Sant-Germainus said nothing, watching as the body slid down the after-deck; the oar-master caught it by the ankle, and let the next wave that broke over the ship carry it off.

◆ ◆ ◆

Dark water heaved around them, changing from mountain to valley and to mountain again in restless progression, but the wind had died down, so that the waves no longer piled up like hissing battlements. The ship was still afloat, but half the oarsmen were on the mid-deck, helping to bail out the holds on a bucket-chain. A wan swath of reddish sunlight smeared the eastern horizon off their port side ahead, its light revealing in the distance the suggestion of an island. Sant-Germainus hung over his steering oar and regarded Khafir-Amun, who held the other next to him. "I think the captain will relieve us shortly." He spoke the Egyptian tongue with an old-fashioned accent.

"A foolish, frightened creature, not worthy of this ship; he makes no offering to Poseidon," said the Egyptian, a tall, wide-shouldered, leather-skinned man with arms as tough as tree-trunks from his long years at the steering-oar; he had a wide, irregular scar along his jaw and another cutting through his eyebrow, and his left hand was missing its little finger. "What made him think he could command a ship, let alone a band of sea-robbers?"

"A family trade, perhaps?" Sant-Germainus ventured, making himself stand upright in spite of the ache in his limbs; his sodden dalamatica adding to his chill. He rarely felt cold, but combined with damp, Sant-Germainus was now distinctly uncomfortable.

"Then he should have left the trade and apprenticed himself to a camel-drover," said Khafir-Amun. "Ynay is better suited to this work than the captain will ever be."

"That is often the case," said Sant-Germainus, thinking back to the many times he had seen outwardly powerful men who were supported by more capable assistants. "Ynay is a true sailor, and sensible."

"Your man—Rutgeros?—volunteered to watch, but the captain wouldn't allow it, nor would he allow anyone who had been among your crew. He said you and they would hatch mischief if you were allowed to work together." He glanced toward the island in the distance. "Do you know where we are?"

"I know we are not at Naxos, or Paros. We cannot have been blown as far as Crete. Amorgus or Ios, perhaps." Sant-Germainus squinted in the increasing light, his skin starting to feel tight, as if he stood too near a flame.

"Amorgus is long and thin, and much too far south," said Khafir-Amun. "From here, that island looks small and probably fairly round. There are no very high peaks I can make out." He thought a moment. "The small island east of Naxos—what is it called?—that might be it."

"We may be east of Naxos," Sant-Germainus conceded. "Not so far south as Koufonisia or Karos, I would reckon."

"Dhenoussa," said Khafir-Amun. "That's the island. I wish I could see it more clearly. I am almost certain I am right."

"I doubt we could have been blown so far to the east," said Sant-Germainus, bur even as he said it, he began to think of the long night and the furious wind. They might well have gone farther than he had assumed. He looked over his shoulder toward the west but could not make out the three peaks of Naxos. "We could have reached Dhenoussa," he said with less certainty; now that they had come through the heart of the storm, he realized he was more exhausted than he could remember being in more than a century.

"It's too big for any of the Makaris, so it must be Dhenoussa.

After such a night as we have passed, I would not be surprised to see Melos ahead, had we gone southwest, or Mykonos, had we been driven backward." He chuckled to show he knew this was impossible.

"With the seas still running so high, I wonder if we will find a safe harbor, whatever island it may be." Sant-Germainus bore down on his oar as the ship crested another wave; his arms shook with the effort and he felt his grip beginning to fail in spite of the manacles holding him in place. "We will see more as it gets lighter. We'll be better able to work out where we are."

"Dhenoussa has two shelters—one on the northwest side of the island, the other on the northeast, and there is a bay on the south-southwest side, and a few coves and inlets as well, but it is much more exposed." Khafir-Amun recited from memory. "The southern inlets can also give protection, but not very good anchorage."

"If we cannot find them, it hardly matters," said Sant-Germainus.

"If the captain would post a watch, we would manage better. We need to know where we are," said Khafir-Amun, repeating the cause of his anxiety. "We needs a man in the bow, and one in the stern."

"Yes; but the captain is not willing to order that," said Sant-Germainus, and after a glance at the brightening sky ahead beyond the bow, added, "And I fear I must rest soon." This admission made him flinch inwardly.

Khafir-Amun nodded. "No man should pull a steering oar longer than a full day or a full night."

"Including the day or night at the dark of the year?" Sant-Germainus asked.

"The days are short now, but in bad weather it hardly matters —every hour seems a day or more." Khafir-Amun looked again toward the island, now appearing a bit larger. "We're getting closer."

"More risks of rocks," said Sant-Germainus uneasily.

"I hope the captain will decide to anchor here. He should order a full inspection of the ship."

"After she's bailed out," said Sant-Germainus, and shoved his end of the oar upward as the ship dropped down a swelling wave; men on deck grabbed hold of the two safety-ropes as water cascaded over them and into the open hold. Shouts from below erupted at once, and Sant-Germainus saw three more oars shipped inside. "One way or another, she will not go much farther."

"No. Nor will the men," said Khafir-Amun.

"The captain will order Dvlinoh to beat them."

Khafir-Amun laughed unpleasantly. "It will do no good. They have no food. All three water cisterns have been breached, so there is nothing to drink unless we open the amphorae for their wine—not that the men would object to that. The barrels of salt pork were washed away some time last night. And the beans are sodden—the cook says they are going to spoil, and must be thrown overboard. He's only going to cook up the few that are dry, and when they're eaten–"

"Then he must reprovision," said Sant-Germainus, holding the shuddering oar so tightly that he felt his manacles dig into his wrists.

"If he wants to get back to Thera," said Khafir-Amun with grim satisfaction.

"Thera: is that where he is from?" asked Sant-Germainus. As another wave slopped over the side of the ship, he wobbled on his feet.

"So he said," Khafir-Amun said, frowning as he watched Sant-Germainus balance himself against his oar. "He could be from there."

Sant-Germainus regarded the men striving to move more buckets of water out of the hold. "It is cold enough that the oarsmen will soon have chilblains, if they do not already. They will have to be given something warm to drink, and soon."

"They are all cold," said Khafir-Amun. "It was folly to set out so late in the year."

"It was that or have the ship impounded and the oarsmen taken as slaves," said Sant-Germainus. "Storms were a more acceptable hazard."

"Storms are one thing, pirates are another." Khafir-Amun nodded slowly.

"The *Morning Star* could weather storms," said Sant-Germainus. "But storms and pirates were beyond her to withstand."

Khafir-Amun touched his hands together. "You did not know about the pirates, or that the storm would be so severe. Every man must decide these things for himself." He narrowed his eyes as the first long rays of dawn broke through the clouds, lighting them from beneath so that it looked as if the sky were afire.

"Then steer for the island until the captain tells you otherwise," Sant-Germainus recommended, then collapsed to his knees.

"*YNAY!*" Khafir-Amun bellowed as he reached to seize Sant-Germainus' oar. "Take Sant-Germainus below and send up another steersman!"

It was Dvlinoh who answered the summons, shoving through the bailers and keeping hold of the safety-rope as he came to the after-deck. He gave Sant-Germainus a thoughtful stare. "Is he alive?" He did not wait for Khafir-Amun to answer, but leaned forward and unlocked the manacles. "Hang on until I come back. I'll take his place at the oar, and the Captain may say what he likes." Without another word, he slung Sant-Germainus over his shoulder and made his way back to the hold.

◆ ◆ ◆

Sant-Germainus opened his eyes; he was still cold and groggy, but he could feel the day waning above him, and although the hold stank of rotting cargo, unwashed bodies, and the effluvia of confinement, it was preferable to being on deck in the fading sunlight. He tried to move and almost fell out of the narrow bunk in which he had been sleeping as the ship weltered through choppy water; he muttered an oath in his native tongue, and heard Rutgeros answer.

"So you are awake, my master," he said in old-fashioned Latin.

"I am," Sant-Germainus responded. "Where are we?"

"We are coming into a small harbor on Dhenoussa. Khafir-Amun found it about an hour ago. It is a small cove on the south side of the island. There are two long crests through the island, one in a straight line, the other curved; the inlet is in the last curve of that second crest. Approaching it is proving difficult: the seas are still high and we cannot use the sail, and the oarsmen are being cautious not to splinter their oars on hidden rocks."

"Did Khafir-Amun have any more information about the island?" Sant-Germainus asked, wanting to concentrate on something other than his discomforts.

"There is no spring on the island, or so the sailors say, so we will have to get water from cisterns on the island, which should be full after such a storm as we have had, assuming the shepherds and fishermen will allow us to have enough for our needs," said Rutgeros. "Also, there is a monastery on the north end of the island; the fishermen are on the south side, so there should be food available somewhere. The monks should be charitable at this time of year, for their faith."

"Assuming the captain is willing to pay for it," said Sant-Germainus sardonically.

"Alas, I fear he has other plans; he intends to seize what he wants and to leave the island before anyone knows we have come." Rutgeros bent down to offer the support of his arm. "And speaking of the captain, I have informed him of the severity of your sea-sickness so he will not expect you to ask for food."

"Prudent of you, old friend," said Sant-Germainus with a rueful smile. "Not that I am not ravenous."

"As is the rest of the crew," said Rutgeros. "If the captain had decided to make for Thera without taking on food and water, there would have been mutiny."

"Or a dead crew," said Sant-Germainus flatly; he would hate to have to drift in a damaged ship with nothing but decaying bodies, and only Rutgeros for company.

"The captain is greedy and foolish, but he knows he could lose everything, including his life, if he starves his oarsmen."

"I should hope so: his men must know it," said Sant-Germainus. He managed to squeeze out of the bunk and get to his feet, but he discovered his head still ached and his strength was at low ebb.

"Hold steady," Rutgeros recommended in Byzantine Greek as he offered the support of his arm to Sant-Germainus; there were other men near them who were listening to their conversation, and would be suspicious of what they did not understand. "I discovered one of your chests in the cargo hold, the only one they took from the *Morning Star*. Apparently the straps and locks intrigued the captain; he couldn't get it open, and so he brought it aboard, hoping he will find treasure inside."

"And so he shall, if only he knew it," said Sant-Germainus drily, still speaking the Latin of five hundred years ago. "If the earth is not soaked, I will take advantage of having it here once we are safe in harbor."

"You might have to wait until the crew is sleeping," Rutgeros pointed out.

"Which most will do, with only a few put on watch through the night. They will not notice what I do, if I am cautious," said Sant-Germainus.

"I could attend to it for you," Rutgeros volunteered.

"It may come to that," said Sant-Germainus as he looked toward the open hold where the ladder was beginning to shake; someone was climbing down. "We will make our decisions in this regard later."

"A very good notion," said Rutgeros. He stepped back as a middle-aged man with Greek features but dressed in Syrian finery came into the hold. "Captain Argourus," he said, effacing himself.

"I see you are awake," said the captain, ignoring Rutgeros and addressing Sant-Germainus; he fingered his curled beard, his lower lip protruding. "May God give you a good day on the Eve of His Nativity." He made a great show of signing himself.

"On this day, we must all be doubly thankful."

"He may have provided our deliverance, more or less." He indicated the pitch and roll of the ship. "We are not safely anchored yet."

"Can you doubt it, on this of all evenings?" Captain Argourus pointed directly at Sant-Germainus. "Do you question His mercy? You will tempt God to allow the sea to swallow you."

"The last few days have been demanding, yet I am still here." Sant-Germainus steadied himself by holding onto the edge of the top bunk of the tier; his Byzantine Greek was impeccable, but slightly accented. "I do not know if this is because of fate or chance or the season; the Christians in this crew must have effective prayers at this time." He paused and added, "If there is reason for thanks, then I am thankful."

Captain Argourus regarded him narrowly, then decided not to make an issue of it. "You did well, they tell me. You kept us from going completely off course. We wouldn't have made this landfall without your seamanship."

"You are mot generous to say so, but it was more luck and the whim of the sea that brought us safely through the heart of the storm," said Sant-Germainus, keeping most of the irony from his voice; only the arch of one fine brow suggested any mordant intent.

The captain studied Sant-Germainus for a long while, and again chose not to argue. "Do you know this island: Dhenoussa?"

"I have passed it many times, but I do not know it. This is the first time I have landed on its shores." He did not add that except for his first voyage to Egypt roughly two thousand years before, in the past he had been in the hold of his ship, atop his chests of his native earth, in a stupor, not struggling on deck, chained to an oar.

"But you are not adverse to going ashore," Captain Argourus said.

"No, I am not," said Sant-Germainus, who was eager to have earth beneath his feet, and the chance to find an animal—a goat or a sheep would do—to allow him to ease his hunger.

"Good. I will send you to the monks; they are more likely to help us than any fishermen — my crew will deal with the fishermen. The monks are supposed to aid seafarers, aren't they? Their cisterns are full, no doubt, and for the monks, these being their Holy Days, they will not begrudge us water and food, in the name of their God. But the request will do better coming from you than from me."

Although Sant-Germainus agreed, he asked, "Why do you think so?"

The captain snorted. "Monks don't like pirates. They're likely to refuse me on that point alone."

"But you think they will provide me with food and water because I am a captive," said Sant-Germainus.

"It would be like them; their faith requires it," said Captain Argourus, his smile widening. "Especially if you tell them I will kill you and all the men from your ship if you fail. They would rather be martyrs than betray their calling."

Sant-Germainus regarded the captain steadily. "And you intend that I should plead for all of us?"

"And the monks, of course, since we would kill them, too, or lock them to the oars if they deny us. They can further their good acts by taking those of the oarsmen who are stricken, and treating their ills. We will lose half a dozen men to frostbite, I fear, and will need replacements for them. The monks could provide us with strong arms." He coughed. "Tell them that during their Holy Days, they should uphold what their founder taught, and suffer for the good of others."

"Ship oars!" came the shout from the rowing-hold.

"We must be close to shore; you can hear the breakers and smell the beach," said the captain. "We will have to use the small boats to get to and from the land; there is no dock or quay at the inlet, not that it would be safe to tie up to any such structure with the seas still so high." He pointed to Sant-Germainus. "Be ready to go ashore. I will not stomach delays. Our need it too urgent."

"I will have to find a cloak. My clothes are not sufficient to keep a mouse warm, not out in the open wind," said Sant-

Germainus. He did not want the clothes for protection against the elements, but to secure himself from prying eyes.

"Your manservant can find that for you," said the captain as he made for the ladder leading to the deck above. "Be ready. I will take your reluctance out on the hide of the oarsmen," he declared ominously as he set foot on the lowest rung.

"I will find what you need," said Rutgeros to Sant-Germainus.

"Thank you," said Sant-Germainus, a troubled line settling in between his fine brows. He stood, accustoming himself to the roll of the ship, trying to put the discomfort of his head-ache and nausea behind him; forcing himself to listen to what the sailors and oarsman were shouting, he was able to reach a point where he could ignore his water-caused irritations, and to put his attention on what was going on around him, so that by the time Rutgeros came back from his search with a fine, if old-fashioned abolla, its deep pleats smelling of salt and rosemary; he was able to pull it on with little more than a wince. Its color—a dark olive-gray—made him seem one with the shadows.

"It is a bit damp," Rutgeros said apologetically.

"What is not?" Sant-Germainus countered with a hint of amusement. "It is mostly dry, and it is heavy enough to keep out the wind." He saw Khafir-Amun descending the ladder into the hold. "How is this anchorage?"

Khafir-Amun was tired; his big shoulders slouched and there were purplish shadows around his eyes. "It is the best we can have in this location," he said. "This ship will not go much farther, in any case. We need food and water and the hull requires patching."

"Is it breached?" Sant-Germainus asked, trying to conceal his alarm.

"Nothing too serious, but the hull must be patched; the damage will get worse if it isn't attended to now. Three of the oars are in need of repair, as well." He rubbed his lips. "I am hungry, and I need sleep."

Sant-Germainus nodded. "As are we all: hungry."

"The captain will have to provide for us, and soon," said Khafir-Amun, scowling as he looked for a bunk in which to nap. "And everyone is tired, I know I am not alone. Some are asleep at their oars."

"Then the captain will provide rest and food," Sant-Germainus agreed, thinking of the errand ahead for him. "If he has any sense."

"Six of the oarsmen have been set to fishing from the fore-deck," said Rutgeros. "They should catch something to cook."

"Octopus," said Khafir-Amun. "I like octopus."

"I suspect anything would do now," said Rutgeros. "Except, perhaps, sponges."

"In storms like this, fishing is uncertain," said Khafir-Amun, no longer paying much attention as he covered his yawn.

"All the more reason for me to make haste," said Sant-Germainus, as much to spur himself on as to explain his mission.

"So say we all," muttered Khafir-Amun.

"Is there a lantern I can take with me?" Sant-Germainus asked, for although his eyes did not require the extra illumination to see in the night, he knew better than to forge off into the fading light with nothing to light his way.

"I'll find one for you," Rutgeros said, and went forward in the chilly, malodorous hold, moving carefully among the groups of worn out oarsmen who sat on the floor, bent with fatigue.

"So you really are going to speak to the monks, are you?" Khafir-Amun asked Sant-Germainus.

"The captain insists," said Sant-Germainus, resignation in every aspect of his body.

"Just like that? On your own?"

Rutgeros returned, carrying a simple oil-lantern, its wick just starting to burn. After blowing gently on the wick to increase its brightness, he held it out to Sant-Germainus silently; Sant-Gemainus took the oil-lantern and studied it for a brief moment, then looked att Khafir-Amun. "He has promised to kill you and all those he took from the *Morning Star* if I do not persuade the monks to feed and help us. I have no doubt he would carry out his threat." His face was impassive but there was a glint in his dark eyes that revealed the contempt he felt for the captain. "That is not the way I would prefer to mark the remembrance of my birth."

"I see. So you aren't likely to do anything other than what the captain requires," said Khafir-Amun. "He's a clever old devil, Captain Argourus is."

"Do you admire him?" Rutgeros asked in disapproving surprise.

"No," said Khafir-Amun. "But many pirates would simply cut their losses and strand the captives and the injured on this island to fend for themselves. At least we have something more than thirst and starvation ahead of us." He listened to the outburst of activity on the deck, and smiled. "Ah. Someone has caught a fish. As soon as the men get the fire going again, we will have a little to eat."

"I hope the fish is of good size," said Rutgeros.

"Or that more are caught, and soon. They will put the fish in with the driest of the beans that are left into the pot, and anything else that we can still safely eat that hasn't been washed overboard." Khafir-Amun touched the charm that hung around his neck on a hin brass chain. "We will not die tonight, or tomorrow."

"If I can convince the monks to aid us," said Sant-Germainus, going toward the ladder, his oil-lantern raised.

Khafir-Amun coughed discreetly. "I have some information to pass to you, which Ynay told me: none of us from the *Morning Star* are permitted to take you ashore, or to go with you. We are hostages, to gain your compliance. The captain said you must stay with his men as far as the shore, and then go on your own. If you aren't back by dawn, he will throw one of us into the sea at noon, and another at sunset, and then he will storm the monastery with his men, and take what they want."

"Why did he not tell me himself?" Sant-Germainus asked, preparing to climb to the deck.

"Because he said there was nothing to discuss, and he wanted no argument from you—it would avail you nothing." He lowered his head. "I am sorry to have to tell you, but it is something you have to know. Ynay insisted that you be informed."

Rutgeros, listening to this, said softly to Sant-Germainus. "If you can escape, my master, do it. We are all dead men in any case."

"This is an island, old friend—where can I escape?" said Sant-Germainus as he began to climb into the brilliant red light of sunset.

◆ ◆ ◆

The boat that provided a crossing from the boat to the shore was small enough to have difficulties in the swells. Six oarsmen tugged and pulled while Ynay held the steering-oar in the stern. The overcast sky caught the low light from the sinking sun; the lambent light making the sky appear to be filled with lava, and lending the land ahead a smoldering shade of orange. Sant-Germainus sat in the middle of the boat, vertigo threatening to claim him as the oarsmen plied their way through the raucous sea.

"There are no houses anywhere I can see," Sant-Germainus forced himself to say.

"Your steersman said that this cove isn't sheltered enough for that. According to him, there is a small village around the point to the west, or there was eight years ago."

"And you're planning to go there, are you?"

"As soon as you are safely landed, yes. I'm sorry you have to go ashore at night," said Ynay to Sant-Germainus, pointing to the eroded peak on the west side of the cove. "They say spirits hold this island at the dark of the year, and not all of them are helpful, or inclined to give aid to visitors."

"I will keep that in mind," said Sant-Germainus. He held his abolla closed; the oil-lantern rested on his knee. As the shore grew nearer, he took stock of the rocky inlet and the narrow beach. "How many of you will remain here while I visit the monastery?"

"Two will remain," said Ynay. "The captain wants the boat to go on to the fishing village as soon as you are landed. They will have something we can eat."

Sant-Germainus thought that over, and disliked the conclusions he reached about this decision. He would have liked to have a knife with him. "Are there wild animals on the island, do you know?"

"Goats and some pigs," said Ynay. "There are also a few sheep; the monks maintain a flock for their own use."

"In folds at this time of year, I suppose," said Sant-Germainus.

"Very likely," said Ynay, and wiped his face as the boat rode through the first breakers.

"Do you know where the monastery is?" Sant-Germainus asked. "I can not see anything from here."

"On the northeast corner of the island, on a rocky crest," said Ynay, and ordered the oarsmen to slow their efforts. "Front oars, prepare to land." The boat rocked up, then down, and as the bow fell, the two front oarsmen jumped out into waist-deep surf. They took hold of the bow-line and began to drag the boat toward the sand while the other oarsmen pulled in their oars. The bottom scraped and the boat leaned to the port side as the two front oarsmen tugged the boat out of the water. Ynay climbed out of the boat and held it steady for Sant-Germainus, who struggled over the side and into thigh-deep water; his senses rocked as he tried to move out of the spent waves and onto the sand. Although the water was unpleasantly cold, it would have been disorienting to Sant-Germainus had it been warm and still. His first stride almost sent him off his feet, and he flailed to keep from toppling under the water. His hands sunk like talons into the side-rail of the boat, and he clung to this as he made his way the five steps it took to get onto the beach where he sat down, panting, beyond the touch of the water. He looked westward where the orange light was now tinged with violet and tarnished silver, and the sun was a brilliant pool of brass hanging just above the horizon, blocked in part by the cliff at the western edge of the cove, and the mass of Captain Argourus' ship.

"Not much light left," said the lead oarsman from his place at the top of the narrow swath of sand. "And the tide is coming in."

"High water should be at the edge of the sand, against the cliff," said Ynay.

"And the tide is coming in," said Sant-Germainus.

"The two of you who remain here should find shelter up there." He pointed to a broad ledge on the face of the cliff, slightly higher than Ynay was tall.

"Is that high enough?" The second oarsman shook his head. "I don't want to be trapped on a ledge for half the night."

"If the winds stay down, you should be fine there," Ynay said.

"There's a shoulder a little higher up. It would provide a little protection, and surer footing," said Sant-Germainus as he studied the rocky face. "You can see that part of the cliff fell in recently, and that ledge is close to the slip; it could also fall."

"So might the whole cliff," said Ynay. "Perhaps we should return to the boat."

Sant-Germainus was not distressed by Ynay's acerbic observation. "The cliff may not be as secure as it seems."

Ynay scowled at him. "If that part of the cliff were going to fall, it would have done so during the storm."

"Possibly," said Sant-Germainus, remaining calm. "But the slope is sodden, and that can loosen the–"

"Very well!" Ynay cut in. "Phaon, you and Kai climb to the shoulder." Having issued his orders to the two oarsmen, he rounded on Sant-Germainus. "There. They will go higher. Are you satisfied?"

"I am reassured," said Sant-Germainus, standing and reaching into the boat to claim his oil-lantern. "Let me get my bearings, and I will start for the monastery. It will take me a good part of the night to get there." This was not entirely accurate, but for most living men it was true.

"You must be here at dawn, or the captain will select who

among your crew is to go into the sea. By noon the first will be drowned. He is entirely serious about this." He looked abashed at this threat.

Sant-Germainus sighed. "What purpose does it serve to kill good men?"

"I told him it would be foolish to waste men, but he is determined not to let you get away from him. He is afraid of what you might bring down upon us."

"I understand that; I will do all that I can to bring the monks by mid-morning. They have dawn rites to perform, and I doubt they would abandon them," said Sant-Germainus, and began to walk toward the cliffs, which were not particularly high—no more than three times his height— but could prove difficult to climb. He found a narrow defile down which a storm-made stream splashed, providing a less precipitous access to the crest above. Little as he liked straddling running water, he began his ascent, sorry that he had not been able to line the soles of his Persian boots with his native earth. The climb was not very difficult and he made good progress upward. In spite of the slight dizziness the running water imparted. Every step on the aneling earth returned a little of his strength. The night would ease his discomfort somewhat, but he would be up the cliff before the sunlight faded, and would need to husband himself against the long walk he was about to make. Grimly he kept on, ignoring the shouts from the men beneath him.

By the time he reached the top of the cliff, he was aching, slightly dizzy, and feeling unusually weak. He coughed experimentally as if to assure himself he could breathe again, then lifted his oil-lantern and cast about for some kind of pathway that would lead him toward his goal. Almost at once he found a narrow goat-track leading northward along the ridge. As the last streamers of sunlight flashed through the clouds, Sant-Germainus began walking, his stamina gradually increasing, and with it, his hunger. On this, one of the longest nights of the year, he took comfort in the dark ahead. The moon would be half-full, he thought, but invisible behind the fading storm, so he would have only the light of the lamp, which for him was more than sufficient; his eyes were little impeded by night. With no one to see him, he moved quickly, covering the ground faster than the living could do. He held the oil-lantern aloft so that he would be readily visible to any shepherd or goatherd; he did not want to seem furtive or surreptitious. There is a great deal of low-lying brush but no tall trees; the few stunted cypress that grew in the clefts and gullies were bent from the constant force of the wind; they offered little shelter. As he walked he smelled thyme and rosemary, an odd perfume in the blowing night. He passed two large cisterns as he followed the path, and noticed both were full, an observation that gave him genuine satisfaction, and the assurance that his journey had not been in vain. He stopped once near a sheep-fold and considered using one of the animals to slake his tremendous thirst, but the sleepy bark of a dog kept him from acting on that impulse, and he went on, promising himself sustenance when he reached the monastery.

Some time later, he topped slight a rise and saw below him a closely locked compound of two long rows of L-shaped cells angled toward a square chapel topped with a drum-cupola and a large crucifix; there were three other buildings, one for poultry and livestock, one that appeared to be a kitchen or bakery, one that was probably a communal hall, and four large cisterns, all within a high rectangular stone wall surmounted at each corner with a Greek crucifix. He nearly smiled. "The monastery," he said aloud, and started down the trail toward the southern gate, the nearest to him; the path was steep, and he went slowly so as not to take a misstep. He was almost at the wall when a bell began to chime its single, monotonous note, and shortly after it began to sound, the drone of chanting arose. Sant-Germainus stopped on a bend in the path, watching intently.

Gradually a number of men formed a line from their cells and walked slowly toward the low building in which the bell was kept. A few of the monks carried oil-lamps, providing light for their slow advance. They continued their three-note chant as they walked, reciting the words of ancient psalms in

Anatolian Greek. At the front of the chapel, all of them knelt, prayed aloud in ragged unison, prostrated themselves, then rose. As they entered the chapel, they fell silent.

After a short while, Sant-Germainus approached the gate again, searching for some means of summoning the monks to admit him. He had almost decided to knock when he heard a shout from inside the walls.

"Glory to God! Glory to God! The Angels proclaim the Birth of the Savior!" followed by a clamoring of the single bell, accompanied by shouts of "Glory! Glory!"

"On this night, God pledges His Love!" cried one bass voice. "In the darkest hour we are redeemed."

"God have mercy on us. Christ have mercy on us," the others clamored.

Sant-Germainus hovered at the gate, his oil-lantern still in his hand. He waited until the exclamations died down and the chanting resumed. Then he used the flat of his hand to pound upon the thick wooden gate in four strong blows. He waited, and when nothing happened, he pounded again, this time shouting, "Help! We need help!"

The chanting broke off, and there was a guarded, listening quiet.

"Brothers!" Sant-Germainus shouted as he bludgeoned the gate more emphatically, using the dialect of Constantinople. "Brothers, lives are in danger! Without your help, men will die!"

This time a deep, rough voice answered. "We are at worship."

Sant-Germainus waited a long moment. "There are sailors and oarsmen in need of food and water and shelter, Brothers. They will perish if they receive none. The storm has deprived them of their food and water."

"Is that what you want us to give?" the gravely voice asked, as if he had not heard.

"Yes: water and food. There is almost none of either left aboard the ship. With your help, we can return to the home port. The men are worn out and they suffer from the cold and two days of heavy weather. On this night of all nights, have mercy upon them, as your god has mercy upon you." He paused, giving the monks time to speak; when they remained silent, he continued. "The ship needs repairs, and there is not much wood on this island to use, so we may ask for your help in–"

"We have no lumber to spare," said the monk who had spoken for the rest. "This island has few trees."

"Then the oarsmen will improvise, if you will let us have a few empty barrels," said Sant-Germainus. "If they have food and water, they will be able to work, and the staves may be enough to hold the hull together." He had to stop himself from thinking what it would be like to return to the boat, and the relentless enervation of the sea.

"It is the Nativity. We cannot stop our worship for such things." The voice had a finality to it that boded ill for Sant-Germainus and the crew of Captain Argourus' ship. "I ask you to leave us to our rites."

Sant-Germainus took a chance. "How can you say this and maintain your faith?" He recalled the many Christians he had encountered in the last five centuries and knew that each group had its own interpretation of the religion, but he persisted. "Charity is a duty for Christians, is it not?"

"We are true to our faith: this is a sacred time for us. This is the time we devote to the birth of the Christ, not to the misfortunes of this world." His tone was becoming testy. "We will be thankful to God for what He has provided to us."

"Yet how better to show your devotion, than to give succor to those in need?" Sant-Germainus countered. "It is what your founder bade you do, is it not? It is what your god did for you in your Christ's birth."

There was a short silence, and then the harsh voice said, "How many men are there on this ship?"

"Thirty-four, counting the captain," said Sant-Germainus quickly. "Five are suffering badly from cold, and all are hungry."

The speaker hesitated, then said, "Where is this ship?"

"At a cove on the south side of this island. There are two

boats left undamaged aboard to bring the men ashore." He faltered, trying to discern the impact his words were having, then said, "If you are willing to help them, some lives will be saved. It will bring glory to your faith. Their prayers of gratitude will be heard in Heaven." He listened closely, trying to be aware of their response.

This time there was a low murmur of conversation before the speaker said, "We will open the gate for you. You and I will speak while the Brothers continue with their prayers. Ordinarily we would not consider dealing with seamen tonight, but, as you say, God provides. Whatever I decide then will be final."

"Thank you," said Sant-Germainus, holding the oil-lantern so that it cast some light on his features.

The gate groaned open, revealing a narrow courtyard and the two rows of cells lined up back from the chapel. A group of about forty monks in rough-spun habits with raised cowl-hoods stood just beyond the swing of the gate. A few carried oil-lamps, but most were nothing more than dark spaces in the night. As Sant-Germainus entered the monastery, one man stepped forward, a thick-bodied man not quite so tall as Sant-Germainus, his features hidden by his hood. "I give you welcome on this holy night," he said, his voice still rough. "Enter and be welcome, if you are unarmed."

"I thank you, good Brother, for your kindness to me and the men of the ship." He held out his right hand, showing it empty. "My mission is peaceful."

"So you have said," the blocky man said. "I am Brother Theron, named for my patron saint, the senior of the monastery. I am leader of these monks. Come with me to our dining hall. There is a fire burning and you can warm yourself while we prepare to fetch your shipmates." His smile was not very convincing, but it might have been because the man had a long scar through the corner of his lip and down to the jaw, which was as much of his face as Sant-Germainus could see. "We will do what God gives us to do."

"Thank you, Brother Theron," he said, going toward the building the monk had indicated. "You are most gracious."

Even as he spoke, he thought the name—meaning hunter—an odd one for a monk, but he kept his reflection to himself; this region was filled with all manner of legends and tales of old demi-gods transformed by piety into stories of saints—undoubtedly Theron was one such.

"It is, as you said, the time of the Christ, and we should emulate Him to His glory." He pointed to another of the Brothers. "This is Brother Hylas. He will help you, and stay with you."

"That is kind, but unnecessary," said Sant-Germainus. "I will take you back to the ship. I can show you the way."

"Nevertheless, he will do it. Together you can offer up prayers for our success. There is no need for you to accompany us." Brother Theron motioned to the others. "You say they need food and water, and that the ship requires repair?"

"I do." Sant-Germainus hesitated. "Some of the oarsmen are captives, others are part of the original crew."

"Ah. Then you must be one of the captives," said Brother Theron.

"What makes you believe that?" Sant-Germainus asked, startled by the observation.

"It is what I would do," said Brother Theron obscurely. "The captain needs his men to contain you captives, doesn't he?"

A cold knot formed itself under Sant-Germainus' ribs and he strove to keep steady. "Yes, he does."

"We will keep the plight of the captives in mind. We may even turn it to our advantage." He signaled to the monks. "We will take as much as we can carry—food and water, and make for the south coast on our mission. We will leave as quickly as we can. Brother Hylas, guard the gate and the monastery while we are gone. Admit no other stranger. You must not mind the care we take," he went on to Sant-Germainus, "but sometimes desperate men have sought to seize this haven through arms or stealth, and to turn it to their own uses. We have become cautious. But, as you reminded us, God provides for those who have faith in Him. Tonight you have brought us a gift from God."

"Caution is wise—guile is often the nature of men," said Sant-Germainus, thinking that Brother Theron was guileful in his own way.

Brother Hylas, who did not resemble the handsome young Argonaut for whom he was named, set a meaty paw on Sant-Germainus' shoulder and prodded him in the direction of the dining hall. "Come. First you will get warm, and I will prepare food for you." There was enough pressure in his grip that Sant-Germainus realized he was under guard; he held his oil-lantern more tightly. These monks, he thought, must have had more than a few encounters with pirates in the past, and had come by their distrustful posture through those conflicts.

"I am hungry," Sant-Germainus admitted, and noticed that the monks were taking up spears. He felt a new certainty come over him: the monks were planning to do more than defend themselves. There had been pirates in these waters for as long as Sant-Germainus could remember, a period of more than twenty-five centuries, and as long as there had been pirates there had also been men who preyed on the pirates, benefitting from pirate misfortunes.

"You will be cared for," said Brother Theron over his shoulder.

Sant-Germainus allowed himself to be ushered toward the squat building with narrow windows along the side facing the courtyard and a door at either end of its length. "Your Brothers are most . . . gracious."

Brother Hylas said nothing, his hand weighing heavily as he increased the length of his stride. He lifted the outer latch and all but shoved Sant-Germainus into the dining hall, then closed the door and set the latch again. "I am going to the bakery," said Brother Hylas through the door. "Stay where you are and you will soon be fed. You have nothing to fear if you are not unruly. But become fractious and I will lock you into the dining hall until my Brothers return and give you nothing to eat."

This reassurance only increased Sant-Germainus' certainty that he was a captive; how much experience the Brothers must have, to have developed such safeguards against attack. "So be it," he said aloud in his native tongue. He decided to take stock of his prison until Brother Hylas returned; he lifted his oil-lantern to begin his exploration.

The dining hall was long and narrow with a single plank table flanked on both sides by benches. The open hearth at the back of the chamber showed only a few glowing embers, and nothing to replenish the fire. Near the door through which Sant-Germainus had come stood a statue, very old, of weathered wood. Studying it, Sant-Germainus recognized the statuary smirk of Etruscan portrait carvings, and the simple coronet offered to athletes and artists of high achievement. The figure held a cup in his right hand; his left hand had been broken off. As always, seeing this art from the descendants of his own people struck him with a profound loneliness, and he turned away. Distantly he wondered if he should expect food, and if any was offered, how he would explain his refusal; he felt more precarious, for if he stayed here, men of his crew would be killed, but if he attempted to leave, Brother Hylas might well do his best to stop him. He paced the length of the room, then returned to the door through which he had been shoved, and called out to Brother Hylas, who gave no answer. For the next while, Sant-Germainus remained by the door, listening intently, curious to know what was transpiring beyond the dining hall. He closed his eyes, hoping to concentrate more fully on listening. Finally he went back to the hearth to see if he might bring the few embers to life.

"I've fired up the bake-oven," Brother Hylas announced from beyond the door. "The dough is rising. There will be loaves ready at the time of first devotions, three hours before dawn." The monk chuckled. "We will have to delay our prayers, but we will say them in gratitude and thanksgiving."

"The men will be grateful for any food you provide," said Sant-Germainus.

"There will be meat, too, once I make the spit ready."

"If you let me out, I might help you," Sant-Germainus suggested.

"I am not permitted to do that, and well you know it," said Brother Hylas. "I am required to keep you where you are."

"Because I might be a diversion, or my story could be a ruse?" he guessed.

"Or you might warn your comrades: we won't allow that," said Brother Hylas; the last of this faded as he walked away from the door.

Sant-Germainus listened to the departing footsteps, his vexation increasing as he considered what he had stumbled into. At least he was on dry land, he reminded himself, and he would not have to deal with the pirates wholly on his own. But there was so much he needed to understand before the monks returned. Hoping to better understand his predicament, he took another turn about the long, narrow, dining hall, making note of the height and condition of the windows—too narrow to climb out of easily—as well as the layout of the room itself: dining hall it might be, but it also served as a prison. Finally he was satisfied that he had scrutinized the dining hall sufficiently—he understood how expertly he had been rendered ineffective. He sat on the end of the long bench and looked toward the far door. What on earth did these monks intend for the men of Captain Argourus' ship? He sighed slowly, letting the possibilities play through his head. "Very well," he said quietly. "Each of them are preparing an ambush, the monks and the pirates."

"You can make a plea to Saint Dismas," said Brother Hylas from beyond the door some little time later. "He may protect you. He protects thieves."

"Saint Dismas?" Sant-Germainus repeated.

"Our patron. We have taken goods and slaves when it has been necessary. Saint Dismas aids us, in the name of Christ. His likeness stands near you. Lift your oil-lantern and see him. You know he is the thief because his hand is struck off. We have made him our protector, and our guardian." He laughed and repeated "He protects thieves."

Sant-Germainus felt himself go cold. "Then I must suppose your Brothers are going to steal or capture the cargo and crew of the ship—as much as is left for the taking."

"Of course: we are thieves in honor of our saint. How else could such a place as this survive on this island? What God sends us, we gladly accept, in the name of our patron." He laughed. "Jesus paid for our sins, and we are redeemed through our faith. Saint Dismas is our provider, and as is his wont, he sends us plunder when we are in need. As to how we live, we live how we must."

"Holy criminals, in other words?" Sant-Germainus asked.

"Some might say so," Brother Hylas said, sounding both proud and amused. "We have often done deeds worthy of salvation, for which we give eternal thanks."

"And the men from the ship–?"

"They will be fed and given water if they will surrender and be sold. If they will not, then the sea shall have them, and God may spare them or leave them to the Devil."

"As has happened to many another?" Sant-Germainus guessed aloud.

"As you say," Brother Hylas chuckled. "You will have the right to choose if you will be slaves or drowned."

"All of us?"

"Yes. All of you." Brother Hylas paused. "In a month, ships will set out from Rhodes, and they will come here. We will exchange you seamen for the food and drink and oil the merchants of Rhodes bring us. There are enough of you that we may also get some gold."

"I see," said Sant-Germainus. "What will you do with us between then and now?"

"Set you to work," said Brother Hylas, as if it were obvious. "There is much to be done to this monastery, and to the harbor in the inlet below. You shall not be kept as hogs, to root and wallow all day. You shall labor as oxen labor."

Lowering his head, Sant-Germainus tried not to give way to ironic despair. After all the sea and pirates could do, that it should come to this! How fitting, he thought, that Captain Argourus would be captured by these Brothers! A pirate seized by thievish monks! He hesitated before he spoke again, for he would have to find a way to keep himself away from the rest of the men in their captivity—he and Rutgeros. He decided to take a risk. "You and your Brothers—do you accept ransoms as well as slave-prices?"

"If ransoms can be got," said Brother Hylas. "Why?"

"I am a merchant with many ships. The one on which I sailed, the *Morning Star*, was taken by pirates, and the crew and oarsmen put to work on their ship, which now lies on the south side of this island. They did not kill me because I have gold in Constantine's City, and in Tyre and Alexandria, which they planned to demand in ransom, and I am the blood relative of a rich widow of Roma: Domina Clemens. If you will keep me and my manservant, and the oarsmen and sailors from the *Morning Star* safe until spring, I will arrange for a handsome payment to you, through this woman, and supplies as well, as much as anything Captain Argourus could gain you."

"Gold in far places is gold on the moon," said Brother Hylas.

"My ships stop at Naxos; I can send word to my captains when shipping resumes. Until then, I will see that my crew and my manservant do nothing against you." As he said it, he shivered a little, knowing how much his men had already been pushed, and how difficult it would be too keep them in order.

"Why should you do this?" There was an edge in his question that revealed how great his doubts were.

"They are in danger from sailing on my vessel. I should do my utmost to see they do not suffer greater harm." He would have to dispatch a letter to Olivia as soon as any ship put in to the harbor; once Olivia knew he was in the hands of these monks, she would order a half-dozen of his ships to come after him, ready to deal with the monastery and its monks.

"Do you have gold to offer while we wait for shipping to resume?"

"I have a dozen jewels," countered Sant-Germainus. "The pirates did not find them because they did not know where to look." He knew Rutgeros would have the hollow brass sea-guide with him, and its concealed contents.

"And these are true jewels, not ones counterfeit?" Brother Hylas made no effort to conceal his interest.

"They are true jewels." Sant-Germainus had made them himself in his athanor. "If you will accept them, and spare my men, I will arrange for you to receive more."

"What is to stop me from taking your sea-guide from your servant and keeping the jewels for our monastery?"

"Only that this is the season of the Nativity, and your god sent us to you," said Sant-Germainus. "My manservant will point out the *Morning Star* crew when he and the others return."

"Brother Theron will have to decide. He rules here," said Brother Hylas, his voice sounding already half-persuaded.

"He would be a fool to refuse jewels, gold, and provisions," said Sant-Germainus.

"He would be a greater fool to keep worthless men about," Brother Hylas countered.

Sant-Germainus was silent for a short while, letting Brother Hylas reflect. Then he said, "Twenty gold coins for each of the oarsmen and crew, forty for my manservant, and fifty for me. It will be delivered on the first ship of my trading company to reach here from Ravenna in the spring." He knew the amount was double what they would fetch in a slave-market, and larger than many ransoms paid in the last decade. "And ten silver Emperors for every day you keep us here." The amount was not so much that it would tempt the Brothers to hold onto them, but enough to make housing and feeding them worthwhile.

"It is a goodly sum," said Brother Hylas. "And a promise easily made. It might not be so easily kept."

"Speak to the men from the *Morning Star* and they will tell you what I say is true. They know my ships and the wealth I may draw upon." He kept his tone level and his words unhurried.

Brother Hylas waited a while, considering. "If we do this, how do we know you will not summon fighting men rather than pay us?"

"I am a merchant, but I am also an exile. If I summon fighting men, they might well turn on me as much as you." It was true as far as it went; he took a deep breath, and added, "I have money enough to pay the amounts I have mentioned. Any ship of mine wintering on Paros or Naxos will be able to give you a first payment. You needn't release any of us until the full sum is paid." He would need to find a way to feed discreetly during the time they waited, but he had endured far worse in times past; he would be able to manage.

"Brother Theron might agree, but he might not: it is his decision."

"Then swear to me you will speak with him," said Sant-Germainus, "so that he may decide."

"If you lie, you will roast on a spit," said Brother Hylas.

"If I lie, I will deserve such a fate. A lie at the dark of the year is a double lie."

Brother Hylas was satisfied with this answer. "Very well. I will tell him." He hesitated. "You cannot escape. Even if you broke out of that hall, you cannot get out of the gate, and if you do, you are still on this island."

"I am aware of that," said Sant-Germainus drily.

"Then you will know that any falsehood will bring retribution, and quickly." Brother Hylas coughed importantly.

"I have more lives than mine to consider; I will not endanger us all," said Sant-Germainus. "I will do what I must to keep every one of my men from harm."

"And the pirates? Will you protect them, as well?"

"The pirates must make their own terms with Brother Theron," Sant-Germainus answered, grimness in his voice.

This time Brother Hylas took longer to speak. "If that is what you wish," he said, drawing his words out, "then Brother Hylas may agree."

"A mercy upon all of us," said Sant-Germainus with only a hint of sardonic intent.

"We are Christians here. We revere mercy, for love of God. We are thankful for Him and all He provides us," said Brother Hylas, apparently sincerely, going on, "I will now fetch a lamb to slaughter, so there will be food when my Brothers and the men from your ship return. If I bring you wood, will you build up the fire?"

"Will you allow me to slaughter the lamb?" Sant-Germainus asked quickly, a surge of energy running through him at the prospect of blood, even lamb's blood. "To give thanks for my deliverance from the storm?"

Brother Hylas laughed again. "You want to slaughter the lamb? I should warn you, it is nearly grown; one of the last from spring."

"No matter," said Sant-Germainus, adding with deliberate obfuscation, "It will suffice."

"I shouldn't give you a knife. Brother Hylas will have me whipped if I do."

"Do not fret," said Sant-Germainus, as if improvising a plan. "I will break the neck and hang it to bleed. I'll use a nail to open its throat." A nail would account for the nip of his teeth in the animal's neck. "There are nails in your benches. I will work a loose one out." He had not checked for loose nails but was confident he could find one or two.

Again Brother Hylas thought over his answer. "I don't see any danger in it. If you make the meat useless, I will tell Brother Theron and he will give you cause to regret it."

"When it is blooded, I will give it to you to gut," said Sant-Germainus, thinking back to the Year of Yellow Snow, when he had lived on less savory blood than lamb's. "The meat will be untainted."

Brother Hylas pondered the possibilities. "I will let you blood the lamb," he said, and was unaware of the sense of relief that washed through Sant-Germainus. "After that, you may turn the spit while I prepare the fish. Bread, fish, and lamb is a fitting meal for any Christian, particularly at the Nativity." So saying, he trudged away from the door, humming as he went.

Sant-Germainus returned to the long table and sat on its edge, his mind intent on the many things he would have to arrange in the next day or so if he, Rutgeros, his oarsmen and crew were to survive until their ransom could be brought. He did his best to ignore the hunger pangs that flared in him at the thought of lamb's blood; he had more urgent plans to make before Brother Theron returned. For an instant he recalled himself as a living youth, going at the dark of the year—the anniversary of his birth—to the sacred grove of his people, to drink the blood of his god so that he would become one of them upon his death, twenty-five centuries ago. With an impatient gesture, he banished that recollection from his mind. With an oath in a language only he remembered, he rose and began to look for a nail he could pull out of the table or bench to account for the holes that he would make in the throat of the lamb.

In a short while, Brother Hylas opened the door. "Come. I've got the lamb for you."

"Very good," said Sant-Germainus, and followed him to the barn at the edge of the monastery wall.

"I should watch you kill him, to be sure you keep your word."

Little as he wanted this to happen, Sant-Germainus feigned indifference. "If you think I have any way to harm the meat, then watch."

"I have work to do in the larder," said Brother Hylas, and shoved Sant-Germainus toward the pen where a small sheep bleated. He pulled the gate open and shoved Sant-Germainus inside. "I'll be back in a while. If the lamb isn't dead and blooded, you will answer for it."

"I will," agreed Sant-Germainus, and set about alleviating his ravening esurience. Only when the sheep was hanging from a rope did Sant-Germainus call out for Brother Hylas to finish the task of butchering the animal. While he waited, he thought again of the irony that had brought him to this place, at this time of year: among the centuries that had passed since his death at the hands of his enemies, few of them had marked the anniversary of his birth so pointedly as this one. No matter how he might end up leaving the island, this first night on Dhenoussa would remain unique and vivid in his memory until the end of his undead life.

TALES
OUT OF
SCHOOL

AUTHOR'S NOTES
Europe in 1325 was experiencing what is sometimes called the Little Ice Age, a period of bad weather that impacted most of the world. Although not so hard-hit as northern Europe, Italy was struck with frequent, severe storms that could and often did lay waste to crops, flooded fields, damaged houses and roads, and killed livestock. The population was higher than it had been since the collapse of the Roman Empire, which made the arrival of the Black Plague, twenty years after this story, so particularly devastating.

Padova (Padua) had become a university town just over a century before this novella takes place, and was feeling growing pains. Town-and-gown problems had arisen and it took more than a little diplomacy to resolve them. The university itself had an Atheneum (administration building and principle lecture hall) on the site of the slaughterhouses at the edge of the livestock market and the barns where soap was made. The university is still there, in a later building than the one of this time, but the stockyards and rendering barns are long-gone— all that remains are the nick-name of the university: the Bo, for beef, and the cow-skull symbol of the university. Although the famous anatomy theater had not yet been built, Padova was already beginning to allow clandestine dissections of bodies for the study of medicine and natural sciences. The Pallazzo della Ragione—the courts building—remains in its original location, but its remarkable roof had not yet been built, nor had the gigantic bronze horse that now stands within it been cast. The city had more wooden buildings than it does now, and few but the main streets were paved or cobbled.

Like many large Italian towns of the period, Padova was run by a Consiglio—a council—which were supported by Artei—Guilds—and Confraterne—fraternal civic organizations. The university had its own Consiglio, similar to a modern Board of Regents. Finding comity among such diverse groups often proved difficult for even the most amiable town leaders, and late-Medieval society was not generally known for its bonhomie.

Language, too, was somewhat different than modern Italian, and I have used the fourteenth century versions of many words for verisimilitude. Most legal documents were written in Latin, but a surprising number of private documents and correspondence remains, using the common language of the time—what is called the vulgate. Fortunately, the university has kept many records and other writing from this time, some of which I have used as a source for this story. In the decades before the Plague, foreigners were welcome at the university, which led to a cosmopolitan environment, more academic than that of near-by Venezia, but still drawing on the wide cultural variety of that city, within whose hegemony Padova flourished as an intellectual center—which it remains to this day.

Thanks are due to Vivian Mecklunder for her knowledge of historical herbal studies, to C. L. Thall for access to information on Italian cities before the Black Plague, and to Margaret Wilkes for the use of her references on 14th century medicine. Most especially, thanks are due to the people of Padova and Gargoyle Books for receiving me and my work so kindly last March. You are truly an inspiration.

—Chelsea Quinn Yarbro
Berkeley, California
August, 2006

ENTRY IN THE JOURNAL of Antonio Vincenzo Mergazza di Aurelio dei Cioventi, recording clerk of the Consiglio Communale di Padova, dated the day before Lady Day, 1325.

There were complaints heard today in the Palazzo della Ragione in the Camera di Imparia, against the teaching of anatomy now being countenanced, if not approved, by the Universita. It is agreed that such instruction has no place in the Atheneum itself, for all that it is built upon a slaughterhouse, and the sight of bones is nothing new there. But such practices as dissections are sins, and those who undertake to desecrate the bodies of the dead face punishment in this life and the life to come, and so all procedures of this kind must be carried out covertly. The covert exercises in anatomical studies are considered an affront to the Universita by a number of their own Magisters. Carlo Zianno, a man I will not dignify with the title of physician, has been summoned before the Consiglio for the purpose of explaining how these charges have come to be leveled at him and his students. They are to appear in three days.

Padre Fiorello Rienetto has informed the Consiglio that he has allocated half of the house he inherited from his uncle to the use of Orazia degli Avei, the widow of his brother Serafino Rienetto, who died in Roma two years ago. Her own family is much reduced by the fever that claimed her own husband, and so can offer her no home with them; it falls to his relatives to provide for her. Padre Rienetto has been advised by his uncle, Alvise Rienetto of Verona, that it is more appropriate for Padre Rienetto to house her than for his uncle, their relationship being closer, and less subject to public censure. Since she is amenable to the arrangement, the Vescovio Strofinaccio has given his approval; the Consiglio received it and endorsed it this afternoon, as was expected. This should put an end to all the gossip about the woman in Padre Rienetto's house.

Leoncio and Lucio Pavona petitioned the Consiglio for the right to divide their father's estate in separate portions, claiming that they are unable to agree on how they are to proceed with the business, and are unable to reach an accord that includes them all working together as their father had intended. Leoncio proposes to continue running the weavery while Lucio will be in charge of the fulling mills as distinct and unconnected ventures. The Consiglio has taken the petition under advisement and will announce their decision in a week.

Enrico Giordianus, as he styles himself, has finally agreed upon a price for the house he built three years ago near the Herb Market. The purchaser is a foreigner from Hungarian lands, a nobleman in exile, Francecco di San-Germanus dei Ragoczy, who has paid the full price in jewels and gold. Consigliero Davinello has witnessed the deed for the Commune and has given full access to the property to San-Germanus, who has proposed building a glass house in the walled garden for the raising of plants, and offered to pay his taxes on such a property for three years in advance. He has also agreed to set aside two chambers on the ground floor of his house for the purpose of making displays of some of his possessions brought from distant lands, and to allow students access to them for the purpose of enlarging their knowledge. He may agree to teach the preparation of medicaments from the herbs he is growing, and those he imports from distant lands.

Aroldo Fiumare, Giusto Stringe, and Uliviero Pradelli were accused of brawling in public. All of them were drunk at the time of their row, and no one was seriously hurt. Since Pradelli and Stringe are students, it will be left for the Universita to deal with them, but as Fiumare is a local vintner, the Consiglio has exercised its right to impose fines on all the men. This is the second time Stringe has been before the Consiglio for fighting, and the punishment he faces is more severe. A brief on Stringe's activities will be sent to the Universita in the hope that the Senior Scholars may prevail upon him to mend his ways.

The weather continues cool for spring, but local farmers report their early crops are taking hold in spite of the lingering chill.

◆ ◆ ◆

As her blood touched his lips, he knew.

Even as he held her naked, vibrant, weeping for joy, replete with passion, and trembling with the force of her fulfillment in his arms, he knew. And more than his certainty, he was aware that she also knew.

Orazia opened her eyes and stared at him. "Dazzled. I am dazzled. I have never felt anything so . . . personal. You . . . you surprised me." Under her gratification, there was a note of unease, an admission that she had exposed more of herself than she had intended, and was now becoming worried about it. She moved back from him half-a-handsbreadth and tried to make out his expression in the enveloping darkness. "And it seems you did nothing for yourself."

"I did all that I am capable of doing, from all you were willing to give; I am as satisfied as you are, for your satisfaction is mine," he said, touching the short curls that had come loose around her face. "I trust you were not—"

From below the shuttered window came the muffled songs of a group of students, merrily drunk, on their way back to their rooms. One shaky tenor led the rest in their serenades. The Latin verses they caroled were scurrilous and salacious; the students laughed at the most reprehensible couplets.

"Oafs!" Orazia said, and pummeled the nearest pillow with her fist. "How can God make such creatures?" Her hair, almost white although she was only twenty-nine, spilled around her shoulders; she tossed it behind her.

"They are like students everywhere," said San-Germanus, his thoughts going back centuries to Egypt, to Athens, to Baghdad, to Lo-Yang, to Paris, to Rome. "All youth is restive, students more so than most. They find a way to relieve the demands of their studies, and to make the most of their maturescence. If they truly want to learn, they must spend their time challenging what they have been taught, and that imposes singleness of purpose upon them that demands much; occasionally that rigor necessitates relief."

"You sound like my uncle, except that he said that God gives all students such temperament so they will be able to pursue their studies. It is the nature of scholars to modify their scholarship with carousal and the solace of merry companions.

None who lacks such a nature can become a student, according to him, and he believes that those who teach them must also protect them. You see, like you, Alvise defends them too, when he can. There are fewer students in Verona, of course, and they are better-behaved, or so he claims. But he does not live near where they do, so he may not know them as well as you must do." She stretched out, neatly and kindly enforcing the distance between them, small as it was. "Some of them may be Fiorello's students, if they are studying law: most of them are—studying law, or so it seems," she said as the voices below were lost in fading echoes. "He will be back in two days."

"From Venezia?" San-Germanus asked.

"Yes. He and the rest of the delegation for merchants' contracts." She rolled a bit of lint into a pill and blew it away.

"He teaches in his house, does he not?" San-Germanus inquired, sensing her preoccupation with the noise from outside.

"Advanced students, yes. Some classes are given under the bull's skull," by which she meant in the Atheneum next to the slaughterhouse. She lay back and extended her arm upward. "What do you think? Have I a few years left in me, or are they fading away already? Am I in the afternoon or twilight of my life?" She let her arm drop.

San-Germanus pushed himself up on his elbow, and looked down at her. "Orazia," he said, to make her turn toward him.

"What?" she asked without any indication of emotion.

"You need not tell me if you would rather not, but do you know what is wrong?" He asked the question so gently that she began to weep, covering her eyes with her hand. For a short while she indulged in tears, ignoring his attempts at comfort, but then she wiped her face and rolled toward him.

"No, I do not know what is wrong, and no physician does, either. They agree I am failing, but none can tell me why, or from what cause. I have consulted with several physicians, from Roma to Milano. All they told me at Bologna is that it was beyond their powers to define." She took a deep, shuddering breath. "Whatever it is, I fear it will be my death."

"It may be, if you do nothing," he said, thinking back to the many times he had encountered this most perplexing illness: low fever, debilitation, poor appetite, pain in many parts of the body, fragile bones, swollen joints, paleness, lethargy, failure to thrive. There were many illnesses that created such symptoms, and all of them were ominous; her whitened hair suggested that she had taken the disease some years before, and that, too, worried him. Yet he had seen others with similar complaints who had survived their maladies; some few, those whose blood smelled and tasted as hers did—more metallic and bitter than most blood—rarely recovered. He knew he would have to make serious efforts if he was to treat her successfully, providing she would allow him to prepare medicaments for her at all, or would accept his care.

"That may be said of many ills," she snapped, the excitement of their ecstasy fading away much too rapidly.

"But with study, something more specific may be learned, and a course of treatment determined," he suggested. "Even unknown illnesses can be made to give up some of their secrets."

"How am I to decide on any course when the nature of the illness is unknown?" she challenged as she turned away from him onto her side once more.

He touched her shoulder lightly. "I have been taught that when the cause is unknown, then one must treat the conditions of the illness, and that I am able to do. You have several symptoms that may be addressed with herbs and a sovereign remedy of sorts. You might be able to lessen the vehemence of the condition with time and the appropriate medicaments. If nothing else, I can ease your discomfort." It was a lesson he had learned at the Temple of Imhotep, and he had followed its principle for more than two millennia. He propped himself on his elbow and stroked her arm. "Orazia, you are not to despair, for that is as deadly as any malady."

"How can you tell? Is it in *you*? Have you taken it from me?"

"I tell you because it is in your blood." He strove to say this as gently as possible.

"My blood is contaminated?" Her face was darkening with ire. "Does that mean I am unclean, like a leper?"

"No, no," he assured her. "No. Some diseases do contaminate the blood, others . . . influence it, give it a different character than is usual." He could see she was not comprehending him. "Some diseases season the blood, as one might season a soup, affecting it but without changing its nature." He had the grace to look abashed at this analogy. "Inelegant and degrading, as comparisons go, but apt nonetheless."

"You tell me this because you have slept with me without compromising my honor? You say that my blood is badly flavored?" She was angry now, trying to hold her desperation at bay by giving free rein to her temper.

"No, I say it because I have tasted your blood and that is the most personal knowledge that I can have of you," he explained patiently, all the while gently touching her shoulder, her arm, her hand. "Your blood is not robust. It has lost some of its vitality. That is one of the reasons you are pale."

She laughed a bit wildly. "How very sweet. I am an unsavory, unwholesome meal."

"I would not call you that," he said, aware that she was trying to provoke him. "And I *did not* call you that, but by way of clumsy comparison."

"Then what? You can't tell me that you are able to get what you require from my ill-tasting blood."

He touched her face, his fingers light but holding her complete attention. "Taste is not what you give me, Orazia, it is something much more important: intimacy, touching, nourishment of the soul as well as body, and these qualities have nothing to do with your own condition, except that I know what you endure because of it; I promise you, I will be alert to your responses to keep you from giving up more than is wise."

"Endure?" She did her best not to sigh. "Is that what I must do? You make it sound so tedious and unpleasant."

"I would hope that you will permit me–"

"Permit?" She broke free of his compelling gaze. "Given who and what you are, you could have been much more demanding—what choice would I have, now that I am in your house, with your servants around us? I am at your mercy, or so it seems. You could keep me a prisoner here, you could debauch me. I don't think my brother-in-law would protest too much, unless you were flagrant about your conquest. He would not bring scandal upon Rienetto for his sister-in-law. It would embarrass him, so he would keep quiet."

"Did you intend that I should abuse you? Is that what you want from me?" In spite of what long experience had taught him, he was stung by her suggestion, but he went on levelly, "I have given you no reason to expect that of me, nor will I ever do so." Those times were many centuries behind him but they still had the capacity to dismay him.

"Oh, very good," she approved, striking her pillow with her fist. "Wounded innocence. How touching."

"Not wounded, and certainly not innocent—not as you intend it," he said softly, no trace of anger or impatience in his words. He bent and kissed her neck, next to the two small holes he had made at the peak of her passion. "You will not drive me off with insults; you have done too much to reveal yourself. You offered me the whole of you, and that is what I know now."

She glared at him, getting ready to banish him from her bed. "You have discerned—I didn't intend to show you anything."

He held his tongue, aware that she was frightened; he smoothed the sheet carefully, waiting for her to speak.

"Aren't you afraid you will take my malady, lying with me in this way?" There was a hidden plea in this sarcastic question.

"No; no disease can touch those of my blood." He reached for her free hand and carried it to his lips. "Do you want my help?"

She glowered at him, then struck the pillow with her fist. "I want to recover," she said softly as if to protect herself from her own desire. "I suppose I must want your help."

"You may have it, to the full extent of my skills, for as long as you require them." He leaned toward her and kissed her, slowly and deeply. "I would not want to lose one moment of time we might enjoy each other."

She tried to glare at him and failed. "You are a strange man, San-Germanus, and not just for the way you take your pleasure."

"So I have been told," he admitted, and ran his hand down her arm. "Think about what you would want to ease your life just now and I will put myself to the task of providing whatever assistance I may."

"This will mean potions and vile-tasting mixtures, and meals of gruel, I suppose?" She sounded disheartened as she asked.

"I will try not to burden you with any of those," he said. "But I will supply you with medicaments, not all of which are sweet."

Orazia slid away from him. "Not just yet, I pray you." She put her hands together as if to hold him off. "Let me pretend for a little while longer that I have just got a slight fever, as many do in April: one that will pass quickly." She smiled at him, her face suffused with a kind of delirium. "Leave me my dream."

He regarded her somberly. "It may be a foolish indulgence."

"I would not think so," she said firmly.

He touched her arm again, his fingers moving as if of their own volition toward the soft swell of her breast. "Do not wait too long, Orazia. I would not like to see you–"

"–suffer more?" she finished for him.

"Yes," he said quietly.

She stared at him, her pulse beating heavily; she tried to smile at him, but her mouth trembled and before she knew what had happened, she was weeping; his arms went around her as if to shield her from her misery. "Saints protect me," she murmured as she wiped at her tears with the backs of her hands.

"Orazia," he said, kissing her brow, "let me help you."

"I don't want to sicken. I don't want to die," she said as if she were apologizing for a great failing.

This time he kissed her eyelids, and promised her, "I will do all I can to keep that from happening."

◆ ◆ ◆

Excerpt from the journal of Filipo Quandt of Avignon, Master of Herbal Virtues, dated April 1st, 1325

The Consiglio Communale here in Padova has decided to expand the license of the Universita to include the study of herbs and all manner of plants, including the insalubrious ones, so that the character of their dangers may be known and catalogued, the better to treat them when they are encountered in patients. I have asked that the advice of the Arte degli Erbei be sought so that a high standard may be maintained in this regard. My years among the Byzantines has shown me all manner of noxious plants not generally known in this part of the world. I have expressed my fear that with so lax a set of terms for the cultivation of plants, those of malign purpose might well take advantage of this new regulation and undertake to supply poisons unknown to many physicians in this country, whereby much mischief can be done. I have been told the Consiglio will make a decision within ten days' time, and that I will be notified promptly of their decision. I will pray to il Santo to guide their deliberations and to grant them the wisdom God gives His servants.

The students say that Fra Jacoppo da Feltre Minore has taken in a six-toed cat against the orders of his Superior, who told Fra Jacoppo that such an animal was unnatural and should be killed to prevent any mischief it might do. Anything so against nature is an affront to God, protecting something like that cat. It is just such cases as this one that the new Arte degli Erbei must seek to contain as it touches the study of plants, for without stringent guidance, it is possible that the interests of scholars would stray into areas of inquiry that might well lead to such knowledge as could corrupt the souls of Christians, for many plants have virtues that quickly lead to vices among errant men.

A Greek scholar has arrived in the town, proclaiming himself as a skilled anatomist. The Consiglio della Universita has agreed to test him and determine if he is as well-informed as he claims. If he is, he may be offered a position with the faculty, if Vescovio Strofinaccio allows it. There is still strong objections to such studies from those upholding the Church's stricture against the desecration of the dead, no matter how noble the cause for doing so may be. With the Church fixed on preserving the body, the Universita exposes itself and all who teach there in any discipline, to the scrutiny of the Church, and the consequence of such heretical tolerance.

◆ ◆ ◆

Rotgiere set down a sack of mulch, looking around the herbhouse with its precious roof of glass; two of the panes were open, propped by braces designed for that purpose, to let in breezes and to adjust the heat inside. He glanced toward the cloudy sky and said to San-Germanus, who was busy with a pot of seedlings, "I think we could have rain this afternoon."

"I would not be surprised." The Latin they spoke was that of Imperial Rome, not that of modern scholars or the Church.

"Shall I close the roof windows?" Rotgiere asked.

"Let me attend to it," said San-Germanus, somewhat preoccupied.

"As you wish. The air is freshening."

"So it is," said San-Germanus. "It smells of rain."

"And at least we are upwind of the soap-makers," said Rotgiere with the suggestion of a smile.

This got San-Germanus' attention, and he gave a quick nod in agreement. "Pardon me, old friend. I want to get these transplanted this afternoon; I have lost track of time."

"Just so," said Rotgiere. He patted the sack. "They say they've removed all the weeds."

"As well they should. Thank you," said San-Germanus, looking over at the sack of mulch. "You had that—"

"From the clearing of the stand of trees by the stream just east of the town, as you requested. I gave the landowner a good price for this, and arranged to get more, if this proves adequate to your requirements," said Rotgiere. "Pigs have been kept in the confines of the woods, and with the trees cut for more houses, the land will soon be tilled." Rotgiere made a sign that meant they were being overhead; San-Germanus nodded his understanding.

"Very good," San-Germanus approved, though whether of the mulch or the warning, he did not specify. "Dead leaves, old brush, and the effluvia of hogs. The plants should flourish."

"The mulch will hold moisture through the summer and stop the plants from freezing in winter," said Rotgiere.

"Always something to be desired," said San-Germanus, going to fetch the long pole with the pruning hook on the end that he used to close the open windows. "How long do you suppose the rain will last?"

"They say in the herb-market that it will rain through the night."

"And through tomorrow, I should think," said San-Germanus. "The weather is heavy, and the clouds are very dark."

"And, as you said, the air smells of rain."

"And as you said, better that than soap."

Rotgiere untied the cord at the mouth of the sack of mulch. "Do you need me for anything more, or have you other duties for me?"

"I would appreciate it if you and Orso would go around to Fedele, the wine-merchant, select the best bottles and casks of their stock, and bring it back here. I want to have ample drink for the banquet I am planning for next Tuesday. Now that we have settled upon a date, we must make the most of it. With Wednesdays fast days and Fridays meatless days, Sundays reserved for religious exercises, and Mondays for public hearings, there are few days left to extend hospitality to the masters of the Atheneum."

"Tuesday it will be. You have dispatched your invitations?" Rotgiere asked out of habit; he was certain that San-Germanus had done so.

"Adrasto carried them for me yesterday: you were out at

the wool-market. There are sixteen invited, all men of good standing, and all on good terms with one another. Two of them have minor titles, so I will make no mention of my own, except as an exile." He thought for a long moment. "I showed you the proposed guest list three days since, did I not?"

"Yes. I'm sorry; I should have remembered; I have been preoccupied with the joiners and builders, the glazers, and the mercers." He made an impatient motion with his hand. "I apologize, my master."

"You have no reason to do so," said San-Germanus. "I, too, have been preoccupied. I am grateful you are willing to attend to the changes in this house."

"I still should have been more aware of what you had arranged," said Rotgiere, dismayed at his failure to anticipate San-Germanus' needs.

"After we considered so many different days for the banquet, I am surprised that you can recall which one we settled upon."

"Do you suppose you will want to add any more guests?" Rotgiere asked.

"Probably not, unless half these men decline my invitation." He went to the opened sack and reached in to finger the mulch. "Very good. I may want another sack before the week is out."

"You have only to tell me and I will procure more."

"I will do," San-Germanus said. "But it will be for later—once the banquet is finished."

"As you wish," said Rotgiere,

San-Gernanus continued his work with plants for a short while, then said, "I should think of what gift I will present my guests,"

"Useful seedlings might be welcome," said Rotgiere, "or a pouch of spices—not too much, or you will be thought rich."

"But I am rich," said San-Germanus with the ghost of a smile.

Rotgiere did not allow himself to respond. "You also have vials of your sovereign remedy that they might value."

"All of those would do," San-Germanus agreed, "But I would like to find something remarkable to offer, something that would incline them to extending more than courtesy to me."

"Padova is not like Venezia—what they value here is more knowledge than foreign markets, so you may want to give them the maps you have from your eastern travels, or a few of the small brasses you have imported from Madras," Rotgiere observed. "Tell me what impression you seek to make and I will try to recommend that which will achieve your ends."

"I would like to have full access to the Atheneum and the right to import all manner of books without the permission of the Church censor. I would like to have access to the libraries at Bologna and Fiorenza." He spoke so quickly that Rotgiere was certain that San-Germanus had been weighing his options for most of the morning.

"Others have received such permission; there is no reason you should not."

"So I think, but it will depend upon how I am assessed by the men attending the banquet. I am a foreigner, and that makes it more difficult to persuade them to accept me except as an instructor for the students." He reached over and plucked a small bud from a spiky stem. "This will be used for an infusion. If you will bring spirits of wine?"

"Of course," said Rotgiere, knowing that San-Germanus would say nothing more about the guest-gifts for now. With a single nod he left San-Gernanus to fetch the keg of spirits of wine.

◆ ◆ ◆

Excerpt from the journal of Flavio Castrabella, student of herbs and other medicaments, dated April 9th, 1325.

Magister Quandt has gained permission for me to study with the foreigner, San-Germanus, who is said to have access to many spices, gums, resins, and roots from as far away as China, and who is known to provide medicaments to those in need of them for no cost; he is rumored to be associated with the Eclipse Trad-

ing Company in Venezia, which would account for his obvious wealth. Having permission to study with him will provide me a great opportunity to expand my knowledge, as well as to have the opportunity to gain skills I might not otherwise acquire thus early in my studies. It is also a good opportunity to establish good relations with the traders with whom I will have to do business in future. In return for this splendid propitiousness, I have pledged to report to Magister Quandt on everything I learn from San-Germanus to the Magister, a more than fair exchange to my way of thinking.

In preparation for becoming San-Germanus' student, I have purchased a large shoulder-wallet for collecting herbs, barks, and roots in order to accommodate the nature of San-Germanus' instruction, which is partly discussion and partly preparation demonstrations. I have also purchased jars and vials for tinctures, unguents, and lotions, and another substance we may make. I do not want to appear lax in my determination, so I am doing all that I may to be ready to undertake everything this course may require; thus will I show Magister Quandt and San-Germanus that I will fulfill my obligation as a student.

◆ ◆ ◆

San-Germanus stood over a large pot in which contained a viscous green liquid from which a strong-smelling steam arose. "This," he announced to his four students, "must be kept over hot coals, not boiling, but so that the steam may come off it, as you see it is doing now. Once the desired thickness is attained, then the substance must be removed from the fire and cooled slowly, but not allowed to stand uncovered for more than an hour. The final decoction should be the thickness of syrup, and as densely colored as Indian emeralds."

Andrea Vecchiato looked into the pot with interest. "How long will preparing this decoction take?"

"Done properly, and in this amount, two days," said San-Germanus. "If the weather is damp, it may take longer." He nodded to Enzo Grimanni, the youngest of the four. "Do you have any questions?"

"You put much importance on washing the leaves in vinegar-water before putting them into the spring-water to simmer. Why must they be washed?"

"To remove the atomites that live on them, for minuscule creatures live on all things," said San-Germanus promptly.

"Why should that be?" Enzo asked; he was fifteen and easily bored. He pulled at his fashionably long hair and strove not to roll his eyes.

"How can you be certain they are there?" Silvio asked nervously, being unaccustomed to challenging an instructor.

"You have only to look about you and to observe with care; there are many things we must infer rather than examine; one day closer examination may be possible, and our diligence now may speed later discoveries," said San-Germanus, undeterred by Enzo's apparent lack of concern, and Silvio's edginess. "All things in nature have smaller creatures that live upon them, and can, in so doing, corrupt them: think of the fever-bugs that are found in our beds if we do not take measures against them." He had learned this theory in China, eight hundred years ago, and over time had wished he had some way to investigate the extent of the teaching, some technique for exposing the atomites and to learn their natures; he put his curiosity aside. "The same is true of plants. You do not want to compromise the efficacy of the decoction through such minuscule vitiation."

Enzo shook his head. "A strange principle, if true."

Flavio Castrabella was frowning. "You said that the buds were not to be used, only the leaves. Doesn't that limit the generative principle? Surely the buds would provide the impetus to accumulate the restorative properties of the plant?" He had done some reading already and was eager to show off his knowledge.

"Not for this preparation, no. But you want to release all the virtue in the leaves, which is why you must bruise them with a pestle before setting them to simmer."

"What about the Syrian clarifying gum?" asked Silvio Mordero, the son of a minor aristocrat who had more ambitions than means to help his sons. "Is there nothing else we can use?

It is hard to come by and expensive."

San-Germanus removed the pot from the glowing coals and set it on an iron cooling-stand. "No, unfortunately not when making this decoction; nothing I have found supports the decoction as well without giving the patient discomfort, which is not advisable. Thrice-strained honey may be used for other decoctions, but not this one. Fortunately, Syrian gum it is very powerful, and you will not need much of this decoction to treat the eruptions I have described; in fact, small amounts are more efficacious than large ones when dealing with rashes and hives. Also, there is a tincture using Angelica root that may stop itching and burning." He wiped his hands carefully. "This should be ready to be sealed in glass containers by the end of the day."

"Must the containers be glass?" Flavio inquired, determined to challenge San-Germanus on every point of his instruction.

"I believe so, yes," said San-Germanus. "The glass has fewer flaws than most sorts of vessels that could allow the substances of the container itself to leach into the medicament, a process that may taint the decoction."

"Would you recommend this for the treatment of children? They often have youthful poxes and require something to lessen the inflammation and itching of the eruptions." Andrea, who was somewhat short-sighted, bent over to peer at the substance in the pot. "How would you administer it to a child?"

"This is not the medicament you may want to use for children; it is too intense for their tender bodies. There is an ointment that will reduce the degree of swelling and the discomfort of youthful poxes and similar conditions. You may use it with confidence on all but infants of less than a year. But I will demonstrate that later, when you have mastered a few more techniques." San-Germanus pointed to the athanor at the end of his laboratory: made of brick it resembled a bee-hive, coming to a rounded point on the top, and having a double door of iron on its side. "You will need one of these to prepare that remedy."

"One needs permission of the Consiglio della Universita to own such an oven," said Silvio, looking dejected. "They are not likely to grant that to us."

"Perhaps not," said San-Germanus, "but it would be appropriate to inquire; to assume that it is impossible and therefore to do nothing, guarantees that it is. I have asked that you four be allowed to own one jointly for the duration of your studies with me, and the Consiglio della Universita has granted permission." His donation of one hundred ducats to the expansion of the Atheneum library had helped to secure the license.

The four young men exchanged glances, each trying to discern how much excitement was appropriate for them to express. Finally Flavio could stand it no longer and asked, "Where will this athanor be built?"

"I have arranged with Baltasarre Procoppio to build one in his bake-house, reserved for you. You may not use it in the early morning when his ovens will be fired for the day's bread, but once the main baking is completed, you will have access to the bake-house, with the approvals of both the universita and the Commune. So long as you do not interfere with the bakers, you will be permitted to continue your experiments." He noticed the light of mischief in Flavio's eyes, and held up a hand in warning. "Since the permission is conditional, you would be wise to be punctilious in your observations of the advantage the baker is granting you. If you cause difficulties for him, the Consiglio della Universita will rescinded their license and it will be unlikely that anyone else inside the city walls will do so much for you, except, perhaps, the soapmakers, if you wish to study in their rendering barn." He did not mention the ten ducats he had paid to the baker to secure this opportunity, or that he would expect the four young men to visit the rendering barn as part of their alchemical studies with him.

"In all that stink?" Silvio was shocked at the notion.

"Rendering is important to more than soap, and you will need to know how it is done," said San-Germanus. "You will need to know in order to secure certain necessary substances for your various concoctions."

"And we will need soap, as well," said Flavio. "All the writing says so. Hands must be washed at the conclusion of every step of the alchemical process."

"I will show you how to improve soap so that it is less harsh and smells more pleasant than what you have available now," said San-Germanus.

"That may all be very well," said Flavio, "but I want to know more than how to perfume rendered fat."

"And so you shall," said San-Germanus.

"How soon?" Enzo inquired.

"By the end of summer, before you go home for the harvest, you should know at least seven procedures," San-Germanus paused and added, "That is, if you have been diligent in your studies. I am prepared to teach you a procedure every ten to fifteen days if you are willing to learn at that pace. I will suit my instruction to your comprehension."

Flavio and Andrea chuckled, Silvio looked embarrassed, but Enzo brazened it out. "I will do what you require, Magister," he said in Latin. "So long as it leads to learning."

"Of course you will," said San-Germano, with only a faint suggestion of irony in his voice.

Flavio spoke up. "So when must we begin with the athanor? Do we need any special clothing or supplies?"

"It will be May before you work with the athanor. I have to build it first, and may only do so in the night, when the bakers are gone," San-Germanus reminded them. "By the time it is built, you will have learned enough to use it properly."

"You will build it, not bricklayers?" Andrea asked, startled into speech.

"This is not a task for bricklayers," said San-Germanus. "Very few of them know how to created the interior of the athanor so that its heat is uniform."

"Why do you say so? Why do you have to lower yourself to the work of uneducated men?" Enzo demanded. "We are not craftsmen, we are scholars."

San-Germanus turned his dark eyes on Enzo. "No, Enzo Grimanni, you are not scholars. You are students who aspire to scholarship. It will be years before you are truly a scholar. So long as you keep that in mind, you may one day be worthy of that appellation; for now, concentrate on being a pupil, and you will make progress." He stopped, then went on less intensely. "If you are interested in learning to build an athanor, you may join me to work on it. You would be well-advised to wear a workman's leather smock and gloves. The mortar I use is too corrosive for hands."

The four students shifted uncomfortably, trying to discern the thoughts of their comrades before expressing any opinion or asking anything more. Andrea and Flavio considered the other two as if to try to think them into inquiry. Finally Andrea said, "Is there any crime in using such a device? Is its use prohibited?"

"Not that I am aware of," said San-Germanus. "Not in this city at least; in Spain it could get you flayed, but we are not there."

The students looked about uneasily, unsure if he was joking or not. They fidgeted and tried to assume a calm they lacked. Flavio spoke for them all when he said, "If you will secure a bona fides copy of your license, we would all appreciate it."

San-Germanus nodded slowly. "I will do so, of course. I would not want to expose you to any consequences that would compromise your scholarship."

Silvio ducked his head. "We would be grateful, Magister," he said, and managed to keep his attention on the substance in the pot.

"If you will also inform Magister Mencigo that you have permission to teach us these things, I will be grateful." Andrea seemed abashed by his own request.

"I will," said San-Germano; Redentore Mencigo was known to be a stickler for form, and never more that when the topic studied might clash with his own teaching in Christian philosophy.

"Do we meet again on Friday?" asked Enzo.

"Yes, we do," said San-Germano. "If you will come after Mass, we can begin in the glass-house; I will show you how to prepare pots for planting, and how to arrange your herbs to gain the most from the sun. That is important now that there are so many storms."

"It is a judgment upon the earth," said Flavio. "Fra Gualtiero spoke on Friday of the dangers around us, showing the Apocalypse is upon us."

"It is certainly unfortunate, but no more a judgment than a–" San-Germanus could not think of a natural disaster of phenomenon that was not presently seen as a judgment, so he stopped and began again. 'Weather is changeable, that much is obvious, season to season, year to year. But the degree of change is always an element in its severity. This is a time of volatile change: another time may present less fluctuation than we see now."

"But why should the weather change? The world is made to balance perfectly—could a perfectly balanced world have unbalanced weather, but that God makes it so?" asked Enzo. "The Church says that severe weather is proof of God's displeasure in man."

"Weather has no temperament, it has only wind or stillness, damp or dry, hot or cold," said San-Germanus, and then, seeing the distress in the young men's faces, went on, "A storm is a storm, not a manifestation of wrath or disappointment. Think of the distant lands of India and Arabia, where the air is hotter than here, and where storms come with sand, not rain. A sunny day is a time when the winds keep the skies clear." He realized he would have to modify his position a little more. "At least for the purposes of your studies with me, consider it so."

Flavio mulled over San-Germanus' remarks, saying, "This is a most irregular approach to learning, but for now, I will try to comply with your demands."

"That is very good of you," said San-Germanus, amusement hidden in dignity.

"The universita was founded by those seeking liberty of inquiry," said Silvio, reminding them all of the story of the Universita di Padova, spoken of with pride to this day.

"If you teach heresy, we will have to report it," said Andrea, unable to look directly at the foreigner in black.

The four muttered their pledge to guard against unorthodox teaching.

"What do you think you will ask us to prepare next?" Silvio seemed eager to change their awkward topic.

"Let us complete this first, and then I will tell you," said San-Germanus, touching the side of the pot he had been using. "You can determine for yourself that this is nearly cool enough to strain into a glass container."

Spared any more ineptitude on philosophical matters, the four students gave him their full attention, glad that they would not have to address issues they felt might overwhelm them. For now, the basic principles of alchemy were all they wanted to deal with.

◆ ◆ ◆

Excerpt from the journal of Rotgiere da Cadiz, written in Imperial Latin and dated April 14th, 1325.

The river is still running high, and floods are reported in some low-lying parts of the city. They say the mountain passes are still filled with snow, but that the thaw is progressing quickly, which could bring more flooding. Some of the farmers from around the city have asked for permission to bring their animals inside the walls if there is any more high water. The Consiglio Communale has agreed to permitting a limited number of sheep, goats, and hogs to be kept in the pens of the stockyards until the waters subside, which means the university is constantly being serenaded by the bleats and grunts of the beasts. Stables and pens have been filled to capacity and may still be insufficient to the needs of the local farms.

With the rains continuing so late into the spring, planting has been delayed, and in some instances, buds have taken rot on the branch, and may not fruit for the summer. Perhaps a dozen farms near the city are late in being able to plant. Word came from Rovigo that many fields there are not yet fully drained of floodwater. Three vinyards are now considered lost for this year's vintage. *Also a bridge at Rovigo was knocked down due to fallen trees being washed against the supports. It will take months to repair the crossing, and already some are muttering about the damage this could do to trade in the next months. If Rovigo is hard-hit, what must be the case in smaller villages? By summer we may see the beginning of famine in the countryside.*

My master has offered the town two barrels of wheat and another of oats for the summer, in case there are food shortages. I will deliver the barrels tomorrow, on his order, to the Consiglio Communale for disposition. Had we lived here longer, there would be more we could offer, but as it is, this gesture is at least a gesture.

I was visited earlier by a Felipo Quandt of Avignon, who has been authorized by the Consiglio della Universita and the Consiglio Communale to review the instruction my master has been providing his students regarding herbs and their uses, so that no unacceptable teaching is provided to them. The man is officious, but beyond that, I suspect he is greedy, and not for advancement alone, but for influence. He would like to see himself a member of the Universita as well as the Arte degli Erbei. It will be prudent to be attentive when he makes inquiries. I cannot help but worry that he might decide to magnify some minor infraction to the level of heresy and sedition.

I am bidden to carry some medicaments to Orazia degli Avei at her brother-in-law's house; it is the thrid time I have done so. She remains pale and has days of listlessness, but she no longer languishes as she did when she first sought out my master to ask him to treat her. If she can increase her strength, perhaps her blood can be fortified. I will report my observations upon my return, and I will hope that the woman may improve; she has a quick mind and a fearless nature, both of which are engaging to my master. The amelioration of her malady will lighten his heart as few other things could.

◆ ◆ ◆

Orazia stared at San-Germanus, her face concealing her emotion as she summoned him into her brother-in-law's house.

"Yes, Magister. Please come up the stairs. Thank you, Pompeo," she said to the footman who minded the front door. "If you will, inform Padre Rienetto that I have admitted Magister San-Germanus to my apartments?" She was model of decorum, dressed in a dark-red belucca with elaborate pleats at the shoulder and bosom, open at the corsage to reveal her camisa; this was proper attire for the reception of visitors, nothing to suggest that there was any untoward conduct to fear.

"Bondamma," said the servant with a bow as he stood aside to permit San-Germanus to climb the steep, narrow flight to the upper floor.

As he reached the top of the stairs, San-Germanus in his long-skirted purpoint of black-silk damask over a camisa of fluted red-linen, offered Orazia a bow, one that showed respect as well as good manners, just as his clothing did. "Do I see you well?" he asked, as was expected of any man treating the health of others.

"Not well, but I think a little better," she answered carefully as she took his hand to lead him down the hall. "I am working in the solarium today. Let us talk there."

"Sunlight can improve vitality if taken sensibly," he said, the last word lost as she pulled him into the north-facing room with three tall windows; she pressed against him, kissing him, her lips almost hard with need. "Oh, I have missed you," she whispered. "I have wanted you beside me every night." Two more determined kisses stopped her flow of speech. As she wrenched free of him, she went on, "I dream of you, that you are with me. I tell myself I feel your hands on me, making me more alive than I've been in months. Your hands"—she took his hands in hers and ran them over her breasts to her waist— "are magical. You are a feast of all delights."

He turned his hands and caught hers in his own, lifting each in turn so he could kiss her palms. "Then do not gulp it down—savor it." Her frenetic demands muted the passion he sensed in her, the passion he answered with his own.

She blinked her eyes, astonished that he would not simply plunder her body. "Have I displeased you?"

"No; no you have not." He took her in his arms, holding her close to him. "I can feel your pulse. It fills you with a music all your own."

She started to kiss him again with the same insistence, but he turned his face so that she struck his cheek with her mouth. "You do not–"

He released one arm from her but only to take her face in his small, elegant hand and lingeringly engage her lips with his. The slow, thorough exploration left her at once more excited and calmer. "You have no reason to rush," he said softly, his dark gaze fixed on her eyes. "You will deny yourself what you seek most if you hurry our meeting."

Her face softened again. "I'm sorry. But it has been so long. You send only your servant, with potions and remedies. You are the remedy I want."

"And now you have me," he said just above a whisper.

"So tell me, if you will, why you have kept away from me for seven whole days together?" She seemed about to weep, but she continued to smile resolutely. "Seven days!"

"You want to avoid gossip, and so do I," he said, his voice deep. "If I am here too frequently, your health must not improve, or there will be scandal. Since I wish to diminish your illness, I cannot attend you too frequently."

She pursed her mouth in displeasure. "I am only starting to improve. Can you not come here more often? May I not come to you, as I did the first time?"

"Perhaps," he said. He kissed her once more, without haste, until the tension went out of her and she answered his kiss with yearning instead of anxiety.

"Oh, Numi," she murmured, then sank into his kiss again. Gradually she lost the tension that had possessed her and she leaned into him, her passion growing more intense than her dismay.

"I hear a footstep on the stair," he told her as the kiss ended.

She straightened up and touched her barbete to determine that it was still covering her hair properly. Next she tugged at the front of her belucca to be sure it was not rumpled. Stepping back quickly, she was almost to her chair when the door opened and Padre Fiorello Rienetto stepped into the room, a genial smiled fixed on his mouth. "Brother-in-law!" Orazia exclaimed. "I thought you were otherwise occupied."

"I was preparing my lesson for tomorrow," he said, "when Pompeo brought me word that this good man had arrived." He turned and made a gesture of greeting to San-Germanus. "Magister. Let me thank you for the care you have been extending to my sister-in-law. You are the first who has shown any ability to relieve her suffering."

"I thank you, Padre, for telling me so." He ducked his head. "We are just beginning, but it is good that you are encouraged."

"You manservant tells me that you have been studying such remedies for more than half your lifetime. If that is the case, you are a most devoted pupil, and one whose dedication must be viewed as a sign of excellence." Padre Rienetto touched the crucifix that hung on a gold chain around his neck. "You must be favored in Heaven."

"If I am, then I am doubly thankful," said San-Germanus.

"How is that?" Doubly thankful?" Padre Rienetto asked.

"If I am twice-blessed, by knowledge and the approval of Heaven, then I am doubly thankful," said San-Germanus with slight, self-effacing smile.

Padre Rienetto laughed. "Humble, and clever as well. No wonder the Universita is glad of your work with them." This time San-Germanus said nothing, but waited for Padre Rienetto to continue. "One day when I am not overwhelmed with the instruction of youths, I would appreciate a conversation with you, Magister." He looked at Orazia as he said this. "If you will be good enough to let me know when you will next call?"

"Certainly," said San-Germanus, his genial outward demeanor giving no sign of his sudden concerns; he disliked being monitored so carefully, no matter how good the intentions behind the monitoring might be.

"Most kind," said Padre Rienetto, who sketched a blessing in San-Germanus' direction, and then one for Orazia. "I will leave you to your ministrations."

"They may take some time," San-Germanus informed him, not quite apologetically. "I am still new to this case, and I have many things to determine before I prepare the next medicaments for your sister-in-law."

"Then I will see you are not disturbed," said Padre Rienetto, and withdrew, closing the door behind him.

Orazia dropped into her chair, and started to speak, but remained silent as she saw San-Germanus' hand raised, warning her to be silent.

"Bondamma," he said, loudly enough to be heard by anyone listening at the door, "I must see your arms and your neck. If you want your maid to attend you?"

"No. You have done nothing to make me think you would dishonor me in my own home, with my own servants around me." She smiled as he nodded his encouragement to her.

"Then I will shortly ask you to remove the upper part of your clothing." He came closer to her and lowered his voice. "We must be very silent."

"Do you think we're being spied upon?" Her voice was little louder than a breath.

He thought of the many, many times he had had to contend with household spies, and knew this was no different. "I think it is best to assume it is so."

Her eyes widened. "Then is it safe to . . ." She finished her thought with a gesture.

"It may be, or it may not." He touched her barbete and pulled out three of the pins holding it in place. "At least you may show a slight disorder in your dress when we are through." The folded linen fell off her hair as he removed the last two pins, revealing her pale hair in a single braid wrapped around her head like a coronet. "The gorgiat as well. Your brother-in-law expects me to remove it."

"Why am I so nervous?" she asked in an under-voice.

"You fear we will be discovered," he said.

"Don't you fear it, too?" She stopped still, as if transfixed by her own dread.

"I do." He looked around the solarium and saw, in the far corner, a Turkish couch. "This should suit us very well." He went to move it toward her. "That chair will not do half so well as this couch. How did you come by it?"

"My husband bought it before he died," she said, rising and coming toward him. "On hot nights he would sleep on it; we had a summer-house in the garden, and he went there."

"But you did not?" He helped her to loosen her laces.

"No." She realized she had been too abrupt, and added, "He said it was cooler sleeping alone."

"He may have been right on that point," said San-Germanus, beginning to open the front of her belucca so that he could move the gorgiat aside. He worked quickly and efficiently, aware that her brother-in-law's intrusion had upset her; her strain had made her flesh taut again, like a bowstring about to loose an arrow. "Recline, Orazia, as comfortably as you may."

She stared at him. "But we could be interrupted."

"We could be, but I doubt we will be," he said, kissing her exposed shoulder lightly.

She reached for the lacing of his purpoint. "Then we must hurry."

He contained her hands. "No, we must not. Haste and apprehension work against us. They would sap all delight from what we do." He dropped to one knee at her side. "If this distresses you, then perhaps we should postpone–"

"No," she cut in sharply. "No. You might never want to touch me again if I permit you to leave me now." Again she took his hand in hers and shoved it under her camisa to touch her breast.

He remained on his knee, still and alert. "You will not want to hasten what we do together. It will lessen your joy from it."

"And yours," she accused. "If what you say is true."

"It is the truth," he said. "Believe this."

Something in his deep, steady voice made her stare at

him; with his enigmatic blue-black eyes on hers, she felt new stirring deep within her, and she held out her hand to him. "I'll need a little while to calm down," she said slowly. "If you don't mind?"

"No," he said, and sank all the way onto the floor next to her, legs crossed tailor-fashion. "Let me tell you a few things you must know."

She reached down and touched his hair. "You don't have to entertain me."

"That is not my intention." He took her hand and kissed it. "I should have told you these things before now—"

"You are married," she said, going on hurriedly. "It doesn't matter so long as—"

"I am not married," he said firmly. "Exiles are not attractive prospects."

"But one some women wouldn't mind. Have you *never* taken a wife? Perhaps one left behind when you had to leave, or one who helped you along the way?"

"Many women have helped me, in many ways, but not as wives," he said, thinking back to Olivia, to Ranegonda, to Gynethe Mehaut, and Dukkai.

She laughed softly. "But you have money, and you're titled still."

"But I have no lands, and no likelihood of advancement." He kissed her hand. "That is not what I must tell you." He took a deep breath. "If you could imagine living a very long time, what would you think it would be like?"

"I'm not going to live a very long time, so what does it matter?" She studied him as if seeking to find out why he asked. "My body will fail before I am old."

"But suppose your body did not fail: what then? You say you want long life. I am curious what such a life would mean to you." He kissed her hand again.

"It would mean that I could devote myself to improving my soul. To come before God with so little to recommend me—"

He swung up on his knee again. "You have yourself, and no one can fault what you are." He put his hands lightly on her bared shoulders. "Is that all a long life means to you?"

"Yes," she said cautiously, puzzled by his sudden intensity.

"Then you have not thought about long life as it is." He rose enough to sit on the edge of the couch and went on. "Long life is as demanding as a short one. Fifty years you think is a very long life."

"It is." She felt a distance in him, having nothing to do with nearness but with age.

"Some few men have lived longer," said San-Germanus. "Some have lived a century, or nearly that."

"Enrico Dandolo?" She laughed. "One bellicose Venezian Doge is not 'some' but one man."

"There have been others." He carefully opened her belucca and bent to kiss the swell of her breasts.

"Everyone hears stories about this one's hundred-year-old great-great-grandmother, or that one's one-hundred-ten-year-old great-great-great-great uncle, but no one brings them to visit. They are fables, as the story of talking foxes is." She gave a languorous sigh, but did not relax. "I wish you and I were alone. I worry the door will open again."

He was already aware that her arousal had waned, and so he sat up straight again. "No matter. We will have another time."

"You aren't going to stop," she protested, trying to take hold of his hands.

He looked down at her. "We will meet again, soon, at my house, where you need not be vexed by spies or well-meaning relatives."

"But how can you do that and avoid scandal?" she asked, feeling a bit light-headed still.

"I will explain to your brother-in-law that I wish to do a study of your malady and will need to have you call at my house for several hours in order to complete it." He stood, and held out his hand to help her sit up. "You are a most enticing woman, Orazia. I will not diminish you by attempting to share a hasty satisfaction. When we lie together, I want you sated with your fulfillment."

She was working her laces, and could not help but feel slighted. "If you want to stay away from me, I suppose you will."

"But I do not want to stay away from you. Quite the contrary: I want to have nothing that could interrupt our dalliance." He assisted her to stand and put his arm around her waist. "Here you anticipate all manner of disruptions, and in the end, whether such occur or not, the effect will be the same—you will lose your elation."

"And so will you," she said wistfully.

"And so will I," he agreed, and kissed her. It was a kiss to be lost in, one that promised visions and ecstacy, and it lasted until Orazia grew short of breath. As they moved apart, he touched her white braid. "Shall we say four days from now?"

"I don't want to wait so long," she said. "But my brother-in-law is likely to approve it."

"Ah," said San-Germanus, tying the lacings of his purpoint and adjusting the pleating of the collar of his camisa. "Shall I offer to include your maid?"

"It would suit him better than not," she said, adjusting her gorgiat. "He is a priest, and a Magister. He has much to maintain."

"Then I shall do so. My manservant will see she is occupied while you and I are alone." He lifted her hand. "The things I said about being very old: think about them, Orazia. Think how it would be to outlive all your siblings and friends, all your children–"

"I have no children," she said curtly.

"You have nephews and nieces," he reminded her.

"All right; yes, I have nephews and nieces. Two nephews and three nieces, God be thanked. I take your point. And I will think about it." She stared at him, her emotions welling with feelings she could not yet identify: her skin felt as if it had been scrubbed, at once tender and stimulated. "I wonder why you ask me."

"I'll explain that to you in four days," he promised as he lifted her hand for a final kiss.

◆ ◆ ◆

Text of an entry from the journal of Antonio Vicenzo Mergazza di Aurelio dei Cioventi, recording clerk of the Consiglio Communale di Padova, dated April 19th, 1325.

The flooding is finally ended. The livestock held within the city walls are being returned to the farms and fields, which is a welcome turn for Padova. Euginio Circando of the Confraternta degli Angeli has supervised the moving of the animals, and Padre Amerigo Matagni has come from il Santo's Basilica to bless them. Four drovers have been retained by the Consiglio Communale to see that all animals reach their owners without mishap.

A group of farmers from the immediate region today presented a petition to the Consiglio Communale asking for a grant of monies to enable them to rebuild and replant; they claim that since Padova is the main beneficiary of their labors, it should assist in supporting their efforts. This request has been scheduled for discussion in five days, and at that time it will be determined if such a grant is appropriate and can be afforded by the Commune. The positions of the Consiglierei are much divided and it may take longer than is planned for a final decision to be made. There may be a civic meeting called if the Consiglierei are not in agreement by the beginning of May.

A group of old houses have sagged and collapsed on the west side of the city. They had been little more than hovels and the flooding weakened them to a point that the ground beneath them gave way and the roofs cracked. The Consiglio Communale is now attempting to decide where to house those displaced by this event, and what to permit to be built in that location.

Martino Ebro has filed a request to be allowed to take down four houses he owns near the church of Santa Sabina. The houses are old—two hundred years at least—and in very poor condition. Ebro claims that they are in danger of burning, and also may collapse. The tenants of the buildings say that they are not in repair and most of them want the buildings improved rather than taken down, but that would require a very large investment which may not justify such costs. For the time being, Ebro has been ordered to have new roofs installed and the stairs shored up.

Manrico da Valle has been admitted to the Universita as a favor to his father, who has recognized this bastard son due to the young man's clever mind and promising intellect. He will reside at the Inn of la Santa Antica, and will commence his instruction at the beginning of May. Padre Fiorello Rienetto will be his master for his studies in jurisprudence. He will be allowed to enlarge his studies over the next two years, assuming his father is willing that he continue his education. Some of the Consigliere disapprove of admitting a bastard as a student, but as Magister Fontana observed, "Many a man may be a bastard and not know it, so it is unfitting to exclude those who know their heritage."

There was a small fire near the soapmakers' barns last night, but it is put out now, with only a small amount of damage, although the odor is still hanging over all of Padova like a miasma, and some are afraid that there may be ills carried in its stench. A goodly number of monks have devoted themselves to more prayer in order to keep such a misfortune from taking place. Two of the Magisters of the Universita have said that prayers are not needed, and that they do not believe that disease is contained in bad odors, but others disagree. We will discover in the next month which of the opinions are correct. For once I would like to take the part of the Magisters who claim there is no connection, but I will offer more prayers tonight and until May is almost finished, in case those whose beliefs are more in accord with most teaching are correct, after all.

There is a procession scheduled in three days, from the Basilica of il Santo to the Monasterio degli Evangelisti. Most of the Consiglio Communale will attend, as will the Consiglio della Universita and many of the Magisters. Only the foreigners have been asked not to participate, this being a local celebration. So far as I am aware, no one has objected to this, and that means the procession should have no unpleasantness to mar the occasion. The Console will have a dozen musicians to play for them, and three wagons drawn by Hungarian ponies to carry the images of the Evangelists. It is a fine, solemn occasion, one that will draw all the nobles from the region to be part of it. A civic banquet will follow the Mass and procession, and it will mark the feast-day of Santa Pherbutha the Martyr, whose death marked the spring festival of the Persians, when Christians were killed to satisfy their demon-gods, or so Vescovio Strofinaccio has taught. If only the weather will remember the holy young woman and remain clear and warm.

◆ ◆ ◆

Outside the house the streets were crowded, students and townsfolk mingling with unusual amity as Padova prepared for an evening of feasting and revelry. With the civic procession over, the city was caught up in all manner of festivities, from the official banquet to the improvisations of the students and people of Padova. The sky had turned a glowing gold as the sun dropped into the west, and the air freshened with the first of the night breezes, smelling now of growing things and blossoms, an aroma mixed with grilling meats from the fires in the piazze where small bonfires provided the opportunity for the butchers to turn sides of goats and hogs on spits, from which they sliced portions for hungry celebrants. Most of the houses on the block were dark, only lanterns shining at the doors, for their occupants were enjoying the festivities. Only the house of San-Germanus had light shining from the small room in the upper story, and one on the ground floor at the side of the house that looked out on a narrow passage between buildings.

"Do you think she will come?" Rotgiere asked as he entered the study where San-Germanus had just set aside the book he had been reading.

"I hope she will, old friend; we shall see." San-Germanus glanced toward the door. "The servants?"

"They are all gone for the evening. I have said you do not expect them until midnight, and that I will admit them to the house by the garden door." His face revealed little of his thoughts, but he added, "If they are sober enough to find their way."

"There may be difficulty," San-Germanus agreed. "Are you planning to go out, yourself?"

"For a while. I will let myself in and keep watch." Rotgiere pledged. "If there is anything you require, you may summon me."

"Thank you, old friend. I think I can manage this well enough." He ran his finger along his jaw. "I will need to be shaved in a few days, I think."

"Of course. And you will want your hair trimmed, as well." Rotgiere paused. "Which room will you choose tonight?"

"The room next to the garden, across the hall."

"I will be sure nothing disturbs you," said Rotgiere. "It is about time that you found a woman you can seek wide awake."

"And so I have," said San-Germanus.

"How much have you told her?" Rotiere asked.

"About my true nature? not enough. I should tell her to-night, and about the decisions she will have to make."

"This is the third time you will lie with her, isn't it?"

"The second, actually. Last time there were too many distractions to make any intimacy possible." He went to the rush-light that burned day and night, took a long, thin, dry reed from the vase next to the light, and touched it to the little flame. As soon as it was alight, San-Germanus handed it to Rotgiere. "If you would take care of the lamps in the room across the hall?"

"How many do you want lit?" Rotgiere asked, taking the reed.

"All of them, since there will be no fire lit in the grate. If the room is too dark, she will be more inclined to be fearful than if it is glowing with lamp-light." San-Germanus held up his hand, unmoving. "I believe she has come."

"Then I'll be about my chores," said Rotgiere, and left the room; a moment later, San-Germanus, too, had closed the door. He went along to the passage-way door and lifted the iron latch: a figure in a long, hooded cloak waited, huddled against the wall as if determined to be invisible. San-Germanus opened the door wide enough to give her room to step inside. "How good of you to come, Bondamma."

Orazia's answer was muffled by her hood. "The streets are frantic tonight. I very nearly didn't leave my brother-in-law's house, except that he is at the civic banquet and I had only Pompeo to guard me."

"Did you have any trouble getting here?" San-Germanus asked. "Did the crowds bother you in any way?"

"I was jostled, but so was everyone else. I kept out of the most crowded places and held my hood closed. I spoke to no one."

"All the more reason you and I will be unnoticed." He stood aside and held out his hand to help her step up into the house. "Do you want me to take your cloak?"

"No. Not yet. If your servants should see—"

"My servants are at the festival. Only my manservant is here, and he will ensure our privacy." He indicated the corridor. "The first door on your right," he said, making no attempt to delay her; he fixed the latch before following her.

"I almost feel myself an adulteress, doing this, not a widow. I believe my brother-in-law would think me such, if he knew I had come here, and would treat me as an adulteress is treated—cast out with nothing but the clothes she wears," she said as she opened the door carefully, to be met only by the shining lights of the oil-lamps and a low, broad Turkish ottoman on which a blanket of Ankara wool had been spread. "But I am a widow, not a wife. This cannot be adultery."

"No, I should think not," said San-Germanus, reaching to take her cloak after he closed the door. "If you are hungry or thirst–?"

She shook her head. "I am, but not in the way you mean." She relinquished her cloak to him, revealing a plain, old-fashioned houppelande beneath, made of blue-green linen, the large, triangular sleeves lined in cotton the color of love's lamps blossoms with inner sleeves of a soft blue-grey; her hair was uncovered, braided and wrapped in her preferred coronet. Although the room was not cold, she clutched her arms across her body as if to preserve her warmth. "All today, I could think of nothing but you. I tried to imagine what this night would be like. The sun is down, and now I entrust my hopes to you."

He draped her mouse-colored cloak over the rack by the door. "You humble me," he said, coming back to her side.

"My brother-in-law has told me that you and he are going to meet to discuss my case in a few days." She held up her hands as if to implore a favor. "Do not tell him anything you do not tell me. Please, San-Germanus."

"I would not do anything so deceptive," he said.

"No matter what he tells you," she added sharply.

"You are my patient, not he," San-Germanus assured her.

"But he has command of me."

"Under the law, yes, he does," said San-Germanus. "And you live in his house. But what has that to do with you and me here, and now?"

She regarded him with surprise. "Nothing," she told him. "Nothing."

"Then do not worry about priests and rules, Orazia, but give yourself over to apolaustic delight. Your brother-in-law will never know of this from me, nor from my servants." He stepped behind her and moved his arm around her waist. "If you will permit me to serve your pleasure, Orazia."

"If I must die soon, then let this be the best of what I can have." She leaned back against him, feeling her pulse race; she whispered, "Unfasten my laces." Her houppelande was laced up the back, the lacings tucked in at the neck.

He took the laces in hand and worked the knot out of them, then pulled them loose enough to enable her to shrug out of the garment and let it fall to her feet, revealing her knee-length camisa of fine dove-colored Antioch silk. "Shall I–?" he offered, touching the shoulders of the garment, lifting them a bit.

"Not yet," she said, bent down to toss her houppelande aside, then rose and leaned back against him again. "I want you to do all the things you did the first time."

"I will strive to do that for you," he vowed, kissing her forehead.

She looked at him curiously. "You haven't removed your clothes. You didn't the first time, either."

He had given answers for this so many times that he did not hesitate to tell her, "There is no need. My pleasure comes from your pleasure. And there are scars on my body that might be upsetting to you. It will be better this way."

"Are you a eunuch?" It had never occurred to her, but she knew what those scars looked like, and admitted to herself she would dislike them in a lover.

"No, but my capacities are severely limited in that realm. I told you before that I have lost the power to penetrate a woman." Since he had wakened from death thirty-three centuries ago, he had not been able to stiffen his organ; for a long time this had caused him embarrassment and distress, but those emotions had ended in the Temple of Imhotep. "It is part of my true nature."

"That you gain your satisfaction through me?" She had begun to twist a small tendril of hair around her Jupiter finger, a lazy, preoccupied motion that protected her from saying too much.

"Yes."

"Then I want to feel everything that I can, everything wonderful." She gazed steadily into his dark eyes. "I want to feel these things with understanding."

"If that will gratify your senses, I will do my utmost to make it possible," he said, and encircled her waist with his arm once more, then bent to kiss the nape of her neck so lightly that a feather would touch her skin more heavily than his lips.

Orazia sighed, and lifted her camisa so that his hands were beneath the silk. She let the fabric fall as if to contain him within her clothes. The texture of his damask-silk sleeve was exciting against her bare skin. "I want this to be my se-cret—mine."

"Here it is only between us," he said quietly as his hands began, with tantalizing slowness, to move up from her waist to her breasts, never hurrying, never pressing, taking time so that she could relish each touch; his caresses were thorough, sweet, and evocative, promising more and better rapture. He felt her shiver as he fingered her nipples to tautness even as the rest of her began to melt into the first transports that shot through her from his hands to the limits of her body. His esurience answered her arousal, and his hands ventured down over her abdomen and into the secrets at the top of her thighs. He eased open the petal-soft folds and found the hidden bud; with minute, delicate strokes he brought the bud to quivery life. Orazia was breathing deeply, her hands flexing and loosening as a cat might knead the air. The air was alive with her increasing exhilaration, with the delirium growing from her heightened receptivity; she was sensitive to everything, from his magical hands to the errant breeze flickering through the room. Her senses fused, her sight becoming hearing, her touch becoming taste, and all the while her body gathered its release deep within herself, coiling deliciously until she broke away from his persuasive hands but only to turn about in his arms and to pull him down onto the ottoman with her, gasping with the onset as her spasms shook her. Her rapture seemed at once endless and too brief. She longed to envelop San-Germanus, to contain him while her fulfillment consumed her, but her release quickly drove wishes from her mind, giving way to the fervor of her exultation. In an unexpected way, she felt him leaning over her, not lying upon her, but enticingly near. "How do you do that?"

He smiled at her, a warm, haunted smile. "I do nothing but love you—it is you who achieves your gratification. I share in what you experience. I can only know what you know."

She stretched suddenly, and just as suddenly relaxed. "You would appear to be a most accomplished teacher."

"Because I learn from you." It had been true of all his partners over the centuries, and not one had faded from his memory.

"Well, I never had such . . . such . . . I don't know what to call it." She saw now that he was holding himself across her, supported on his arms. "Women rarely . . ." Again she could find no words to describe her culmination of desire.

San-Germanus moved and sank down next to her, his arm still across her waist. "Sadly, yes. Women rarely."

"And you know because you have sampled many?" An unexpected surge of jealousy made her question harder than she had intended.

He did not answer at once, occupying himself with stroking her sides lightly. "You know that I have: I told you so."

"And I am just one among many?" She could not believe that she was behaving so badly. Why was she being so accusing, she wondered, when she wanted to continue the feeling of elation and receptivity for as long as possible.

"You are Orazia. You are not one among many." He kissed her cheek, noting that her skin was unusually rosy. "You need not think that you will ever be forgotten."

"Do you say this to comfort me?" She wanted to bite her tongue, to take back the hurtful words, but could not.

"I say this because it is true." He touched the two bright dots on her neck where his mouth had been. "You are part of me and will be always."

"Or at least for a few more years, and then it will no longer matter," she said, and put her hand to her lips to stop herself from saying anything more.

"It will always matter to me," he said.

She began to weep silently, tears running down her temples and into her hair. "I don't mean to be hateful."

"You aren't," he assured her.

"I hear myself and I am abashed that I should speak so." She stared at him. "You won't upbraid me, will you?"

"Why should I?" He wiped her tears with a careful touch, sympathy suffusing his features with an expression she had not seen before. "You are afraid that your life will end and no one will notice or care, and that wounds you."

She regarded him with fascination. "Yes. You *do* understand." This realization almost brought her to tears.

He kissed the edge of her mouth. "I know you are ashamed that you could not carry a child to delivery, and that you felt you had failed your husband."

"Four pregnancies, all coming to nothing." She stared up at the painted ceiling. "And then Serafino died, and I had nothing."

He drew her a little closer to him. "You need not be afraid."

"Why not? Can you tell me I will not die? You said yourself that my blood is no longer . . . healthful."

"And that is what I am treating," he reminded her.

"So that I may eke out a few more weeks when there is nothing left of me? So that I can wither and dry, like an autumn leaf? So that I can have days of pain and–" She turned her head away from him, determined to fling no more delations at him when he had done nothing to deserve them. She went on more plaintively, "I would rather spend my time with you, like this, until my flesh is no longer capable of fulfillment. If I am to die soon, let me die with bliss, not anguish."

San-Germanus heard in this a distant echo of Thetis in Sarai, eight hundred years ago, following the Year of Yellow Snow, when all the world seemed about to perish. "I would hope you will improve your health."

"And I, but I know it is not likely to happen." She turned back to him. "Will you do this for me? Will you love me until I can no longer endure it?"

"If you will understand what the consequences of such acts may be." He ran his fingers lightly along her brow. "If we lie together as we have done this evening for another four times, your fate will be different than you anticipate." He saw a mix of hope and distress in her eyes. "I want you to know what can happen. Then you may decide how you wish to continue, if you do wish to continue."

"Why would I not want to continue to the end as we have done already? Why four more times?" She gave him her full attention, her eyes keen on his. "What do you mean by this?"

"You know I am a foreigner, an exile," he said carefully.

"From the Carpathian Mountains." She nodded, her full attention still upon him.

He paused. "I told you when we first met that my father's

kingdom was over-run by his enemies?"

"I recall that. My brother-in-law cursed the Turks for their beastliness." She was curious to know what he was trying to tell her, but she was reluctant to urge him on.

"But it was not Turks who killed my family," he said. "And Turks did not kill me."

"No, of course not," she said, baffled by this comment.

His compelling gaze became more intense, the blue light shining in his black eyes. "The Turks had not left their traditional home when mine was destroyed." He waited for her to speak; when she remained silent, he continued, "I became a slave, and was placed at the head of my soldiers who had been captured with me, to provide something for other soldiers to mow down in battle. I kept most of my men alive and we routed the foe from the field. And for this, I was disemboweled and left exposed."

"But you must . . . you could not live," Orazia whispered.

"And I did not." He felt her wince. "They killed me improperly, for what I am, and I did not stay dead very long."

"You're telling a tale, aren't you?" Her words were slow and hushed.

"I'm telling you my history," he said calmly.

"Your history," she repeated, dazed.

"Since that day, I have existed on the blood of the truly living, and I have remained alive." He contemplated her face. "And if you allow me to taste your blood four more times, then you will rise when you die, unless your spine is severed or you burn."

Her breath almost caught in her throat. "You mean I will not die?"

"You will die, but you rise."

"My brother-lin-law would call that blasphemy, but I don't think you mean it as an affront to religion." She touched his silken sleeve. "You are not what I would . . . How do you mean, rise again?'

"You will not be held by death, unless your spine is broken or you burn to death, and you will live as those of my blood live." He spoke quietly, his voice deeply musical.

"In taking blood?"

"In touching life."

"But you say my blood is not salubrious," she said, astonished to hear herself speaking so tranquilly about such astounding revelations.

"It will not matter when you rise. No disease will touch you." He kissed her hand as he contained it in his own.

"Ever?"

That simple question held all the dread the living had of illness, and his unbeating heart went out to her. "As long as you do not die the True Death, you will be proof against all disease."

"Including the one I have now?" The recriminatory tone was back in her voice.

He understood the fear and despair in her question, and he answered her as he could. "I can alleviate your suffering, but I cannot stop the disease entirely. But if you decide to come to my life, it will not follow you beyond death."

"You mean I am dying, no matter what you do," she muttered.

"Eventually you will succumb to your illness, or to something brought about by it." This was the most difficult admission he could make, and he said it reluctantly.

"Succumb. You mean die." She felt her eyes fill with tears again.

"If you will take what I can provide you, that will not last." He saw she was wavering, and went on, "I do not want you to do anything against your will or your character, but if you wish to live beyond the time you have left, I can offer you the means to do it."

She shook her head slowly. "I don't know. How long would I live if I accepted your offer? A long time?"

"That would depend on many things," he said.

She shivered and huddled into her camisa. "Then I would die."

"Everyone dies eventually," he said.

There was doubt and hope in her eyes as she looked at him. "Must I decide now?"

"No, of course not," he said, and drew her closer to him.

"What do you find hard about your life?" Her words were very soft.

"Loneliness," he answered.

"Everyone is lonely some time," she said.

He said nothing for a moment, then began, "In this life you have only those who are willing to be touched by you, and to accept what you offer. Without intimacy, there is limited virtue in what we do, and that can prove as isolating as the passage of time. There are no family, no friends, no companions, no one from the life you knew before you change. Touching such as we have will be the whole of your true society, and those of my blood treasure the gift it is." He strove to block the memory of Csimenae from his thoughts. "That constraint is not easily accepted, nor is this life a way some are willing to live." His voice was as warm and caressing as his words were bleak. "Consider well what I tell you, and do not think it is a minor thing."

For a short while she was still, feeling the last tremors of fulfillment echo within her. Then, when the last sparks of pleasure had left her, she said, "I will tell no one of what you said; not even my Confessor."

"Thank you," he responded with genuine gratitude. "Such knowledge can be dangerous, as much to you as to me."

"Then I will be especially careful." The next question came from her as if compelled by inner fire. "If I decide not to live your life, what will you do?"

"That will depend on you. It will not make me love you less." He could feel her twist under his arm.

"Will you mourn me when I die?"

"I will mourn the loss of you no matter what you choose to do," he said.

Hearing this, she wriggled in his embrace and began to kiss him in desperate haste, as guilty lovers might kiss, fearing their doom was near.

◆ ◆ ◆

Text of an entry in the journal of the student Enzo Grimanni, dated April 26th, 1325.

Tomorrow is the first time we will be able to use the anthanor Magister San-Germanus has constructed for us. We had all thought it would take longer for him to build it, but he told us yesterday that our next lesson would be with the athanor, and advised us to purchase padded gloves and a leather apron. Flavio is all excitement, and Silvio has been boasting over his cheese-bread that he will have one of his own: we all know that his father cannot afford to dower his daughters, so there is no hope that he will spend money on an alchemical oven for his son. Andrea says little, but that is nothing new; he's as closed-mouthed as a turtle.

I have managed to make a tincture of milk thistle which the Magister says will help fortify the sinews and strengthen the liver, to be used in case of fever, sprained tendons, those given to drunkenness, and those suffering from antipathies to foods. It is not given to those with sudden headache or pains in the chest, or spasmodic coughs. It is the first time I have a result he approves of. He tells me I do not pay enough attention to his teaching, and it may be that I don't, but with the days so warm and pleasant and so many things to do in Padova, how could it be otherwise?

In little less than a month I will have to be gone for two weeks; I have sent my acceptance off today by messenger. My cousin Giuliano is getting married and I am asked to be part of the wedding-party. My father tells me that it is an honor, and that he will expect me to conduct myself as befits a man of his position. I think my father is hoping to find a suitable bride for me in the next year or so, one with a fortune so that we need not be so that our estates need not be encumbered and my sisters can be dowered. I wish he would delay for a year more; I am not yet ready for a wife. So long as I have been sent to study, I might as well do so. Eighteen will be time enough to marry. For now, I want to learn, as my father expects me to do, even if my mind occasionally wanders.

◆ ◆ ◆

"Padre Rienetto is waiting in your book-room," Rotgiere said as he entered the glass-house where San-Germanus was trimming back the growth on a few small trees. The day was warm, so the upper panes were open, making the most of the sunny morning. "He claims it is urgent, but his sister-in-law is not with him."

"If you would provide him refreshments and tell him I will be with him directly?" San-Germanus said as he set aside his shears and reached for a rag to clean his hands.

"I take it this call is expected?"

"Yes, it is," said San-Germanus; he indicated his dirty linen smock. "I will put on fresh clothes and join him directly."

"So I will inform him," said Rotgiere.

"Very good; thank you, old friend."

Rotgiere left San-Germanus in the glass-house and went to the kitchen to order wine, bread, and cheese for Padre Rienetto, then went on to the book-room where he found the priest inspecting the contents of the shelves and reading-desks. "My master will be with you directly. He wishes to freshen his clothing before greeting you."

Padre Rienetto nodded as he continued his inspection. "Your master has a most remarkable library." He stroked his spade-cut beard, contemplating the variety of subjects represented. "Many schools would be proud of such a collection."

"He is fond of books and values information," said Rotgiere.

"He is also willing to spend money on his interest," said Padre Rienetto. "My sister-in-law tells me that you stand unusually high in your master's esteem and confidence."

"I have traveled with him a long way, over many years," said Rotgiere.

"Then perhaps you can inform me on the history of the acquisition of some of these volumes," the priest said, putting his hand on an old Greek missal. "This, for example, is a rare find, indeed."

"The Magister bought it from a monastery on a Greek island, many years ago," said Rotgiere.

"It is surprising that the monks would part with such a treasure." There was a tinge of inquiry in his remark.

"He took it in lieu of a jeweled crucifix of gold," said Rotgiere.

Padre Rienetto considered this, and said, "Not many men would prefer the missal."

Rotgiere responded with deference. "My master reads: many men do not. For them the crucifix would be the greater treasure."

"True; very true," said Padre Rienetto at his most lofty. "But I wonder at the monks who sold it to him."

Before Rotgiere had to supply what would probably be an unsatisfactory explanation, a tap on the door announced the arrival of the refreshment tray; Rotgiere went to relieve Gemignano of the tray which he carried to the table in the center of the room. "Padre, if you would like to select what would please you?" There were two kinds of bread, two kinds of cheese and a bottle of straw-colored wine. A plate, a knife, and a glass awaited his use.

"Very handsome," the Padre approved. "But then, all I learn of San-Germanus makes him out to be a man of good conduct and respect. That is why I have entrusted my sister-in-law to his care. Not that this is any concern of yours."

"No, Padre," said Rotgiere, ducking his head as he withdrew.

Left alone, Padre Rienetto filled his glass with wine, broke the smaller loaf in half and cut a wedge of cheese. Selecting a high-backed chair, he made himself comfortable for his little meal. He murmured a blessing and set about eating, aware as he did that the bread was excellent and the cheese among the finest made south of the Alps. He was into the second loaf and the second cheese when the door open and San-Germanus, elegant in a skirted purpoint of black silk with dagged sleeves, came into the book-room. He had his eclipse device depending from a heavy chain of silver links, and he carried a small silver box, which he put on the high table in the center of the room. His manner was stately without being imposing. He offered a dutiful bow to his guest as the priest rose to his feet and said, "I am pleased to welcome you to my house, Padre Rienetto. Pray do not let me interrupt your repast."

"You do not interrupt me," said Padre Rienetto.

"Then continue," San-Germanus said with a gesture that was grand without arrogance.

"Thank you. I will." He sat down again. "I am sorry it has taken me so long to act upon your invitation."

"The demands of teaching and your calling must impose heavy demands upon you," said San-Germanus.

"They are both demonstrations of my devotion to God," said Padre Rienetto. "I assume them gladly."

"No doubt they do you much credit," said San-Germanus, watching the Padre more closely than he knew.

"But you wish to inform me about my sister-in-law's malady, and I am desirous to know what you have learned." He coughed importantly. "Your treatment has done her good."

"That was my hope," said San-Germanus. "And I hope her improvement will continue."

"May God and His Angels say Amen." Padre Rienetto crossed himself.

San-Germanus echoed the gesture as he regarded the priest for a long moment, then said, "Then I hope I will not cause you distress when I tell you I am not sure that a complete cure is possible."

"But why not?" Padre Rienetto asked, his pleased expression vanishing.

"She has had this condition for a long time, or so she tells me. As this is the case, it means the illness has established itself in her for a considerable portion of her life, and under such prolonged infection, the body–"

"–takes on the habit of the disease. I have heard many of the Magisters say so." He considered more cheese. "I will admit this does dash my best hopes for her."

"That does not mean that she must waste away," San-Germanus said quickly. "But she may not ever be entirely rid of her ailment."

"Have you told her?" Padre Rienetto gave him a sharply accusing stare.

"No. Nor will I until I am more certain that this regimen has reached the limits of its efficacy."

Padre Rienetto made a gesture of resignation. "Then I will continue to urge her to enter the convent so that she may prepare herself for the end, with her soul cleaned no matter what becomes of her body." In an abrupt movement, he cut more cheese and began to eat it. "All is in God's Hands, and we must accept His Wisdom in these matters."

"Padre, let me ask you to wait a while before you discuss such things with your sister-in-law," San-Germanus said with a nod of respect. "I know you care only for the preservation of her soul, and that is as it should be. But there as much medicine in optimism as there is in ointments and decoctions; if your sister-in-law fears she is ailing still, it may bring about a dejection that would allow her ailment to once again dominate her body."

"Then she should pray for a better state of mind," said Padre Rienetto. "Surely you would not have her turn away from Salvation for the relief of her body?"

"I would want her to have the best opportunity for the greatest degree of improvement possible."

"Which will come by the Grace of God," said Padre Rienetto, getting to his feet. "Nothing happens in the lives of men but God makes it so. God, or the Devil."

Knowing it was useless to argue the point, San-Germanus said, "Certainly that is the teaching. But might not God extend his guidance to letting us decide for ourselves, once he has given the discretion to choose?"

"Among men, perhaps, although it is a dangerous gift. But women? Ever since Eve, women have chosen unwisely. It cannot be left to women to chart the course of their lives. For their sakes and the sake of all mankind, they must be protected from their own capacity for evil. The Greeks were very wise for all they were unredeemed pagans, to describe woman as the beautiful evil. Without the example of Eve, the Greeks discerned the irresolute nature of woman's heart. It is for us to guard them, to preserve them, and to correct them when they err." Padre Rienetto set his cheese aside. "It is easy for men who read too much to fall into error."

"Must all knowledge be forbidden fruit?' San-Germanus asked, taking care to keep any suggestion of challenge out of his tone.

"If it supercedes the teaching of God, then yes, for it corrupts faith and leads to damnation." He frowned at San-Germanus. "Why do you ask?"

San-Germanus shrugged. "I have often found that the demands of faith are hard to explain to those who are oppressed and suffering."

"Such as my sister-in-law," said Padre Rienetto.

"Yes; such as she," said San-Germanus.

"I had hoped she had overcome her doubts, but I gather not." Padre Rienetto nodded, concealing a sigh. "I understand you now, and although I do not entirely agree with you, I will concede you have helped her when no one else could." He crossed himself and whispered a brief prayer. "Very well, I will postpone my next discussion with her until it seems that she is improved enough to be willing to think about the benefit of her soul."

"I think that might be wisest for her at this time," said San-Germanus. "If she is improving, it will be likely that she will want to enjoy her improvement before contemplating what she must face before long. Unless the Greeks were also wise in calling hope the last evil loosed on the world: what do you say?"

"I will adhere to your plan unless I see that she is falling into error; if that should be the case, I will have to remonstrate with her for the preservation of her soul, a concern in which the Greeks of old were strangely lax." He took a long drink of wine, swallowing as if his throat were parched.

"Should she reach such a decision, I hope you will inform me, so that I may encourage her to be watchful of her interests, and provide her with regimens that might help her." San-

Germanus thought of Olivia, now at Lake Como, who chafed under the constant intrusion of men in her life through the law and the Church; when Olivia had been alive, women had many of the same rights as men, but over the decades and centuries, those rights had eroded to nearly nothing.

"You seem distracted, Magister," the Padre observed.

"I was recalling one of my blood, a widow, who has had much to contend with in this world." He paused. "She has no brother or son to protect her, and her father is long dead. She has found it hard to deal with all the demands upon her." Over the centuries, Olivia's articulate complaints had kept San-Germanus keenly aware of the erosion of the position of women.

"Does she have a fortune, or property, or is she without means?" Padre Rienetto inquired.

"She has lands—which she is not allowed to control—and some money, presently administered by the local Bishop." It was true to a limited extent, for Olivia had several estates from Rome to Brabant, and a great deal of gold and jewels hidden away.

"An excellent executor, and one who must encourage her to take the veil and gain the protection of the Church," said Padre Rienetto.

"Alas, she has no vocation," said San-Germanus, knowing that Olivia held the Church to be the principal instrument of the deprivation of property and autonomy for women.

"Then she should marry," said Padre Rienetto. "Still, it is sad business." This was a standard observation, more a courtesy than a sentiment.

"It is difficult when women must rely on men so completely." San-Germanus said this as if it had just struck him.

"But it is the way God has told us to live, and those of us who follow His Word may gain the glory He offers in Heaven," said Padre Rienetto, going on in a more practical tone, "If you are her kin, why do you not open your doors to her?" The implied criticism in this remark made it sound insulting.

"I would were I not an exile. She does not need that taint

added to her difficulties."

"So she married well," said Padre Rienetto.

"Some might say so," San-Germanus agreed, thinking back to the savagery of Senator Cornelius Justus Silius, who had been Olivia's husband in her breathing days, and who had treated her in ways he would not have dared to treat a Roman whore.

"What would you say?" There was an incisive shine in his eyes.

"I would say her marriage benefitted her parents more than it benefitted her, as is often the case when fortunes are involved."

"But it gave her security for her children," said Padre Rienetto.

"Unfortunately, she had none." He paused, "His previous two wives had also failed to produce any offspring for him."

"Ah. I can understand your misgiving on her behalf." He took a last gulp of wine. "Do you think my sister-in-law is likely to have children if she remarries?"

So this was what the man wanted to know, thought San-Germanus. "It is too soon to tell, but from her history, I would think it unlikely. I am sorry to tell you this, but you say you want my honest opinion."

"Yes, I do." Padre Rienetto sighed. "That is unfortunate." He picked up a last morsel of cheese but did not eat it. "Is there any chance that she has been cursed?"

"I see no indication of it," said San-Germanus cautiously.

"The Devil is very subtle, especially in women's flesh. It was Eve who embraced the Serpent in Eden, and it is women who are led into error, as she was. I would be remiss as Orazia's brother-in-law and as a priest not to consider this possibility. I should think that you, with your medical studies, have reached the same conclusion."

Aware that he was being tested, San-Germanus made a show of weighing his answer. "I am not a man of religion," he said, "although, as a youth, I trained for the priesthood. Circumstances intervened to prevent my completing my training. I have no pretensions to your degree of understanding. " That the priesthood he had trained for was ancient and vampiric, he did not mention, nor that the intervention had occurred more than thirty-three centuries ago. "Lacking the full appreciation of possession, I would not be so proud as to assume I can recognize all signs of demonic presence. However," he went on more forcefully, "I have seen religious men, zealous in their faith, who were quick to assume the devil was responsible for the state of a luckless soul when, with more circumspect inquiry, it could be discovered that the sufferer was disordered in her wits or had contracted a malady that made her see visions. Fevers can bring about delirium and certain herbs can summon up demons and angels for those who employ them. Those unfortunates bitten by mad dogs see visions before they die that come from their infection, not from anything the devil need bother to do."

"That may be true, but visions are very dangerous, for who knows what evil may disguise itself as the very center of Paradise?" He lowered his head. "I fear that my sister-in-law, in her weakness of body may also acquire weakness of spirit, and thereby endanger her soul. If her suffering on this earth can save her from the perils of Hell, it may be that God intends her to endure her pains in order to cleanse her soul of evil."

Without being obvious about it, San-Germanus studied Padre Rienetto closely. "Has anything she has done caused you anxiety?"

"To the extent that her better health has brought about a certain lightness of manner, no, there is nothing. I have made allowances for her lapses in conduct, knowing that it has been long since she was able to indulge herself." His frown deepened. "But I know that there are acts that contain great evil that appear to be nothing more than a minor flaw. God has brought her to the pass for a reason, though I may not discern the reason for it, I am disinclined to go against His Will."

"I would not regard the treatment she is receiving as indicative of anything but a lessening of the discomfort of her condition. If God had not wanted her to have such relief, he would not have brought her to you, in this city." San-Germanus waited a moment, then went on, "If you have any doubts about my treatment, I would be glad to submit the regimen I have initiated with her to any Magister at the Universita who studies medicaments and the human body. If my methods are not approved, then I will withdraw from treating your sister-in-law and you may place her in the care of a practitioner more to your liking."

"It would be irresponsible for me to take such action when she is clearly feeling better," said Padre Rienetto, waving away his generous offer. "I will keep your proposition in mind, should her malady return."

San-Germanus made a slight, graceful bow. "I thank you for your good opinion."

"Thank my sister-in-law. Were she not so much improved, I might well subject your treatment to the review you suggest. I will still watch her, to see if her improvement is ephemeral, or she does not continue to practice her faith. For now, I will follow your recommendations." He stood, brushing bits of bread from his beard. "You have done well so far. I pray you will continue to have so much success with her."

"You are most gracious, Padre Rienetto."

"Keep in mind that she is a fragile vessel and must not be allowed to work against her recovery, nor is she to do anything that would exclude her from salvation," said Padre Rienetto, starting toward the door of the book-room. "If I may, I would like to come again, when I might peruse your collection more thoroughly."

"If you will tell me what time is convenient, I will be glad to show you what I have." San-Germanus began to follow him.

"When will you next want to see my sister-in-law? And how long will your treatment take?" He asked it candidly enough, but there was something in the Padre's manner that made it clear that he was testing San-Germanus.

"If her condition continues as it has been, then a week until her next treatment should suffice. If there is any change—to the better as well as to the worse—send me word and I will examine her as soon as possible. I may adjust her medicaments and the amounts she takes from time to time." He paused. "I cannot tell until I examine her myself how long I will need to complete the treatment, or if she may need to continue on treatment for years to come."

"Then I will send her maid with her," said Padre Rienetto, apparently satisfied with the answer.

San-Germanus closed the door behind them and escorted Padre Rienetto to the front door, an unusual courtesy, but one San-Germanus guessed the priest expected.

◆ ◆ ◆

Text of an entry from the household journal of Niklos Aulirios, bondsman to Atta Olivia Clemens, currently at Lecco, Lake Como, all but the final paragraph written in the vulgate and dated May 6th, 1325.

Spring has finally taken hold after two false starts, although it is somewhat cooler than it was at the same time last year. Fruit trees are in bud at last, and there is a field of oats and a field of wheat showing promise of a good harvest. There are six foals newly in pastures with their dams: four fillies and two colts. The two foals who died in March may be the worst losses we see this year. One more mare is still to deliver, and since she is waxing, it cannot be much longer.

Bondamma Clemens has expressed a wish to return to Roma in the next five years or so. She says she is again feeling the absence of her native earth. Assuming that there is no reason not to travel at that time, I know it will ease her spirit to walk those streets again. Sanza Pari nay have an excellent caretaker, but it is not the same as having the owner in residence. Also, she claims that she wants to do all she must for Villa Ragoczy, which had its fields struck by a blight, or so the caretaker has claimed. Bondamma Clemens tells me she is suspicious of Coriolano Soave, and not without cause. I, too, have found his claims on costs higher than seem justified, and I suspect he may be doubly lining his pockets.

Tomorrow we take a dozen lambs and fifteen shoats to market, the first major venture since the last market of the past autumn. It has been said that there will be less livestock available this spring than last not only because of the harsh weather but because many farmers are keeping their flocks and herds in higher numbers in case another hard winter lies ahead. Bondamma Clemens certainly supports this notion, for she had done a great deal to protect and enlarge her flocks and herds. She is planning to purchase more goats, for they, like pigs, can manage on poor fodder. If the weather is against us for another year, the people of her estate will not starve next winter. We will be gone four days, and will take six men with, and three ox-carts so that we may bring back what we have secured, including grain and hay. We need to supplement our own stores of both until summer. Prices may be high at the market, for we will not be the only ones looking to augment supplies of fodder, but Bondamma Clemens is planning to bring six pieces of gold for such purchases which should suffice. She is sewing them into the lining of her market-garb, an old-fashioned houppelande with closed sleeves and a high corsage. As she describes it, worthy but not grand. With her widow's coif in black-linen, she will be shown respect for her position in life if not for her generosity.

The monks of Santa Croce sul Lago will be here shortly to collect Bondamma Clemens' donation to their monastery: a barrel of wheat, a barrel of oats, ten laying hens, and a barrel of wine. In the autumn we will also provide a barrel of oil and four bushels of onions. I must supervise the loading of the barrels, to be sure the monks have full measure, or there could be unpleasantness later, of a sort that neither Bondamma Clemens nor I would want. Such scrutiny as might come from questions asked about our reneging on our pledge to the monstery would be likely to cause trouble for us both. So the monks are accommodated, and we do not have the Church nipping at our heels.

Upon our return from the market, the spring inventory will begin, and a copy provided to the Prior of Santa Croce sul Lago will be given it, to compare against our inventory at the end of harvest, from which the monastery and the local officials will once

again arrive at our taxes for the year. Since there are many who
seek the favor of the monastery, Bondama Clemens always insists
that the accounts be as accurate as counting can make them, no
matter what other landholders may do. She lives in fear that the
Church will claim this land and she will once again be forced to
move before she is prepared to do so.

◆ ◆ ◆

Four large cauldrons boiled over rock-contained fires in the largest of the three soap-makers' barns; the odor from the scraps and bones supplied by the slaughterhouse was as intense as it was unpleasant, a kind of thickening of the air, made worse by the warmth of the day, a noxious mixture of half-rotten meat and old blood along with the smoke from the fires that bloomed under the cauldrons, and the stink of partially rancid fat. Smoke hung in the rafters and dropped specks of oily soot on the men beneath. At the other end of the cavernous building, men with wooden paddles were stirring vats of rendered fat, lye, and saponic gum, creating soap.

San-Germanus, dressed in a tent-like canvas soap-makers' smock and surrounded by his four students, stood beside the largest of the rendering cauldrons; the young men had wrapped cheese-cloth doused with essence of jasmine around their mouths and noses in an effort to reduce the eye-watering stench, but it was clear from their expressions that this precaution was not truly successful in blocking the pervasive odor.

"This is the first stage," said San-Germanus. "If you look to the other cauldrons, you will see the second and third stage boiling. In the end, the rendered fat is of a clear yellow with a center the color and consistency of soft butter." He looked at the soap-maker. "How long will you work at this cauldron to finish this first rendering?"

"Today and tomorrow. Tonight our two night-minders will bank the fires and keep watch to be sure the fat doesn't burn, or the barn," said the man in a thick Alpine accent; his thick shoulders and muscular fore-arms proclaimed his profession as much as the odor of his clothing did. He was middle-aged, his hair badger-grey, his face ruddy from heat and effort.

San-Germanus pointed to the other cauldrons. "Will all of them be tended in that way?" He knew the answer, but wanted his students to know.

"Of course," said the soap-maker. "We will have to make ready a new load of soap to send to Venezia in another five days. The oils from fishes make very poor soap, so the Veneziani must depend upon us." His chuckles took the four students aback.

"True enough," said San-Germanus, smilling. "And it is a lesson these youths may well take to heart. Every skill has its uses; it is only a matter of finding them."

Enzo coughed once, then muttered, "I think I'm going to be sick."

"Go out around the side of the barn," the soap-maker recommended. "And drink some wine before you return, to steady your guts."

Enzo nodded and bolted, his hand clapped over his mouth, leaving the other three students to be embarrassed for him.

"Do any of you want a little time to yourself?" San-Germanus asked, aware that Flavio was also looking a bit queasy.

Andrea ducked his head and rushed out the barn-door.

"Flavio? Are you certain you will endure this?" San-Germanus inquired, taking care to make no sign of disapproval. "Silvio?"

"No; I can stay," said Flavio in grim determination. He kept his breathing shallow. "It's a . . . foul odor."

"It is the odor it is because of the nature of dead bones," said the soap-maker. "You must render the bones and get the fat from them." He looked upwards. "The rafters and beams and planks are so filled with the steam and smoke from our rendering that I could probably render fat from them, given enough time and a big enough cauldron."

"Do you always crack the bones?" Flavio asked.

"It helps to put more in the pot," the soap-maker said, beaming again at his cleverness. "Some of the large bones of cattle have to be struck with a sledge-hammer, but for the most, a metal mallet will do the job."

Silvio, who was looking pale, said, "Which bones give the best rendering?"

"Now that's a good question," said the soap-maker. "For our work, I'd say pigs are the best—more fat and the bits of meat are easily skimmed out of the cauldron on the second rendering. Cattle have fat, as well, and render fairly easily. Sheep are plentiful in fat, but they are the most malodorous of all to render, and the soap their bones provide is greasy as well as unpleasant to smell. Goats have relatively little fat and are not often worth the trouble. Ducks and geese have a lot of fat, but you need dozens and dozens of them to get a proper rendering, and the quality of fat is not so good. Dogs and cats are also too small to be useful to us. We do not often get horses or mules or donkeys, but they can provide as much fat as cattle." He nodded to San-Germanus. "Your Magister knows as much as I do about the various animals, if not more. You should ask him."

Flavio stared in surprise. "You make soap?"

"Upon occasion; there are formulae for medicinal soaps, as you will learn, and for perfumed ones," said San-Germanus. "Most of the time the rendered fats are used in preparing lotions, ointments, and unguents. Two medicaments require thrice strained as well as thrice rendered fats. But that is for later."

"Does it always have to smell so awful?" Silvio asked.

"Yes," said the soap-maker, "but in time you get used to it." He beamed and took a long, deep breath. "So."

Silvio almost laughed but gagged instead and clapped his hand to his mouth, pressing the cheese-cloth to his nose as well.

The soap-maker wagged a finger at Silvio as he shoved his wooden paddle into the cauldron to stir the bones. "You have a strange view of the craft if you cannot see that the smells it generates gives strength to the soap when it is complete."

"This stink makes it better?" Silvio gasped.

"It is not a stink," said the soap-maker patiently. "It is the necessary odor that releases death from the bones and leaves the virtue of the fat."

"Is that true?" Flavio demanded of San-Germanus.

"It is said to be so," was his answer, one that earned a glare from Silvio.

Before Flavio could pursue the matter, Enzo tottered back into the soap-makers' barn, his face still with a greenish tinge, his eyes blazing with mortification. "Andrea will be back shortly," he announced as he wrapped his cheese-cloth around his nose and mouth.

"Did you have a cup of wine?" the soap-maker asked kindly.

"I did not," Enzo said defiantly. "I will contain myself." His glance at Silvio and Flavio challenged them to contradict him.

"Let us look at the second-stage cauldron," San-Germanus suggested, stopping any argument from growing.

The soap-maker removed the paddle and summoned one of his apprentices to take over his stirring. "Mind you don't let anything burn, or we'll lose the whole."

The apprentice was a bit younger than Enzo, but his manner seemed older, for he conscientiously copied the demeanor of his master; he took the paddle as San-Germanus led his students along to the second cauldron where two of the soap-maker's sons were minding the cauldron, one working the paddle, the other tending the fire to keep it balanced in heat. This part of the barn seemed smoky from the carefully maintained fire.

"In this boiling, all forms of detritus is removed from the rendering, and the fat is made ready for the final stage," the soap-maker explained. "This rendering must not be allowed to boil too roundly, nor to cool too much, nor too rapidly."

"How do you manage that?" asked Flavio.

"See what Umberto and Buovo are doing? How steadily Umberto plies the paddle? How Buovo uses charcoal to keep the heat even?"

Dutifully the three students watched the soap-maker's sons at their task.

"It is important that you do not skim the fat until it is hot enough to show the rise of heat," said the soap-maker. "You will rob it of much of its virtue if you do that."

"All right," said Enzo, trying to look composed.

"And when the second stage is finished, you must let it cool down slowly before the third stage; if you hurry it, the clarification will not be achieved," said the soap-maker. He pointed to the next cauldron along, one set over a slow fire. "This is the last stage before you stir in the lye and saponic gum." Near the rear door of the barn, another cauldron sat over slow coals, three men taking turns stirring and removing the greyish substance that formed on the top of the mixture. This was taken off by three mold-men who strained the soap into arm-long, narrow wooden molds where the soap would harden. There were already seven molds set on racks, and another ten were laid out for filling.

"It is a complicated process," said Silvio.

"But not impossible," said Enzo, determined to lessen his abashment.

"No—as you see," said the soap-maker. "You understand our work better now, I am sure."

"Can you make soap without triple rendering?" asked Flavio.

"Of a sort, but not very satisfactory," said the soap-maker, "and surely not good enough for lotions and unguents."

San-Germanus indicated the mold-men. "See how they stir the soap in the mold, to rid it of any bubbles or poor consistency."

"They are being very thorough," said Silvio.

"That is their job," said the soap-maker. "If the molds are done poorly, the soap will not harden evenly."

"That could be inconvenient," said San-Germanus.

"All that work wasted! Inconvenient!"

Silvio did his best to ask his question with a show of interest. "How many molds can you fill in a week?"

"In warm weather like this, perhaps one hundred fifty or a few more. In cold weather, perhaps ninety: we have fewer carcasses to render in the winter and the cold makes maintaining an even heat in the cauldrons difficult, so it takes longer to produce the soap. It is worst when it rains, for sometimes the soap will not set in the molds."

Andrea came stumbling back into the soap-makers' barn, an empty wine-cup still clutched in his right hand. He blinked twice and swallowed hard. "I ask your pardon, Magister."

"You have no need of it, but you may have it if you wish," said San-Germanus. "When we are through here, I will give you a composer."

"I hope I will not still need it," said Andrea. He came up to the mold-men and watched them at their work. "Pray God I may never have to do such labor."

"Amen," said Enzo, and endured the sudden glower of the soap-maker.

"It is good work, honest work, worthy and needed," said the soap-maker.

"That it is," said San-Germanus, his attention on the soap-maker. "You are most generous to show us how you prepare your soap. Your example will stand these students in good stead when they come to making their preparations." The money he had paid had smoothed the way for this visit, but he made no mention of it.

Somewhat mollified, the soap-maker said, "We will be packing a crate of molds to go down-river and on to Venezia in four days. Eighty long bars, enough to last them until winter."

"Why Venezia?' asked Enzo. "Can't you find buyers enough in Padova?"

"Why should I turn away such a good market? In Venezia, their laundries need soap just as everyone else's does. These days even some ships carry soap among their provisions. Our dealer there has increased his order from two to three hundred molds per season. We will ship more in a month." He was not quite boasting but he was able to inspire astonishment in two of the students, which pleased him.

"How long will it be before he orders more?" San-Germanus asked.

"A month, perhaps two, with a larger order to come at the end of the year," said the soap-maker, and was delighted to see how astonished the students were to hear that. "Yes, youngsters, this business does very well. If you can but ignore the smell, this business pays well. Not all of us can be scholars."

"No, not all," Silvio admitted for all four of them.

San-Germanus motioned his students to follow him, saying as they started out of the soap-makers' barn, "We thank you for all you have shown us, and hope that your example will imbue our work with like care."

The soap-maker smiled again, and went back to the first rendering cauldron; by the time San-Germanus and his students were out of the door, the soap-maker once again was busy stirring the bones in the huge pot, humming to himself as he did.

◆ ◆ ◆

Text of an entry from the journal of Alassandro Sen, factor in Venezia for the Eclipse Trading Company, dated May 15th, 1325.

Three ships have arrived this week: the Princess of Navarre, *the* North Star, *and the* Corinth, *all well-laden and requiring only minor repairs. The Captain of the* North Star *has brought a dispatch from Captain Emerenzo Mutore of the* Boreas, *now lying at Varna for repairs, announcing a delay in his return until August or September. The inventories from these three ships have been submitted and checked, and the taxes paid on them.*

Petro Angioli has returned from Milano, Verona, San-Giusto-in-Monte, and Padova, having turned a handsome profit for Eclipse Trading Company, and for himself. His journey was safe enough, for he traveled with bands of monks for almost every part of it, and dressed as a lay-brother. Few brigands bother with monks, and so the spices Angioli carried were safer than if he had gone in the company of armed men. This is a clever move, and one I will recommend to others of our overland agents, so that they, and their consignments, are safe. The same may be said of the gold he gathered; I will recommend that all subsequent deliveries of spices be made in this way,

He made his delivery in Padova to Magister San-Germanus, and has reported that he saw the man, very briefly, for the first time; in his previous two deliveries, San-Germanus has been away from his house, but this time he had a bag of saffron to be carried back here to Venezia, and presented it personally, as if it were gold, which it very nearly is. Angioli was much struck at the strong resemblance he has to his kinsman, Conte Ragoczy, who founded Eclipse Trading Company nearly twenty-five years ago. In his days as an apprentice clerk, Angioli saw Conte Ragoczy, and was much-impressed with the man, and so was astonished at how much San-Germanus resembled the Conte. This man, San-Germanus, is much the same age now as the Conte was then: middle-aged, average height—not quite so tall as the Conte, deep-chested and strong, with attractive rather than handsome features, and eyes of black shot with blue. For that reason, Angioli says that he supposes that line has a prepotent sire among their ancestors, to put such a distinctive mark on those who followed, although he also admits his memory may not be as accurate as he could wish. Still, he said the man had the same striking presence as his relative, so it may be a mark of their blood, after all.

In two days the inspection of the returned ships will begin, and such repairs as we may find are needed will be commenced. I am satisfied that the ships need only minor attention, but it is required that we take this precaution every time, and that any improvements in ship-building be incorporated into maintenance and repairs in order to make sure that the ships are in the best possible condition when next they set out.

When the ships are being readied, I will make my report to Conte Ragoczy's factors in Genova and Trieste—pray God that will be ahead of the autumn storms—so that by next spring I will know what routes the ships are to take once the storms are over. God willing, the winter will not be as fierce as it was this last year, and the pirates will not be too numerous or greedy. In the meantime, I will do what I can to make the most of the summer. There are five more ships due back in port before September. I hope the success of these first three is an omen of success to come.

◆ ◆ ◆

"You have not ground the rosemary leaves sufficiently," San-Germanus told Flavio as he looked into his mortar at the slightly oily smashed herb. "They must be almost a paste before they will infuse the ointment properly. This, as it is, will not relieve tired muscles or induce sleep, and the ointment will be of an unpleasant texture." He looked around his laboratory at the other two students. The shutters were raised and the windows propped open on this day that was turning hot although it was only mid-morning; the sounds from the near-by herb-market echoed along the arcades, making a roar like the ocean in the narrow streets.

"But we have the camphor lotion to relieve tired muscles," Flavio protested. "And I am not a cook, to spend my time with grinding herbs."

"If you wish your ointment to be efficacious, you will," said San-Germanus levelly. "The camphor lotion is a much stronger formula, and one you would not use on children or most women," he reminded Flavio, then added. "Do you have a head-ache: you are squinting."

"Perhaps a slight one," said Flavio.

San Germanus observed him closely. "What is recommended for a headache?"

"An infusion of willow-bark and pansy," Flavio responded sullenly, as if he resented being right.

"You know where these things are kept—go and make your remedy; eat a lemon, too. They are in the bowl in the corridor." San-Germanus took the mortar and pestle from Flavio and set them aside. "They will be here when you return."

Andrea snorted, but whether in amusement or derision, not even he could say; Flavio glared at him as he made his way down the room toward the old-fashioned red-lacquer chest that stood next to the open window at the far end of the room.

"Mind you use the boiled water," Enzo called after him.

Flavio swung around. "I *know*. I *listen*." Then he turned his back on his fellow-students and trudged on toward the chest.

"I want you to consider this," said San-Germanus to Enzo and Andrea, ignoring their exchanges. "This may be the beginning of something more than a headache and you should observe your comrade closely for the rest of the day, and tomorrow, to be sure no other signs of illness have developed. If you notice anything that troubles you, tell me at once. It would be disrespectful of me not to look after the health of my students. Little as he may like it, this is a good step to prevention of a more serious illness, should he be touched by one."

"But mightn't we get something from him?" asked Enzo. "If he is ill, we may take his disease from him."

"You might, but if you fortify yourself with rose-hip tea, you should not suffer as he is suffering now." San-Germanus looked at the two young men. "If you wish to know apothecarial skills, you must be prepared to treat those who may be much taken in fever or flux. Neither is pleasant, but it is the intention of your training to bring you into such hazards as sickrooms and hospitals in order to provide succor for your patients."

"But must the study of herbs lead to that kind of danger?" Enzo asked.

"It is the nature of the study. Your mothers know how to dry lavender to freshen rooms, and she can make a mustard poultice for a cough. Your fathers have wanted something more for you, something that will provide you an honorable living as well as an education, all without turning you into monks," said San-Germanus.

The two youths exchanged glances. "But we could become ill."

"Yes, so you could," said San-Germanus. He had seen that happen many times in his centuries at the Temple of Imhotep, and had learned how much courage living physicians and apothecaries needed to do their work. "But I will teach you to make a sovereign remedy that will prevail against all manner of infection and contagion."

"Why do you not begin with that remedy?" Enzo asked.

"Because you have not enough knowledge yet," said San-Germanus, deliberately ambiguously; his sovereign remedy was made from moldy bread, and the wisdom of the time taught that moldy bread was unwholesome.

"Then what benefit is acquiring this knowledge if it only serves to expose us to risks?"

San-Germanus laughed once. "Living is filled with risks. Potential calamities await you at every turn, and even an innocuous act can lead to disaster; a man out on a stroll may be set upon by thieves or fall and break his ankle. The most we can hope for is that we are able to deal with all but the worst of the misfortunes we encounter." He could see that this had not persuaded the two students. "Suppose a man arrives in Padova, a scholar of good repute, but suffering from a cough from days on the road. It may be due to all the dust he has breathed, or he may have a fever that can develop a miasma of contagion. But if a physician with some apothecary skills should visit him upon his arrival and give him the medicaments his fever requires, then the scholar will recover and no miasma will spread through the city. The man who treated him will have delivered the people of Padova from danger as surely as if he had manned the Guard or put out a fire, would he not?"

Enzo shrugged. "I suppose, if anyone thought of it that way."

"If you limit what you do to those things that bring you praise, you will never–" He stopped and rephrased what he had been going to say. "You will never be worthy of Heaven."

Andrea looked abashed. "But still, it is a risk."

"So is walking the streets after dark, but most of us do it," said San-Germanus.

"God's Angels guard us," said Andrea.

"But men are attacked and women raped, good men and virtuous women," San-Germanus said, realizing he was coming close to heresy. "Those who live as they were made to live follow God's plan for them. Yet even they are tested."

At the far end of the room Flavio slammed down his empty cup on the small end-table that stood under the open window. "There. I have drunk it."

"Very good," said San-Germanus. "Take a mint-leaf and

chew it—that will sweeten your mouth."

"Tell me," said Andrea, "why do so many medicaments have unsavory tastes?"

"They have such accumulation of medicinal virtue that their strength makes them unpalatable to those in health, so that they will not consume the medicinal herbs and spices and thereby harm their health through untoward fortification. There are safe levels of many healthful plants that will aid as a general tonic against disease, and I will teach you about them later." San-Germanus watched Flavio as he came back to them. "Have you been eating well?"

Flavio shrugged. "Well enough."

San-Germanus handed him his mortar and pestle, saying, "Resume your work. All three of you." As the three young men set about reducing their rosemary to paste, San-Germanus went to ring the bell by the door, opening as soon as Rotgiere tapped on it; when he spoke it was in the language of the Copts. "Tell Orso that I want to provide a meal for these students today: ask him to go to the herb-market and get spinach and onions, and then to the meat-market and bring some veal-ribs and cream. I will open the spice-chest for his skills to employ. I think young Castrabella is starving himself to save money, and it's making him ill."

"And the other two?" Rotgiere asked.

"It would be unwise to single out Flavio; it would embarrass him before his comrades. At this age, that would be a great disadvantage for him. I am sure we can afford to feed them all. Please ask Orso to plan meals for the students for every day they study here. You had better ask Fedele to send over a dozen bottles of his best wines—no telling what they may be drinking in their inns and taverns." He was about to close the door when he added, "Oh, and bread. We will want two loaves, I think."

"For a man who doesn't eat, you are a most careful host," said Rotgiere. "Two loaves it will be, and butter as well."

"I am a careful host, am I not. It makes my not eating less conspicuous, particularly to these students." He glanced back over his shoulder at the three young men. "I will use the time they dine to tend to my plants."

"Is there anything more you require?" Rotgiere asked in the Padovan dialect, aware that the students were listening.

"Later today I will ask Adrasto to carry a message for me; at present, nothing more is needed." He had changed language as well, giving Rotgiere a single nod as Rotgiere withdrew from the doorway.

"What tongue was that?" Andrea asked.

"One that is spoken in Egypt," said San-Germanus. "I have spent some time there, and my servant with me." The servant he meant was Aumtehoutep, dead since the reign of Vespasianus, but he did not mention that.

"Is it as remarkable as the Venezians say?" Enzo asked, holding out his mortar. "Is this enough?"

San-Germanus took the mortar and looked into it. "Almost. Another dozen turns of the pestle and it should be ready." He paused. "Egypt is a most ancient land, with monuments to their kings and gods that are two and three thousand years old." When he had first seen the land of Khem, Hatshepsut had been Pharaoh, and he had been a slave, sent to tend the dying in the Temple of Imhotep.

"If it were not ruled by the followers of Mohammed and the Sultan, I would like to see it," said Enzo, a bit wistfully.

"If you travel there, you will see only a bit of what it was, centuries ago." San-Germanus stared at the red-lacquer, seeing things in his memory that he could not reveal to these students.

"But it is still worth seeing, isn't it?" Enzo persisted.

"It is," said San-Germanus, "to my mind."

"Then I am sorry I cannot see it."

Flavio, still a bit pinched-looking, said, "You could go aboard a Venezian galley. They trade in Alexandria, don't they?"

"Many do," said San-Germanus.

"It would be dangerous," Andrea observed, and held out his mortar for inspection. "Have I done enough?"

"This is ready to be added to the ointment," San-Germanus told him. "You know where the rendered fat is kept. Go and fill this jar to the black mark inside, and bring it back. You will want your ivory stirring fork for the task."

"Yes, Magister," said Andrea. As he left the room for the supply closet behind the glass-house, he marked his departure by saying, "God has abandoned the people of Egypt. It would be folly to go there."

"There is much to learn in Egypt," said San-Germanus, and added, "Some of what I know of medicaments I learned there."

"How can you be sure the medicaments are wholesome, in that case?" Flavio asked.

"I have had time to test them, and to improve upon them as I learn more." He thought of the herb-woman he had known, almost six centuries ago, when he had lived in a small, remote fortress in Poland. Old at thirty-eight, she had spent most of her life studying medicinal plants, and her knowledge was staggering. "It is always wise to learn from others who know more than you."

"If what they know is Godly," added Flavio.

San-Germanus did not respond to that prod, but looked at the contents of the two students' mortars. "You may go fetch the jars and the rendered fat you will need to complete this." He indicated the door; once the two young men had left, he opened two more windows and found himself wondering if he were under scrutiny, and if he were, who was watching him: the Consiglio della Universita, the Church, or the Consiglio Communale di Padova.

◆ ◆ ◆

Text of an entry from the journal of Filipo Quandt of Avignon, Master of Herbal Virtues, dated May 23rd, 1325.

The summer is producing many herbs; already the market is full of beneficial plants of known medicinal properties as well as many good plants to eat. The Arte degli Erbei has made its first assessment of the summer and have determined that nothing being sold is of inferior quality. Despite the flooding of two months ago, the farmers have been able to plant and harvest much more than I anticipated would be the case. Anyone coming to Padova for table-plants or medicinal ones will be more than satisfied with what he finds, with the possible exception of mushrooms, for some that have sprouted so abundantly are not safe to eat. The Arte is assigning two of their experts to inspect all questionable mushrooms to determine which may be consumed without harm, and which are dangerous.

Magister Sesto di Acquapura has suffered a sudden illness and there is talk that he may have to discontinue his teaching. He lectures in his rooms at the Inn of the Two Lambs, on the northern side of the city; his servant found him this morning collapsed, pale, sweating, and almost fainting. He has sent for San-Germanus to treat him—not a man I would recommend in spite of his knowledge—and has decided to remain in his care until his crisis has passed. I think he may be putting too much faith in San-Germanus because he is an foreigner and an exile, and because his skills are endorsed by the Consiglio della Universita, factors that make San-Germanus intriguing. I have sent word to magister di Acquapura that the Arte degli Erbei is ready to treat him as soon as he requests our presence. There is more to treating disease than the anatomists know, whether or not they recognize our abilities and training.

The heat has increased since yesterday and the city is all but basting in its own juices. Everyone complains of it, and most of the farmers are saying that their produce will wither if the heat lasts much longer. The greens they have brought to market do wither quickly The soap-makers' barn has been ordered closed so that its noxious fumes and heat will not add to the woes of the city. The Consiglio della Universita is anxious to have the barns taken down and reerected outside the walls, so that no miasma may become hidden by the stink of the rendering cauldrons. The Consiglio Communale has not agreed to that plan, not liking the cost of such a project, but as the Herb Market is not far from the soap-makers' barns, we of the Arte degli Erbei have stated that we are certain that a decrease in the stench will lessen the dangers to the city, and to the quality of the plants sold at the market. Pray God, the summer will turn milder shortly, or there may be more than a miasma to deal with.

◆ ◆ ◆

"The heat has taken a toll upon me," Orazia said as she was admitted to San-Germanus' book-room; behind her, Rotgiere closed the door. "I hope I'm not interrupting you. I felt . . . I felt it was wiser to come to you than lie down at home." She was deeply flushed but no sweat showed on her face, and she was warmer to the touch than she ought to be. Her lightest-weight houppelande dragged from her shoulders. "I was feeling so much better, but since yesterday, the heat has sunk into my bones. This afternoon, not even my nap served to improve me, so I have come here."

"I am thankful that you did. This is not a condition to be neglected." San-Germanus put aside the tome he was reading and came to her side. He took her hand, noticing the puffy state of her skin and the white line around her mouth. "You say you have felt like this for more than a day? Why did you not send for me?'

"My brother-in-law says that all men suffer when heat comes." She was glad of his help as she sank into the Turkish chair near the window. "It is God's Will that we endure heat and cold."

"Your brother-in-law is not a physician, and he knows nothing about the treatment of heat-fever. I have encountered it before, in Ottoman lands." He put his hand on her forehead, and removed her linen hood. "When did you stop sweating?"

"This morning, I think; it is when I became flushed," she said, her face showing nothing more than fatigue. "Is that a bad sign?"

"It is not a good one," said San-Geramnus, his mouth thinned by worry. "Have you been drinking water?"

"With my hands like this, and no sweat? Certainly not." She laughed a little wildly. "I already feel like a goat-skin filled to the breaking point."

"You will need to drink."

"And make the condition worse? How could drinking water help me?" She made a half-hearted attempt to rise, giving up almost at once.

"I know it is unpleasant, but you will need to drink water, treated water." He studied her hands again, and shook his head in increasing alarm. "I would like you to lie down, if you would, and allow me to put a damp sheet over you, to help cool you."

She frowned. "Am I so feverish that this is necessary?"

"You are feverish, and as you are not sweating, we must do what we can to keep the fever from rising." He kissed her quickly, then went to summon Rotgiere.

"But won't the fever remain, unbroken, if I am cooled?" Her question followed him to the door.

"I will explain," San-Germanus promised.

"She isn't doing well," Rotgiere said in Visigothic Spanish as San-Germanus opened the door to his knock. "I have set Gemignano to making up a bed for her in your study. It seemed the best place. And I have sent Adrasto to the New Moon Inn to borrow one of their maids, so that her brother-in-law will have no cause for complaint."

"Ah, old friend," said San-Germanus in the same language. "You anticipate me at every turn. Thank you. I suppose she came here alone?"

"Her maid wasn't with her," said Rotgiere. "Do you want me to send word to Padre Rienetto that she is here?"

"As soon as we have her laid down, then I'll write him a note explaining her condition." He rubbed the line of his jaw with his thumb, and said, "We'll need juniper-water. A great deal of it. And a latrine pail for her use. How much of the Chinese tea do we have left?"

"Not a great deal. I can prepare some for her, if you think it wise," said Rotgiere.

"The pale, not the dark, with a very little honey. Alternate it with juniper-berry-water. You know where it's kept. In an hour, she will need a few of the salt-wafers from the pantry. As soon as possible, she will also need a sheet, wetted and wrung half-dry, to encourage her to lessen her fever. I know heat-fever of old, and it is not like other fevers."

"I will give the orders." Rotgiere stepped back from the door.

"I will bring her to the study in a short while. As soon as the maid arrives from the New Moon we'll have Orazia undressed and wrapped in the damp sheet. That should improve her state fairly quickly, particularly if she has drunk the juniper-berry water. " He was once again speaking in the Padovan dialect. Rotgiere ducked his head and turned away, and San-Germanus went back to Orazia's side. "In a short while we will have you feeling more comfortable."

"Is this my malady, returning in strength?" she asked, a slight tremor in her breath revealing her fear.

"No, it is not, but that you have your malady makes it more difficult for you to withstand heat-fever." He did not add that it made treating her more difficult. He took her pulse and found, without surprise, that it was rapid and thready.

"Could this kill me?" It took all her courage to ask.

"It is possible," said San-Germanus quietly, his hand resting on her shoulder. "But I doubt it will happen, since you have come to me before the heat-fever can take hold too deeply. Your muscles are not cramping and your skin is not hard to the touch. If you will, sit quietly for a little while longer and you will have some relief. I will begin with easing the tautness in your body, indicating an accumulation of debilitating humors." He went to the fireplace and the large ewer of water that stood next to it to put out any sparks that might endanger the precious books. He poured off a little of the water into a shallow basin in which the ewer usually stood. This he took back to her, saying, "I am going to remove your shoes and put your feet in the water. I will massage your legs and feet, to activate the humors of your body, which have become stagnant."

"All right," she said, moving so he could kneel down at her feet. "I fear my ankles are as swollen as my fingers."

"Your ankles are swollen," he said in an unperturbed way.

"It is to be expected in heat-fever." He unfastened her shoes and pulled them off, setting them next to the Turkish chair. He moved the basin into place and lifted her feet to put them into the tepid water. "Just relax and let the water work."

"But won't it make the swelling worse?" she asked even as she did as he told her. "If I am already bloated, will not water make that worse?"

"No, not in this instance," said San-Germanus. "Heat-fever is unlike most fevers in that it does not break from within but from without. We must cool you until you are once again without elevated inner heat." He picked up her right foot and began to massage it, not too deeply, but with sufficient pressure to make her hiss in response to his ministrations. "You have accumulated humors in your muscles in your feet and legs, and this will help them be released. As that happens, you will be able to sweat them out."

"Then the fever will break," she said, sighing as his expert touch found a tender knot in the sole of her foot.

"No, it will diminish, and then you will sweat again, as do all creatures in hot weather."

"You do not sweat," she said.

"No; nor can I weep. Those are two things we lose when we come to this life." He started to work up her leg, feeling more tension in her calf.

"I will not be able to weep, then?" She shivered at the thought.

"If you decide you want to return from the dead, no, you will not."

"There are times that must be most welcome," she said.

"Not so many as you might think," he told he as he continued to knead her calf. "Have you had cramps in your legs or your guts?"

"Yes. Most of all in my guts." She leaned forward in the chair. "That is painful, just where you are pressing."

"Then I will not continue there," he said, and moved his hands to a little below her knee. "When have you had the cramps?"

"The first were last evening. I could not eat anything with-out cramping. I drank a little wine, and it helped for a while, but then the cramps returned." She shuddered.

"The wine may not have helped. Sometimes, when sweat is held in the body, strong drink serves to prolong the retention. I saw this happen many times in my travels."

She allowed herself to relax more as his hands worked on her calf, then moved down again to her foot. "Whether it helps or not, it feels wonderful," she said.

"That, in itself, is helpful," said San-Germanus, and ex-changed her right foot for her left. "Is there any room in your house that is cooler than others?"

"We have a small cellar, and it is fairly cool." She shivered as something a bit more than pleasure ran through her.

"Not a cellar, I think. What of a spring-house? Is there one you may use?"

"I . . . I don't know," she said. "Perhaps my brother-in-law would know of one."

"If you would, ask him about it," he said, surprised to feel her flinch as he pressed the arch of her sole. "Is this part of your foot tender?"

She nodded. "I stepped on a faulty paving stone coming here."

Although this explanation did not satisfy him, he said, "Very well. You will want to favor the foot until you are better."

"I will," she promised.

He worked his way up her calf to her knee, then back down again, all the while noticing how taut her skin was. He was again massaging her foot when there was a tap on the door. With a murmured apology, he rose and went to answer it.

Rotgiere was at the door with a large glass drinking-jar of water. "With the juniper-berry infusion; I will have a second one ready when the Bondamma's bed is ready, and will start a third," he said as he handed the jar to his master. "The tea will be steeping shortly. Should I bring it hot or wait until it is cooler?"

"Let it cool. For now, she should not be allowed anything

hot." San-Germanus took the drying cloth Rotgiere offered. "Will the bed be ready for her—"

"Shortly, my master. I will let you know as soon as the maid arrives." He ducked his head and stepped back.

"Thank you, old friend," said San-Germanus as Rotgiere closed the door.

Going back to Orazia, San-Germanus held out the drinking-jar. "I know you would rather not, but for your own sake, I want you to try to drink half of this now."

Orazia made a grimace. "If I must." She sat up a little straighter and reached out for the drinking-jar. "You have done well by me so far."

"Take steady, small sips," he recommended. "You will not want to drink too quickly."

She tried to obey, and coughed a little as she took her first large sip. "Smaller," she said as she recovered.

"Smaller," he seconded, and watched her drink at a more circumspect pace.

"What does this contain? It's strange."

"The berries of the juniper plant," he answered. "It should help you to pass water." He regarded her thoughtfully as she continued to drink.

When almost a half of the water was gone, she set the jar aside. "I can't manage any more, not now. I fear I will have knots in my guts if I drink more."

"All right," he said.

"How long does this take to work?' she inquired uneasily.

"Usually an hour is sufficient for the body to respond, but given that you are so feverish, it may take longer." He took the drinking-jar from her. "As soon as you are ready for more, let me know, if you would."

She tried to smile, but could not quite achieve it. Tears started in her eyes, "I fear my death is coming."

"Everyone's death is coming, Orazia—even mine," he said gently.

Before she could explain, another tap on the door was followed by the announcement that the bed was ready for her, and the maid had just arrived from the New Moon Inn.

◆ ◆ ◆

Text of an entry in the journal of Julot Jeremias, anatomy student at Padova, dated June 2nd, 1325

Last night a fire started in a horse-barn three streets away, and it took down four houses and the barn before it could be stopped. Today the air smells of soot and charring, and there are men stirring the ashes with rakes to be sure all the embers are out. The fire seems to have started during the lightning storm, for there were brush-fires seen beyond the city walls. Most of the fires were put out by the rain, but the barn gave the sparks shelter, so that the rain was over by the time it burst to fury. A hod-carrier and a muleteer are missing, and three bodies have been found.

I will have to Confess it, I suppose, but I want very much to study one of the burned bodies. We are being taught the workings of the body, and in so doing have seen some of the ailments that contribute to death—a liver as speckled as a painter's smock, lungs the color of tar, a burst blood-vessel in the abdomen, ruptures in the stomach—but we have not seen anyone burned or badly mangled. Of course, the Church would not permit us such license, and the Consiglio della Universita would not allow it, either. As it is we are going against all law that the Church has long since established, and we are very much at risk doing these studies. I have urged our Magister to find one of the physicians who have treated soldiers wounded in battle to come and describe the wounds and his methods of treatment so that we may incorporate his methods into our understanding. The most the Magister has done is ask that foreigner, San-Geramnus, to discuss his methods of diagnosis and treatment of conditions that surgery cannot improve. While it was interesting in its way, and the man's experience appears to be very broad, it is not truly part of our anatomical studies, and more of a curiosity than worthwhile instruction. Such is university life, however: the Magisters will always introduce more information than any student can wholly take in.

Benjanino Gilbrano and Fausto Cercicchio are going with me to the fair at Santa Romola to help me choose a horse. My father has finally agreed to give me the money for one, and admonished me to choose wisely. The purse was delivered not two hours ago. My father has also made arrangements with the innkeeper here at the Two Rams to stable the horse. He says this will more easily permit me to visit his old uncle who lives near Santa Romola, and who, as it turns out, is wealthy. Since my father cannot easily leave Avignon to visit his uncle, I am to do so in his place. So I will call upon my great-uncle once a month and for this, I am provided my own horse. As soon as I return from Santa Romola, I must consult a saddler.

◆ ◆ ◆

Clouds dark as ink billowed on the afternoon sky, occasionally muttering with distant thunder. Beneath them, the land was hot and singing a high, persistent whine that made waiting for lightning more nerve-wracking. San-Germanus had dismissed his students early, for all three of them were out-of-sorts and unwilling to concentrate on what he was trying to teach them.

"I am going to get a ladder to put planks over the glass-house roof," San-Germanus announced.

"Lightning may still strike it," said Adrasto as he went to fetch the tallest ladder.

"It isn't lightning that worries me," said San-Germanus, "it's hail."

"In June?" Adrasto asked incredulously.

"It happened last year," said San-Germanus.

"The weather was strange last year," Adrasto said as he hefted the ladder from its hooks on the wall outside the pantry.

"It has been strange this year, as well, and may be so again," said San-Germanus, who had seen the climate change many times in his more than three thousand years and was no longer surprised by it. He opened the door for his footman; Adrasto nearly dropped the ladder, he was so surprised. "Better to protect the glass and not need to have it, than to need it and not have it."

"As you say, I suppose." He frowned as he jockeyed the ladder through the door.

"But you are concerned," said San-Germanus.

"I am," Adrasto admitted, going on in a burst of candor, "Some would say you don't have enough faith."

San-Germanus had encountered this doubt many times in the past. "Those men would have to know me very well to make such an assumption."

Maneuvering his way down the narrow alley, the ladder balanced on his shoulder, Adrasto tried to recover himself. "This is not to say that I would think such a thing. But there is always talk."

"No doubt," said San-Germanus, indicating the long chest on the side of the glass-house. "I have the key and will open it."

Adrasto put down the ladder where San-Germanus indicated while San-Germanus worked the key in the heavy padlock that closed the chest. "If there is no hail, what then?"

"Then we will remove the planks and store them until the worst winter storms come in." He pulled open the top of the chests. "I'll climb the ladder and put the planks into position as you hand them up to me."

"Wouldn't you rather wait until Rotgiere returns?" Adrasto suggested, looking up at the darkening sky.

"Yes, but the weather may not hold off to suit me; Rotgiere will not be back until morning, long after the storm is over." San-Germanus pointed at the western horizon. "This is no squall coming, this is a proper thunderstorm, of the sort that sometimes contains hail. If the roof is broken, most of the plants will be damaged by the glass and the ice." Over the centuries he had learned the difference between all the varieties the weather could spawn, and this was so typical that he had very little doubt that in an hour the rain would begin, and the lightning.

"If you are certain," said Adrasto, watching while San-Germanus set the ladder in place and began to climb. "Which planks do you want first?"

"Start from the tops of the two stacks and work down," San-Germanus said, beginning to feel the separation from the earth, no matter how slight it was. He held onto the ladder more tightly and continued his dogged climb. At last he reached the roof and called down to Adrasto, "Hold up the first of the planks."

Adrasto did his best to oblige, but found the plank awkward to balance, and heavy enough to strain his back. "Here, Magister."

San-Germanus took the plank and pulled it up with the appearance of more effort than was actually required. He slid the plank into place above the far side of the largest skylight window and called down for the next plank.

They worked steadily for almost an hour, by which time the day was sunk into a twilight caused by the advancing clouds. The sound of thunder was louder, and occasional patches of lightning lit up the thickening clouds from within. "Magister," called Adrasto, "we should go inside."

"I agree. If you will hand up the last plank?" A long, slow roll of distant thunder was loud enough to echo along the streets.

"But the storm?"

"It is still some leagues away. It won't take much longer to complete the work, and I am up a ladder, not you. Hand up the last plank if you would." Although his words were unrelentingly courteous, his tone brooked no refusal.

"All right," said Adrasto sulkily, and hefted the last of the planks. At the top of the ladder, San-Germanus clung to the edge of the roof as he angled the plank into position. Then, giving the roof a last review, he moved carefully down the ladder, hardly pausing when the first loud crack of thunder announced the storm was about to break. He reached the stones of the street and discovered that Adrasto had retreated to the safety of the house. Undismayed, San-Germanus lowered the ladder and carried it back into the house, putting it away and closing the door to the outside as the rain began, suddenly and voluminously.

"A dreadful thing," said Orso, bent over the carcase of a goose that was laid out on his largest table, plucked and dressed. Next to the bird lay a bowl of stuffing made from sausage, onions, mushrooms, chopped greens, and chopped figs, ready to go into the cavity.

"That bird?" San-Germanus asked as he came into the kitchen.

"No; the storm," said Orso, his face pale with fear.

"It is only a storm," said San-Germanus, watching the cook shake his head.

"No. It is the proof of God's Wrath," said Orso, looking toward the shutters as the city shook under the strongest peal of thunder yet. "The ungodly work of those heretics sheltering at the Universita are bringing judgment upon us all."

San-Germanus was alarmed by these sentiments, but responded levelly, "Universita or no Unversita, there are thunderstorms every year, and not just in Padova."

"But they have been growing worse because we remain in sin." Orso crossed himself, looking toward the shuttered windows as if expecting to be seized by the force beyond. "Magister, I must go. I have to pray. If I am not in church, who shall protect me?"

"This house is as safe as a church," San-Germanus said, "at least where lightning is concerned."

"No. No. I have to get to a church. I am exposed here." He looked about, his consternation increasing. "We are all exposed."

Thinking back to the many, many times over the centuries he had seen frightened people seek protection in temples and churches, he said, "Go, then—but when you return, I will give you two months' wages and dismiss you from my service. It is up to you." He spoke calmly enough, but Orso glared at him.

"You try to keep me from my faith?"

"No, of course not," said San-Germanus. "But I would prefer you leave my service if you cannot feel safe within it."

"I shall seek a hearing in the Palazzo della Ragione, if you turn me off," he warned. "You cannot keep me from the Church."

"Nor am I trying to. You may do as you like," said San-Germanus, seeing Orso blanche still more as a loud bang of thunder shook the house. "If you are leaving, best to go now, before the storm gets much worse, or you may not reach your destination. You may collect your property and your wages in the morning."

"If you shut me out, I shall tell the Consiglio Communale."

"You may complain of me to anyone you like if you believe I shall have mistreated you, including your God and the Santo."

"You blaspheme!" shouted Orso.

"You are free to pray here in the kitchen—which is just as safe from this storm as a church—or any other part of the house. But if you leave, you will have to go elsewhere for your living. The Church may seek to assist you to find other employment, or take you in, as you prefer," San-Germanus told him quietly. Gemignano had heard the commotion and had come into the kitchen, doing his best to remain unnoticed. He sank down on a small stool and crossed himself. "You see? Gemignano can do it—he prays here."

"More fool he!" Orso said, his voice rising in pitch.

"Then leave," said San-Germanus, "but the rain will quickly turn to hail, so you had best leave at once."

"You are sending me out into danger," Orso shrieked as the first of the hail spattered on the shutters.

"I am not. You have asked to do so." San-Germanus knew the man was terrified and that his terror was fueling his panic.

"*No-o-o-o!*" Orso ran toward the cellar-door and all but dove through it as the thunder boomed overhead, accompanied by the rattle of hail.

"Gemignano," said San-Germanus calmly, "will you follow him to be sure he doesn't do himself an injury?"

In answer, Gemignano rose and followed after Orso. His eyes were distant and his kept his hands together so that he could continue praying as he went.

San-Germanus wondered briefly where Adrasto had gone, and for a moment wished he had not sent Rotgiere to Venezia; neither of them could have anticipated such a storm as this one, and the *Sunrise Angel* was due in port with the medicaments from Alexandria that could help alleviate the worst symptoms of Orazia's malady. "I would not have asked any other to do this," San-Germanus said to the goose.

A sound of breaking glass came from the open cellar door, and a shout of alarm from one of the two men who had gone there.

"Four wine-bottles have broken," yelled Orso defiantly.

"I am sure you will deal with them," San-Germanus answered.

"We must!" shouted Orso.

San-Germanus did not bother to respond, but gave his attention to the goose laid out on the table. He had not had to prepare food for such a long time that he faltered as he realized that the stuffing would fill the interior of the goose because it had been eviscerated. For an uneasy moment as the hail battered down on the shutters and the wind moaned in the chimney, he touched front of his purpoint, over the scars from the disemboweling that had killed him; he felt an uncomfortable sympathy with the bird. Then he took a handful of the stuffing and shoved it deep into the goose, repeating this action until all the stuffing was in the bird, then he used three metal pins to close the opening. By the time he finished, the wind was rising and the house moaned and whistled. From the cellar came loud hymns, the melodies unsteady and the words slurred; these accompanied San-Germanus as he built up the fire and spitted the stuffed goose. Only when he had set it in place to roast did Adrasto appear, shamefaced and deferent.

"I shouldn't have gone—"

"But you are here now, that is what matters," said San-Germanus, pointing to the goose. "That spit wants turning."

Glad to have something to do to make up for his poltroonish behavior, Adrasto set to work at once. "How long do you think this will last?"

"Not much longer. The thunder and lightning is diminishing." San-Germanus glanced toward the cellar-door as another bottle crashed.

"Are they–"

"They are breaking the necks of the bottles. I suppose they're drinking from the mixing bowls stored down there." San-Germanus shrugged. "This is their sixth bottle, by my count."

In spite of his chagrin, Adrasto laughed a little. "That is three apiece."

"Even accounting for spillage, they must be quite drunk," San-Germanus agreed.

"Will you dismiss them for drinking your wine?" Adrasto inquired as if to separate himself from the conduct of the other servants.

"No; not for drinking my wine."

Adrasto turned the spit a little faster. "Then . . . why do you permit them to do it?"

San-Germanus considered his answer. "They didn't ask me."

Adrasto stared at the turning goose. "Oh."

San-Germanus realized he had added to Adrasto's distress. "Don't fret. They have taken little from me. I do not drink wine."

"I know," said Adrasto. "Your guests and students do." And he went back to cooking the goose.

◆ ◆ ◆

Text of an entry from the journal of Cecilio Benedetto da Parma, Magister of Law at the Universita di Padova, dated June 13th, 1325.

I had set this day aside for the pleasure of reading and playing music, but it has turned out other than I had intended. A servant named Orso came to me, to reveal what he considered to be the treachery of his recent employer, a man so well-regarded by the Consiglio Communale that this Orso has persuaded himself that he cannot get a fair hearing in the Palazzo della Ragione. He claims he is afraid of the foreigner San-Germanus, who has taken in students for instruction in alchemical and apothecarial arts. This Orso claimed that San-Germanus prohibited the practice of religion in his house and when Orso attempted to attend Mass, San-Germanus confined him to his cellar before sending him away with nothing but his belongings. It was apparent that Orso thought himself hardly used, and that he was determined to exact as much satisfaction as a servant may from a master. Seeing that I was not sitting at the Atheneum today, I dispatched a servant to the house of San-Germanus, requesting that he present himself at my house to explain himself. As an affiliated Magister of the Universita, it behooves San-Germanus to submit himself to my assessment of his conduct.

San-Germanus arrived promptly, with his household servant, Gemignano, in his company. San-Germanus recommended that I speak to Gemignano alone before I examined San-Germanus, so that the man would not be influenced by any considerations but the truth. He also advised that Orso be sent out of the room, and for the same reason. This seeming to be a prudent approach, I agreed to conduct the interview in that manner, and had Gemignano brought to me. He swore before God that he would not lie, and answered my questions in a frank and direct manner that made his story more creditable than the rantings of Orso.

I must state that the story Gemignano told was a different one from what Orso related: according to Gemignano, Orso wanted to flee the house during the terrible thunderstorm of last week—when the bell-tower of San Eusibio di Vercelli, the old Lombardian church near the Flower Market, was struck by lightning and collapsed—convinced that he would come to harm if he remained in San-Germanus' house. Within Gemignano's hearing, San-Germanus advised Orso that if he left the house, he would also leave San-Germanus' employment, an assertion that Orso resented, but took seriously enough to remain within doors, in the relative safety of the cellar. Gemignano admitted that both he and Orso spent most of the storm in the cellar, where Orso had fled, driven by the ferocity of the thunder; they passed the time drinking some of the wine stored there, and emerging only when the storm had passed. He told me that San-Germanus had gone to gather up the hailstones from the courtyard and so did not speak to either Orso or Gemignano at that time, but later in the evening, when the storm had ended and the servants were dining on stuffed goose—a most lavish dish for them, to be sure—San-Germanus appeared and told Orso that he would have until morning to collect his things, receive two months' wages and depart. Orso protested that he had only wanted to seek the protection of a church, a sanctuary of which San-Germanus had deprived him. According to Gemignano, during the time he was with Orso in the cellar, Orso declared his intention to demand a goodly sum from San-Germanus, and then to denounce him as a heretic, which Orso was certain he is.

I then summoned San-Germanus to explain himself, and he told me that, as he is a foreigner, he knows that servants are often wary of those not of the city. Orso had on several occasions voiced his suspicions to the other servants about his employer, not only on account of his foreignness, but because of the skills he teaches his pupils, which this Orso claims may be diabolical, and might lead to corruption of the young students through San-Germanus' machinations. Orso, being a cook, was certain many of the combinations of herbs and other substances must be poisonous, or at least insalubrious. San-Germanus assured me that the formulae were medicinal and offered to provide them for the review of the Magisters of the Universita.

When he resumed his account of the events, San-Germanus said that as soon as the storm came and Orso insisted that he be allowed to leave during the height of it, San-Germanus warned him that such an act would end his employment, for it demonstrated the complete lack of confidence Orso had in San-Germanus. He observed that a servant who feels in danger is one who cannot be trusted to stand by his master. When I asked about his willingness to continue to employ Gemignano, San-Germanus said that the young man had not lost his conviction in the decisions San-Germanus had made, and therefore was part of his household in every sense of the word. When I asked him *if he had paid Orso's wages, San-Germanus said he had, and provided two months' extra to sustain him until he should find another master. When I asked him why he had been so generous when Orso had not conducted himself properly, San-Germanus remarked that he had long since learned that if a servant was discontented, there was no reason to provide more of it through avarice. Having heard all that seemed to bear on the dispute, I dismissed the three men and retired to my study, where I have spent a goodly time considering what is to be done.*

Tomorrow I will announce my decision in this matter.

◆ ◆ ◆

Orazia regarded the bottle San-Germanus held out to her with suspicion. "What is it?" In spite of the brilliant summer sun pouring through the windows, turning the warm morning into a hot afternoon, she was pale, her face seeming almost translucent. The soft-blue of her belucca of Antioch silk served only to bring out the faint lines of the veins in her skin. "I have kept indoors, in the coolest room my brother-in-law allows me to occupy. I have done as you ordered, and I drink juniper-berry water through the day. I haven't had another attack of heat-fever."

"I know. This is another matter—a medicament. From Egypt." He unfastened the stopper so she could smell it. "Not the most pleasant odor, but not too dreadful, either."

She leaned forward and sniffed. "Like spinach, only stronger, and with something sour. No, not sour: bitter."

"That is from a very rare mushroom, from Persia. It can be found only in the forests on the side of their tallest mountains, and it is picked only at the height of summer." He replaced the stopper and set the bottle on the low table that stood between the couch and the wall in his small solarium. "If you will take a measure of the liquid with every meal, I think it may speed your improvement. It will certainly do you no harm."

"Why would you say such a thing to me?" she asked, shocked.

"What? That this will not harm you?"

"Yes." She studied his face as he answered.

He moved a step or two away from her, indicating the couch. "There are medicaments that are used only in extreme cases, and with great care, for although they are effective, they are also quite dangerous and can bring about harm even as they cure, although the harm they do is far less than the good. This is not such a medicament."

She shook her head. "Would you ever give such a thing to me—a medicament that harms?"

"If it were utterly necessary, yes, I would, if it would trade a great malady for a lesser one," he said. "And I would tell you why I was doing it."

"Yet you say this is not such a medicament," she prompted.

"It is not. It is a compound that serves to fortify the blood when it has become weakened, as yours has. It has been used by apothecaries and physicians for centuries."

"As you know from your own experience," she said, and managed to smile. "Very well. I will have some of it this evening, when I return to my brother-in-law's house."

"Then you and I will have most of the afternoon for ourselves?" He could sense her anticipation.

"I hope so," she told him. "If you are willing."

"My students do not attend me today. They have been sent to collect plants in the woods. They are supposed to return at sunset." He indicated the couch. "You may want to sit, to rest on so hot an afternoon."

"And will you rest with me?" She smiled, this time with ease. "I can think of many things that might while away the time."

"As can I," he responded.

"This is only five times, and I will still be . . . unaffected by our exchange, won't I?"

"Yes. But a sixth will assure your change. After today, if we lie together again, you, too, will become a vampire when you die." He used the word deliberately but without disgust or shame—he had lost such emotions millennia ago; his tone was gentle, for he was aware that despite all he had told her, that the word was still distressing to her. "You will gain strength but will need your native earth with you at all times. You will need it to walk comfortably in sunlight and to cross running water. You will have to seek out knowing lovers to sustain you. Nothing will bring the True Death but fire or the severing of your spine above the heart. You will have to travel a great deal so that your lack of aging will not be noticed."

"I should probably learn to read, if I–" she said as if she wanted to make a joke.

"You ought to learn to read in any case, not just because you may become a vampire."

She crossed herself. "My brother-in-law says all such . . . such beings are creatures of the Devil and condemned for all eternity. I would rather not be damned for all time." This last was followed by a feeble laugh.

"You will be no more damned than I am," he said. "Unless you decide that you must conform to Padre Rienetto's dogma."

"I wouldn't want to," she said. "But if I die and rise, he will surely burn me at the stake."

"Yes, he would do," said San-Germanus with composure. "So you would do well to plan to be buried elsewhere, perhaps in your original home."

Orazia giggled nervously. "First reading, and then my burial. This is a peculiar discussion to be having."

"But a necessary one. I would be derelict in my obligations to you not to bring all this up before you had need of it." He had had such discussions in the past, and witnessed the transformation of four of those who had accepted their change, as well as one who had decided against his life, and one who had ignored his instruction: in their own ways, both Nicoris and Csimenae still troubled him.

"Can we discuss something else for a time? I know we have a long afternoon, but I would like to devote much of it to making love." There was a sudden, hectic flush in her cheeks that spread down to her neck.

San-Germanus bowed to her, his movement graceful and elegant. "It shall be as you wish." He paused, then went on, "Is your maid with you, then, that your brother-in-law will not–"

"I have a new maid. My brother-in-law has chosen a more diligent woman to serve me, which means she keeps watch on me. Her name is Elisia, and she comes from San Michele-vincina-di-Udine." She gave an abashed sigh.

"And you don't like her," said San-Germano.

"I don't like her purpose; I cannot say I know her at all. I won't care about liking her so long as she is my brother-in-law's creature, for that serves only to subject me to his scrutiny through her eyes." Orazia looked about as if she half-expected Elisia to be lurking in the shadows.

"You have no reason to worry on her account. Rotgiere will attend to her." San-Germanus had given no orders to his manservant, but he knew that Rotgiere would quickly discern Elisia's mission and take steps to deal with it.

"Are you certain?" She was growing restive, as if the thought of discovery doomed it to happen. "Why would he–"

He took her hands and kissed them. "Do not fret, Orazia. You may depend upon Rotgiere. He has been with me a long time and understands my nature. He will make sure your Elisia is preoccupied while you and I are alone, and he will reassure her that you are safe with me. He is adept at such diversions."

"That is most consoling, at least so long as I come to no harm; my brother-in-law would beat her if he decided that she had failed in her assigned task. He is her master and will uphold his position," she said, doubt coloring the sincerity of her words. "Do you believe we will be safe? No one will notice how we pass the time?"

"You will not be subjected to surveillance under my roof, my Word on it," he said with stronger purpose than before as he moved toward the tallest window to open it a little wider.

"I can't help but worry," she said apologetically. "I don't want to, but I can't help it."

"And if I assure you that you are safe from any intrusion, will that suffice?" The warmth in his dark eyes took away any suggestion of challenge in his question.

She considered, then shook her head. "I'm sorry, San-Germanus. If we were to begin, I might forget my—but I might not."

"Then, if you are not comfortable, we can postpone our enjoyment until another time when you are not so apprehensive about our privacy." He said this without any trace of condemnation.

"You've said that before," she reminded him.

"I was sincere then, as I am now."

She stared at him. "You puzzle me, San-Germanus," she said.

"Why is that."

"You say you want to lie with me, but it does not trouble you when I vacillate in my desires. Most men would rail at me for provoking them. I don't always know how to deal with your tolerance of my unsteadiness. I have prayed for more diligence of purpose, but I fear that God has not yet moved to strengthen me, nor has He shown me His Will in any of this." Her face clouded as she went on in a rush of emotion. "You say my desire *is* your desire, and you tell me that you know when I am distracted, which lessens the passion we have together. I have tried to understand that, as I have tried to decide if I want to come into your life when I die. I have prayed and meditated, and still I cannot decide, not on any of it."

"You need not decide today, Orazia," he said, and continued patiently, "If you would rather we do nothing more than converse, or spend the time in my glass-house, among the plants, then that is what we shall do."

"Wouldn't that disappoint you?"

"Would I prefer to spend the time amorously? Yes, but only if you would." He returned to her side. "You tell me that you are aware of the risks you run from me, and that relieves me, but I am also cognizant of your reservations, and I respect them."

She sighed. "Must you be so infuriatingly accepting, San-

Germanus? Can you not, for once, bend me to your will?" She rose from the couch and turned away from him. "I would like to be carried away, to be overcome."

"Why should you want that of me?" he asked, genuinely curious; he had encountered such responses before, and they always left him perplexed. "To overpower you would also be to threaten you, and that would awaken fear in you that would blight our touching. Why should a threat entice you to reveal yourself to me?"

"That isn't what I meant," she said.

"Then what do you mean?" he asked, only a suggestion of exasperation in his question. "Why do you want to give up your choosing in preference for capitulation?"

"Because it saves me from having to bear responsibility," she shot back, and put her hands to her mouth, her eyes wide in consternation. "I would not have to Confess it, or do penance for it," she went on softly as the full weight of her words sunk in.

"Do you Confess what we share?"

"No," she admitted. "And I know I should."

"And that is what you want? To be made to feel guilt for being loved?" He held out his hands to her. "It would scathe what we have achieved, Orazia: believe this. You would resent having your autonomy taken from you, and that would keep you from—"

"Oh, you're right, you're right," she said in aggravation. "But if women are known to be tools of deception, and inclined to sin, then . . . it may be better to succumb to the needs of men than to follow my own will."

"Ah," said San-Germanus. "But I am not a man such as living men are."

She turned and stared at him. "I know."

"If that surrender is what you truly seek, I ask your pardon that I cannot oblige you." His voice was low, and his dark eyes somber.

"*Must* you be so . . . so . . . " She struggled to find the word she wanted.

"Compliant? Acquiescent? If I were either of those, I should conform to your wishes." He lowered his hands. "For the sake of the intimacy we have had, I cannot do anything that would attaint it."

Orazia heard him out, her eyes shining with tears. "Then you are more righteous than I am, and truer to your purpose than I can be," she admitted. "I cannot endure that burden with such grace as you do." She sat down, looking toward the tall windows; when she spoke again, it was as if she were addressing the sky. "Why am I treating you so badly? I ask you to love me, and then I upbraid you when you try to comply."

"You are frightened," he said gently.

She wiped the tears on her face with an impatient hand. "Why should I not fear? I am going to die, no matter what concoction you give me. If I am discovered in our love, the least that will happen to me is that my brother-in-law will cast me out with nothing—if he doesn't condemn me to prison or the stake, which will speed my death. He tells me that God has made me frail in mind and body, and that the sooner I am gone from this world, the better my opportunity of entering Heaven, for the longer I remain here, the greater the likelihood of my sins multiplying. "

"If you decide to become one of my blood, your brother-in-law would do worse than condemn you," San-Germanus said.

"That is what troubles me: if I die and become like you, how can I manage in the world? I will be hunted and despised. I can think of nothing that does not lead to death and damnation in anything I have done since I became a widow."

"You are wrong, Orazia. Nothing you have done would—"

"My brother-in-law exhorts me at every turn, telling me that I am in danger of eternal damnation," she declared, half-defending and half-castigating Padre Rienetto. "He prays for God to spare me, to save me from the fire everlasting."

"Why should he do so?" San-Germanus asked. "You have done nothing to deserve his censure."

"I have become enamored of you," she said. "You are a

sickness in my soul."

"What have you told him?" San-Germanus asked with a tranquility he was far from feeling.

"That I want to lie with you. That I am drawn to you, through no fault of yours. Nothing more. Not a breath more," she said. "Elisia found the ruby ear-drops you gave me and asked where I had them. I didn't know she would inform my brother-in-law, although I should have suspected she might." Now that she had told him so much, she could hardly stop herself from disclosing the whole of it. "I said you have given them as a token of my improvement, but Elisia knew that my emotions were caught up in all you had done."

"Then I take it she told your brother-in-law about them," said San-Germanus, thinking of Srau, almost twelve centuries ago.

"She fed his worst fears," said Orazia, her voice hushed. "If half of what he accused me of were true, I would be debauched beyond all hope."

"Your maid said that you admitted to debauchery—to her?" He was at once amused and worried. "Did she happen to explain why you would tell such things to someone new to her service and untested?"

"According to my brother-in-law, she said I boasted of it." She shook her head angrily.

"That you and I were caught up in corruption and lubricity," he guessed, and saw her blush. "That I have provided the occasion for sin."

"So he claims," she said. "He is willing to believe her, that's the most . . . disappointing part of it."

He was silent for a long moment, then said, "If he is so convinced of the worst, how do you wish to change his mind, if you do wish to change his mind? Do you intend to show him his error, or would you prefer he–"

"He has thought me guilty of many faults, my legacy from Mother Eve. I don't know that he would accept that I was not lost to all virtue. Sometimes I think he is looking for sins in me, so that he may not have to pray for my recovery, because he is sure I am dying. It must be God's Will that I die, and to pray against that could offend God." She went to him. "It may be a sin, yet I long for your love, for the ardor you give me. But I am afraid of being accused of greater trespasses than I have already been."

He took her in his arms as much to shelter her as to awaken her desire. "I have a notion," he said, and kissed her brow. "You have nothing to fret about, Orazia. Rotgiere will disabuse your maid of her suspicions." He released her and went to pick up the bell that would summon Rotgiere. "Sit down, and bring serenity to your thoughts," he said to her while he waited by the door.

"If only I could. I tried when I first . . . but I could not sustain . . ." She wiped her eyes again as she sank onto the couch. "I feel such a fool, to be overset by what my brother-in-law thinks."

"Given your circumstances, I think it to your credit that you have withstood so much ill-usage," he said, and broke off as he heard a tap on the door.

"My master," said Rotgiere as San-Germanus opened the door.

"Come in," said San-Germanus, leaving the door ajar and positioning himself so that he could spot any eavesdroppers. "I fear we have a problem to deal with." Then he summed up what Orazia had told him, speaking in the tongue of Persia a thousand years before.

"You want me to persuade Elisia that she has misunderstood?" Rotgiere said at the end of San-Germanus' recitation.

"If you can: nothing obvious, of course, but enough to convince her she mistook the situation." San-Germanus glanced at Orazia. "And, if you would, bring up a jar of wine fortified with mashed plums and cardamom. Tell the maid it is to strengthen the blood, just as the rubies are supposed to do."

"Egyptian secrets?" Rotgiere asked with an amused glint in his faded-blue eyes.

"The more arcane the better, so long as they are not heretical," San-Germanus said. "If you have her prepare the herbs for the infusion, it may increase her belief."

"I will do so," said Rotgiere in the regional dialect.

"Very good," said San-Germanus in the same language. "I thank you, old friend."

Rotgiere nodded. "I will be back shortly with the wine. Then I will leave you to your treatment."

San-Germanus made a gesture of approval as he opened the door for Rotgiere, then closed it and turned back to Orazia. "Rotgiere will tell your maid that–"

"I heard: that the rubies are to improve my blood." She sighed unevenly. "I doubt that my brother-in-law will believe it."

"Oh, he will," said San-Germanus. "Your maid will be heartily sorry that she ever entertained any misgivings about your behavior. Rotgiere will see to it."

"You have confidence in him," she said as if it were surprising he should.

"Rotgiere is utterly trustworthy, and a man not easily turned from his purpose."

Orazia looked startled. "You think highly of a servant."

"I think highly of anyone who has such integrity as Rotgiere has." He came back across the room to her. "You may not understand why I should have such an opinion, but I would trust him with my life—and have."

It took her a short while to consider this. "Is he aware of this?"

"I believe so," San-Germanus said.

"Then I shall trust him, too," she vowed, and looked toward the window. "You replaced two panes of glass, you said?"

"After the hail broke them, yes, I did." He knew she was making social conversation, waiting for Rotgiere to bring her wine.

"And did many other windows break?"

"Two others — none of them in the glass-house, may all the forgotten gods be thanked."

She stared at him. "There is only one God to thank."

"In these times, and in this place, possibly. But other lands and other ages worship other gods," he said.

"In error." She crossed herself. "To worship false gods will lose all hope of Paradise."

"That is what the Church teaches," he agreed.

"And the Universita does, as well," she reminded him. "You mustn't say things like that, or you will not be permitted to have students."

"That would be unfortunate," said San-Germanus.

"Are you making light of it?' She was suddenly anxious, as if she again feared spies. "Don't mock the Church."

"No, I am not: I am reminding you of a truth, one that you should know. Gods come and go over time; they are as mortal as men, and they are born, reign, and die just as all living things do. The ancient statues the Universita has in its courtyard are of gods and goddesses the Romans worshipped, long ago." He saw her fidgety nod and was relieved to hear a tap on the door.

"The wine you asked for. A jar and a cup." He held up the tray. "I have asked Elisia to help me select the ingredients for the decoction you will prepare for Bondamma degli Avei to take with her when she leaves."

"Thank you," said San-Germanus.

"Rest assured: you will not be disturbed by anyone, my master," Rotgiere promised as he closed the door.

San-Germanus carried the tray to the small table, set it down and filled the cup with the wine; the mashed plums made it pulpy, but the aroma was enticing. He brought the cup to Orazia. "Here. Drink. It will help revive you."

She took the cup and drank a little of its contents. "Will this make me more compliant?"

"No; it will lend you stamina and a little well-being to make the afternoon more pleasurable, however you wish to spend it." He studied her face, seeing her doubts and desires in conflict.

The next time she drank, she emptied the cup and handed it back to San-Germanus. While he went to refill it, she said,

"Serefino, my husband? he used to say, when my hair went white, that I was lost in the clouds. He thought it was funny, but my Confessor said that it was wrong to say such things, for it dishonored the Queen of Heaven, Who is in the clouds."

"I do not imagine your husband meant anything irreligious by what he said," San-Germanus remarked as he bore the cup back to her. "I would guess he was saying that he thought white hair becomes you."

"I have thought the same," she said, her demeanor softening, her voice sounding less brittle.

"Do you miss him?" San-Germanus asked.

"I . . . I suppose I do," she said, her eyes flicking away from him.

"It is no slight to me if you do," he told her.

"Then yes, I do miss him, and I am vexed with him for leaving me in such a coil." She drank quickly before she could say any more.

San-Germanus nodded. "Yes. The living are often angry with the dead for dying."

"Even those they love?" Orazia asked a bit wistfully.

"Especially those they love," San-Germanus assured her. "It is a sign of great affection."

"How strange," she said, and set the cup down. "Do you mind if we begin?"

"Are you sure?" he asked as he sat down next to her.

"Right now I am. I may not remain so, but . . . " She faltered, not knowing how to continue.

"Well enough," he said, and took her hands in his, and bent to kiss her palms.

"Do you think I will accept your . . . your life?" The question was out before she was aware she had spoke, and she blinked in amazement at her temerity.

"I don't know," he said, unfazed.

"This time, there is no danger of change—is that correct?"

"Yes," he said, his voice deep and soft, his dark eyes on hers.

She made a sound between a sigh and a call, then went into his arms. "If this is the last time, let it be memorable," she whispered.

Text of an entry from the journal of Padre Fiorello Rienetto dated June 24th, 1325.

There was another fire last night, this one in the houses by the Porta Romana. They were badly burned but not destroyed. Nine persons are now homeless and have taken refuge in Santi Florus e Laurus, in spite of the general objections of the parishioners who worship there. Vescovio Strofinaccio has this evening declared that until those who have lost their homes have found other habitation and have the wherewithal to rebuild their lives, the church, and the Church, will shelter them. He says that charity must include taking in all who have suffered misfortunes, so long as they are faithful to their God.

Elisia has once again defended my sister-in-law's character and her conduct in regard to the foreigner who is treating her illness, Francecco di San-Germanus dei Ragoczy. She insists now that she was mistaken in her first assessment of their relationship, and that there are no grounds for suspicion. Both my sister-in-law and San-Germanus are beyond reproach, having done nothing to earn the disapprobation of worthy men. Elisia says she did not understand the significance of the gift of ruby ear-drops and assumed they were intended as tokens of admiration, not of healing in the manner of the Egyptians, who place great faith in the magical power of stones, much as we understand the holiness to be found in the relics of the Saints. This is the third time she has explained all this to me, and sworn on the Cross that she is truthful, so I am constrained to believe her, little as I like a foreigner using the techniques of the Muslim Egyptians on Orazia. Women are the weaker vessels, and who knows what devilish arts may be contained in those ear-drops, or in the other concoctions San-Germanus provides. Were it not that the Unversita vouches for his skills, I would complain to the Consiglio Communale and

Vescovio Strofinaccio of his treatments.

May it be God Who guides my steps and is with me in all I do, in my waking and sleeping, in my living and dying, according to His Will. Amen.

◆ ◆ ◆

Bells and gongs sounded the alarm, rousing half of Padova from sleep in the hot July night. Shouts of "Fire!" echoed along the narrow alleyways beyond the soap-makers' barns, and across the steps of the Palazzo della Ragione.

"Where!" shouted the Captain of the Night Guard as four men in leggings and night-rails came rushing down the Herb Market piazza.

"The last of the soap-makers' barns is on fire!" one of the men answered. "Water! We must have water!"

The clamor grew louder as more small gongs were hammered into life, and the nearer church-tower bells tolled. Along the streets shutters were thrown open and the glimmer of newly lit lanterns shone from the interior. The streets were beginning to fill as men hurried into the streets, prepared to fight the fire.

From the vantage-point of his book-room window, San-Germanus watched the uproar while he pulled on his tall Ottoman boots with the thick soles filled with his native earth. "Rotgiere," he shouted, hoping to be heard. "Bring the servants and our buckets. Hurry!"

"Yes, my master," Rotgiere called from the floor below. "Directly!"

San-Germanus pulled on his black-damask purpoint over his white-linen camisa as he rushed to the door, emerging not quite dressed into the dark corridor. He rushed down the stairs and was bound for the side-door when he heard a ferocious pounding on the front. He changed directions and went to lift the night-brace and open the door.

"Oh, Magister!" Enzo Grimanni exclaimed as he almost fell through the opening into the small entry-way.

"Enzo!" San-Germanus exclaimed. "What are you–?"

"God forgive us. We never thought–" His face was sooty and his hands were blistered.

"Enzo," San-Germanus said, reaching for the lantern near the door and bringing it up to the youth's face. "What has happened?"

"We didn't mean . . . " He trailed off, ending on a rasp.

Rotgiere appeared in the corridor behind San-Germanus. "I am going out with the others. I'll wait at the entrance to the Herb-Market arcade." He did not wait for a response, turning and hastening away.

"What is it!" San-Germanus demanded. "There is a fire, and I must go–"

"I know there's a fire," said Enzo, and began to cry in steady, gasping sobs. Finally he managed to stop enough to say, "We tried to contain it, but it–" He stopped, holding up his damaged hands. "Flavio . . . he wouldn't leave. He said he would stop it. But it's getting worse, and spreading."

San-Germanus went very still. "What do you mean, you tried to contain it?"

"The fire we'd made."

San-Germanus stared in disbelief. "You tried to render your own fats in the soap-makers' barn?"

Enzo swallowed hard and nodded twice, saying in his own defense, "Well, the baker wouldn't let us render fat in the bakery–"

"Of course not," said San-Germanus.

"And we couldn't do it here, in your house, could we?"

"No, and well you know it," San-Germanus said gruffly to conceal his worry. "I told you I would make appropriate arrangements for you."

Enzo paid him no heed. "And we didn't think the soap-makers would mind, since they do rendering all the time; they boasted to us of how they keep their fires burning. We'd already seen how they managed the rendering in those large cauldrons, and surely something as small as ours–" He looked about miserably. "We brought our own cauldrons, and . . . and our own charcoal and wood." He bit his lip. "We bribed the night-minders to let us set up."

Rotgiere appeared in the entry-way, two buckets in his hand. "Adrasto, Gemignano, and I are ready to go, my master."

"Go ahead," said San-Germanus. "I'll be along shortly."

"Is something the matter?" His long association had taught Rotgiere how to read his master's face.

"I'll tell you later, when the fire is out." He took Enzo's sleeve and tugged on it. "Come into my reception room and tell me as much as you can, and quickly."

"I have so little I can say," Enzo told him, becoming hoarse.

"You had better provide a full account," said San-Germanus, almost shoving him into the handsome reception chamber. "When did you decide to use the soap-makers' barns for your project?"

"Five days ago," Enzo admitted.

"You and Flavio. What about the others?"

"Andrea said he wouldn't. He threatened to come to you, Magister." Enzo looked down at his feet. "I paid him to keep quiet."

"Not a very good bargain, was it?" San-Germanus shook his head. "I will have to report this to the Consiglio della Universita. They will decide what's to be done to you—and to me."

Now Enzo was truly shame-faced. "I . . . we didn't think about that."

"No, I didn't suppose you did." He paused a moment. "You say Flavio remained to put out the fire?"

"He did."

"And you? You came to alert me, but how long did you wait?"

"Not very long. I stopped to get a cup of wine, since I was choking from the smoke— it was greasy and smelled of rotten meat. The smoke, not the wine." He looked down at his hands as if seeking a better story in the charred blisters. "But then I came here as quickly as I could." Enzo suddenly began to weep. "It all went wrong."

"So it did," San-Germanus said, the line of his mouth grim;

he pointed to a chair. "Sit there and wait for me. If there is fire within a block of this house, flee. Do you understand me?"

"Yes, Magister," said the unhappy young man.

"When I return, I will want to have a serious discussion with you."

"Will you beat me?" Enzo asked miserably.

San-Germanus stared at him. "Why would I do that? It would not change what has happened, would it. And you are not likely to make the same mistake again, are you?" He went to the door, where he paused briefly. "There's an ointment for burns in my red-lacquer chest. Soak your hands in cold water with tincture of oregano until all the soot is gone, then rub the ointment in." With that he left his student alone.

Reaching the street, he saw the confusion was increasing, accompanied by the brazen clamor of the alarm bells. The clouds of roiling, malodorous smoke filled the air, and bits of burning embers were falling all through the area. A dozen men were already busy on the roof of the Palazzo della Ragione, emptying buckets as soon as they could be hoisted up to them. A smaller group were providing the same efforts for the Atheneum of the Universita. All through the Herb-Market torches were lit and groups of men from the Artei and Confraternite were managing bucket-chains while houses near the fire were emptying, some of those fleeing clutching treasures and talismans against harm. The noise was loud as a stormy sea, and the unsteady light lent a nightmarish character to the efforts of the people.

Out of the confusion Rotgiere stepped, saying, "I will go as near the fire as the Watch will permit me."

"Thank you, old friend. I am going to see if I can locate Flavio. Enzo said that he—" He stopped.

"Don't venture too near the flames, my master: they are as fatal to you as to any of the living." He ducked his head. "I'll look for you at the house before dawn."

"I will try to be there," said San-Germanus, and hurried off toward the burning barns, his anxiety increasing as he went. He reached the front line of fire-fighters when a Watchman stopped him, shouting to be heard.

"Who are you? Why are you here?"

"I am San-Germanus dei Ragoczy, Magister Apothecary," he answered, raising his voice. "I have come to do what I may to help."

"The flames need to be stopped. Can you do that?" The Watchman, a large, burly fellow with singed eyebrows and a shock of sooty chestnut-colored hair, made himself a barrier between San-Germanus and the line of fire-fighters.

"I can help."

"The roof fell in on the main soap-makers' barn, and one of the other two is likely to have the same happen." The Watchman studied him. "Can you provide ladders, so water can be dropped from above, to keep the sparks from starting new fires?"

"I have three ladders and will gladly provide them all for this use," said San-Germanus, with the unwelcome realization that if Flavio had not managed to escape he was very likely dead under the collapsed roof. This realization distressed him as he rushed back to his house to retrieve the three ladders. He carried them to the fire-line and announced to the Watchman, "I have the ladders here. Use them as you will."

"That was fast," said the Watchman, and began to cough.

"I know you want to save as many as possible," said San-Germanus.

"Nothing left in the barns to save. Or anyone," he added, coughing more harshly.

San-Germanus ducked his head. "I have an elixir that can lessen such coughs. And I have medicaments for burns," San-Germanus offered. "Shall I bring them to help treat those injured by the fire?" He was aware that he could not continue to use his remarkable strength or his speed without drawing unwanted attention to himself. He saw the Watchman nod.

"That would be helpful. The Servite Sisters have set up an aid station on the other side of the Universita. They could probably use your skills," the Watchman growled, and motioned a new gang of men to the end of the bucket-chain. "Better than you remaining here to no purpose."

San-Germanus made a gesture of compliance, and hurried off again. This time when he reached his house, he took a moment to look in on Enzo, who sat in the kitchen, his hands thrust deep into a pail of water; his eyes were red and swollen from smoke and weeping. "Are there blisters?"

"On my arms. My palms are raw." The student could not bring himself to look at San-Germanus. "Flavio?"

He framed his answer carefully, not wanting to provide too great a blow or false hope. "If he remained in the barns, he has perished. If he fled, he may yet be alive." San-Germanus approached Enzo, who flinched and closed his eyes. "Let me see your burns."

Mutely Enzo lifted his hands from the water and held them up to San-Germanus' scrutiny.

"I will bandage them when I return. Make sure you apply the ointment liberally and rub it in as well as you can. You will have scars, but there is nothing that can be done about that." He went out of the kitchen and up to his laboratory where he picked up his carrying-case of medicaments, then swung around and went back down to the ground floor and out through the kitchen door, not to return until mid-morning, to find Enzo asleep in the book-room, and Rotgiere waiting with the news that Flavio's body had been found.

◆ ◆ ◆

Text of an entry from the journal of Sesto di Acquapura, Magister of Natural Philosophy, dated July 7th, 1325.

The damage to the roof of the Atheneum, the result of last week's fire that destroyed the three soap-makers' barns and killed five people, is finally being repaired. The work is scheduled to be completed before the end of the month, for although it is not extensive, a few of the drain-channels were effected and now must be replaced.

One of the dead from the fire, Flavio Castrabella, was a student of San-Germanus dei Ragoczy, who is Magister Apothecary in the Universita. According to what has been reported, two of his students—Castrabella and Grimanni—may have been in the largest barn at the time of the outbreak of the fire, in which case, San-Germanus' responsibility, if any, must be determined by a review by the Consiglio della Universita. All Magisters will have to attend the hearing, and contribute to the decision reached. It is always difficult when a student dies, and when such a death is under questionable circumstances, it is doubly difficult to resolve the situation the death creates. Filipo Quandt of the Artei degli Erbei has stated that he believes that San-Germanus dei Ragoczy must be held responsible for the deaths of his student and the burning of the soap-makers' barns because the student went to the barns on his recommendation; without San-Germanus' instruction, Castrabella would not have come in harm's way, a position flatly contradicted by Grimanni, who has exonerated San-Germanus from all responsibility, and will say so when the official hearing convenes.

I, for one, plan to speak in support of San-Germanus, as an instructor and as a man, for it was he who provided me with a regimen to control the dreadful symptoms that overtook me earlier this summer. He provided me an infusion to drink, and gave me a dietary plan that appears to help, although I do miss having honey and sweet-cakes, and being limited to one glass of wine a day. He has supervised my improvement without undue imposition. I cannot argue with the results of his care: I am glad to say that his subsequent treatment has restored me as no other physician has been able to do. I have incorporated some of what he told me about antipathies of the body into my instruction, for I believe it behooves a natural philosopher to incorporate all observations of the natural world into his study.

The Consiglio Communale will decide in two weeks if the soap-makers' barns are to be rebuilt where they stood, or be re-located outside the city walls. There have been persistent rumors that the fire was started to gain just that result. The Consiglio Communale will hear all the arguments in the Palazzo della Ragione, and come to a decision by the end of the month. I think it is at least as likely that the barns were burned by those wanting them out of the town than burned by a mishap caused by San-Germanus' students. But the Consiglio Communale may prefer to hold a foreigner ultimately accountable than to become locked in disputes with the Artei and Confraternite again. I will make an appearance at that hearing, not on behalf of the Universita but on my own account.

Tomorrow I lecture on Pliny the Younger and his comprehension of the world, and will then exhort my students to learn from his excellent example, but to temper their learning with the precepts of religion as well as knowledge.

◆ ◆ ◆

"Could you really be dismissed from the Universita?"' Orazia demanded, her face pale as she looked directly at San-Germano. Around her, the solarium shone golden in the summer afternoon, and the scent of green things wafted in through the open windows from the Herb Market. "My brother-in-law says it's all but certain." Unable to bear to look at him, she turned around and stared out the window toward the roof of the glass-house.

"It is possible, but no decision has been handed down, and none will be for some days yet," said San-Germanus, coming up behind her and laying his hands gently on her shoulders; he felt her wince. "You have nothing to fear." This was not quite accurate, but it was all he was prepared to tell her.

"Haven't you defended yourself?"' she asked, pulling away from him enough to free her shoulder.

"I haven't yet been summoned for questioning." He could see that more than his predicament was troubling her. "Is something wrong?"

"Nothing. Not because of you, not because of this impasse with the Consiglio della Universita." She turned around to face him, but could not meet his compelling gaze; instead she stared at the intricate fastening of his purpoint as if she had never seen them before and they fascinated her.

"If not from me, then who? and why?"

"It is nothing of importance," she began, and then stopped.

"No. I don't want to misrepresent myself to you." She took a deep breath. "My brother-in-law—"

"Ah," he said.

"—sought to purge me of any evil that might be sequestered in my soul. He said upbraiding me was not sufficient, that flesh is stubborn in its sins, and had to be mortified."

"You mean he beat you," he said directly.

"For the sake of my soul," she replied, trying to sound convinced. "It is his right and obligation to chastize me, to remind me of my errors."

"And which errors are these?" He kept his question calm although he was troubled.

"Errors in judgment, and in conduct. He thinks I have lost my humility." She closed her eyes to avoid the compassion in his gaze.

"Why does he think that?' He knew she did not want to answer.

"He said a beating would restore my conduct to that which is fitting for a widow in my position." She reported this as if she were reciting by rote.

"If only he would not relish his task as I reckon he does," said San-Germanus, and took her hands in his. "How badly are you hurt?"

She shrugged. "It is nothing I haven't endured before."

"That does not excuse it; you should not have to endure such ill-usage at any time," he said, and kissed her hands before slipping his arms around her and drawing her close to him. "He knows he has done wrong in beating you."

"How can you say that?' She was dismayed now, and pushed at his shoulders to break away from him.

"I say that because he did not bruise your face. All you injuries are hidden, which means he was ashamed of them. If he truly intended to provide a reminder of his purpose, your face would be black-and-blue. But he confined his blows to parts of your body that are covered. He is not certain of his actions."

She stared at him. "No. That can't be right."

"I have seen many beatings through my life—" he had received some and delivered a few himself— "and I have come to think that there are many aspects to beatings, not just the infliction of pain, but much more."

Orazia sighed. "You have had more experience, I cannot doubt." There was a fatality in this observation that was disconcerting. "God must have made you to be witness for others on the Day of Judgment."

San-Germanus could feel the inward chill that gripped Orazia; he was aware of her newly awakened dread and realized that she no longer believed he was an ally. "I am sorry you have suffered on my account."

"But I haven't," she protested. "You have been good to me, you have treated my ills, and you have offered me your protection." There was a forlorn sound to these protestations, and it undermined all the staunchness she wanted to assert.

"Thank you for that," he said, so genuinely that she blinked in surprise.

She went over to the couch, and after a brief silence, said, "I'm sorry," before she sat down; she took a square of linen from its place in her sleeve and wiped her eyes.

"You need not apologize," he said, coming to her side.

"I suppose I have made my decision—about your life."

"I suppose you have," he agreed.

"I know I can't be like you. I could never live the way you tell me you have." She shuddered, and drew back from him as if chilled by his nearness. "If I could remain with you, then it might be possible, but since you say you and I would no longer be lovers if I were like you, I have no reason to live your life."

He went to the window, as much as to give her a chance to regain her composure as to look out at the sky. "Then you will not."

"I think I must say farewell today," she went on before her courage failed her.

"If that is your wish," he said, bowing slightly in her direction.

"My brother-in-law has found me a new physician. He has forbidden me to speak to you, even for medical treatment." She got up. "I have told him he has no reason to think ill of you on my account, but he is adamant."

San-Germanus listened to her closely, then said, "You must do as you think right."

"This is right. I know it is."

He went to her and put his hand out. "Will you allow us to part friends?"

"Oh, yes," she said in a rush of relief, laying her hand in his, "I was afraid that you would scorn me. I have been such a coward about my brother-in-law, but I am so wholly dependent upon him, what else could I do?"

He would have taken her in his arms if she had shown the slightest inclination to be embraced; as it was, he bent over her hand. "You may always depend upon my friendship."

She pulled her hand away as soon as he kissed it. "But you will not remain in Padova for all time, will you? You will leave, this year, next year, and you will go about the world to places whose names I have never heard and could never find."

He could not deny this. "Yes. I will leave Padova. But Eclipse Trading Company in Venezia will know where to find me, if ever you have need of me."

"And how will I get word to them—apply to my brother-in-law to write the message for me?" A spark of anger shone in her eyes. "If I could write, I would thank you, but as it is, once you are gone, I am mute."

"You read enough to know—"

"I know what almost every servant in Padova knows: I can recognize letters, I know their names, and I can make out a few words, but my hand has never been turned to writing, so I must accept my silence." She went toward the door. "I am going to miss you, San-Germanus, and not only for the pleasures you have given me, and your care of my malady, but for your kindness and your interest in me. I have never known a man to listen to me so attentively as you have. You have not made light of my ills, nor told me they are a judgment upon me. For that I am grateful, and I will remember you every night in my prayers."

"If that will console you, I thank you," he said.

"And I ask that you do not forget me too soon, like those Greek gods in the courtyard of the Atheneum." The wan smile she offered revealed her sadness.

"I could never forget you, Orazia. You are part of me now." His dark eyes were lambent with unexpressed passion.

"I will ask your man to take me to the door. I am sure he is near-by." She put her hand on the latch. "I am sorry."

"So am I," he said as he watched her go. Only when she was gone did he return to the window and stare out at the bright sky, letting his thoughts drift with the occasional clouds puffing through the afternoon. His reverie was interrupted by a rap on the door. "Come in, Rotgiere," he called, and turned his back on the glorious sky.

Rotgiere entered the room, full attention on his master. "Bondamma degli Avei has left with her maid."

"Yes," said San-Germanus.

"She told me she would not be returning."

"Yes," said San-Germanus.

"She apologized for–"

"Yes; she said the same to me." San-Germanus rubbed the line of his jaw with his thumb. "He beat her, you know."

"Padre Rienetto?"

San-Germanus nodded. "I have become a danger to her."

"And she to you," said Rotgiere.

"I fear so," San-Germanus admitted. "Perhaps it would be wise to prepare a short journey to Venezia."

"Immediately?" Rotgiere asked, encouraged by San-Germanus' plan.

"As soon as I have given my account to the Consiglio della Universita and the Consiglio Communale decides if I am to pay a fine for the damage my students caused." His voice was steady but remote, as if he were discussing distant matters.

"That may take time," Rotgiere cautioned in the language of Persia a thousand years before. "Delay could be hazardous."

"So it could. But if we depart before such decisions are made it would make return almost impossible." San-Germanus let Rotgiere consider the implications of this, and then went on in the same Persian dialect, "We should prepare the household for our absence for . . . shall we say . . . six months? I am known to have business affairs to manage in Venezia, and setting time aside to deal with them will astonish no one."

"How soon will this be?" Rotgiere's calm demeanor almost hid his impatience.

"We cannot be seen to be fleeing," San-Germanus replied. "So perhaps the end of August would be a reasonable time for us to leave."

"Are you sure you want to take that long?" Rotgiere asked.

"Unless matters become more difficult, I believe it would be best to go about our business in the usual manner. I will not have pupils again until the Consiglio della Universita complete its inquiry into the death of Flavio Castrabella; I will have more time to devote to my interests in trade. There will be no surprise at our leaving after I have spent a month and more delving into the state of my trading contracts."

"In other words, you're planning to let half of Padova know of your uneasiness about your business in Venezia." Rotgiere did not quite chuckle but there was a glint of amusement in his faded-blue eyes. "No doubt you will find a way to convince your associates here that you need to confront your Venezian partners directly."

"I should think that likely," said San-Germanus, starting toward the door.

At last Rotgiere asked the one question he was most distressed about. "And Bondamma Orazia?"

"She will not accept help from me, that much she made clear," San-Germanus said heavily. "If I thought I could spare her more suffering, I would oppose Padre Rienetto openly, but that would bring her more beatings, and I want no part of adding to her misery."

"Are you sure you would?" Rotgiere's tone was serious, and

he spoke in the Padovan dialect.

"Oh, yes." San-Germanus regarded Rotgiere levelly. "I have no doubt of it."

"She is aware of your true nature, isn't she?" Rotgiere pursued.

"Yes."

"Then the sooner we are gone, the better it will be," said Rotgiere with feeling.

San-Germanus pulled the door open. "Then end of August will do, old friend."

"And if you are imprisoned by the Consiglio Communale?"

"Then I depend upon you to find me a good lawyer. Padova is full of them, thanks to their school of jurisprudence." He stepped into the hall, Rotgiere right behind him.

"You will make light of your risks," said Rotgiere.

For a long moment San-Germanus was still, then he said, "Morbid worry will not alleviate my situation, old friend, nor will it spare Orazia any pain. If I conduct myself as a man expecting to go about his business, it is likelier that I will not be held or imprisoned."

Rotgiere sighed. "And this is not China."

"No; nor is it Crete or the road to Baghdad."

"Or Leosan Fortress, or Spain," Rotgiere supplied.

San-Germanus stopped at the top of the staircase. "Keep that in mind and we should emerge from our difficulties here without anything worse than a loss of a sack of ducats and the athanor I made for my students."

Rotgiere knew that slightly ironic, unapproachable tone of old, and so said nothing more than, "Minor inconveniences, my master, by comparison," and kept his opinions to himself.

◆ ◆ ◆

Text of an entry in the journal of Cecilio Benedetto da Parma, Magister of Law at the Universita di Padova, dated August 20th, 1325.

Today we heard the last of the testimony in regard to Francecco San-Germanus dei Ragoczy, this being a second appearance by Filipo Quandt da Avignon, of the Artei degli Erbei, who has reiterated his objection to granting San-Germanus the right to instruct students. The others who share my duties to hear and assess the degree of responsibility San-Germanus bears in the death of his student Flavio Castrabella, as well as the destruction of the soap-makers' barns—which will be determined in the Palazzo della Ragione rather than the Atheneum—have indicated that they are unimpressed by the strident denunciations in which Quandt indulges. To demand that the Universita refuse the athanor San-Germanus made for his students on the grounds that it may contain a curse goes beyond the limits of education to the realms of prejudice. Even Sesto di Acquapura, Magister of Natural Philosophy, has said that such concerns are not in the purview of the Universita, and that if Vescovio Strofinaccio is willing to approve the athanor, Filipo Quandt can have no reason to object to its use.

Silvio Mordero and Andrea Vecchiato have addressed the Consiglio della Universita concerning the nature of the instruction that San-Germanus provided, making it clear that he did not endorse any independent preparations of formulae until the four students had had much more experience under his guidance. They both agree that Enzo Grimanni and Flavio Castrabella could not claim that they had ever been given permission to undertake rendering on their own. Both these students say that San-Gemanus is a most prudent and careful teacher, one whose pedagogy is of the highest order. Enzo Grimanni, while not speaking as a witness, but as a student accused of wrong-doing, confirmed all that the other two said. Grimanni is not returning to Padova for study, but will go to Bologna, where his father hopes that the stronger presence of the Church will help to guide his son's errant steps toward better conduct; Grimanni's father has sent a sworn document that declares he holds San-Germanus blameless for the mistakes of his son.

The most disturbing account we have had thus far in regard to San-Germanus was the account of Padre Rienetto regarding the medicinal treatment San-Germanus provided his sister-in-law, which seemed at first to improve her, but then brought about a long period of penance-like fasting, from which she, being already in compromised health, could not recover, and four days ago perished. Padre Rienetto is of the opinion that her death may be laid directly to San-Germanus' treatment, although he concedes that his sister-in-law never spoke a word against San-Germanus, and refused to believe that any of his medicaments were harmful.

I have gone on record today that San-Germanus is in no way accountable for his student's death because he at no time told his students to proceed with rendering without supervision. If they acted from their own decisions, his students must bear the brunt of their actions. The Universita will provide the father of Castrabella the amount of fifteen ducats, the sum he has paid for the education of his son. If San-Germanus is not responsible for the fire caused by his students, he is not likely to be charged for the loss of the soap-makers' barns, which should make it possible for him to attend to his business in Venezia without any unfinished civil matters lingering here in Padova.

In three days, our decision will be published, and the city will know that San-Germanus has been exonerated completely of all complaints against him. This will put an end to what I have felt was an unreasonable attempt to discredit a man who has done much for the Universita. During his absence, he has made his house and servants available to the Universita, not only for Magisters but for students, as we deem appropriate. A man who has done so much for us deserves the benefit of any doubts we may have of him. We have welcomed foreigners in the past, and will surely do so again, without holding their foreignness against them. I will miss my occasional discussions with San-Germanus, whose experience of the world is far wider than my own, and whose understanding is beyond contravention.

Next Sunday, there will be a feast commemorating the restoration of the blameless wife of the jealous man, a great miracle of il Santo. Ten Magisters will join in the procession, and I have been asked to be among their number. San-Germanus has also been invited, but he has refused, saying the place should go to a Magister who will *be here in the winter, and the Consiglio has agreed. So I will meet with him in ten days' time, on the eve of his departure for Venezia, to wish him good fortune and a swift return.*

INTERCESSION

TO THE VERY WORTHY and most faithful Passionist monk, Andres del Cruzado, at the Monasterio de
la Nuestra Senora, la Reina del Gelo at Antioquia,
Audiencia de Santa Fe, the respectful greetings of Rogerio,
manservant to el Conde de San Germanno, currently residing
at Portobello, Audiencia de Panama.

The Church detained my master a number of months ago,
and I have been subsequently unable to locate him or receive
any news of his welfare. Recent inquiries have suggested that
you may know where he is, for you have long kept the records
of incarceration at your monastery and, in that capacity, have
access to many more records of suspected heretics. I am writing to you in the hope that you will tell me where I may find
him, and the reason for his detention.

I must here make bold to tell you that el Conde is no heretic,
although he is not a communicant of your Catholic faith, for
those of his blood come from the Carpathian Mountains in
Hungary, and in such places, the Greek Church is maintaining
the mission of Christ against the forces of the sultan and all the
Ottoman followers of their false prophet. Those of his heritage
have defended that land from the might of Islam and offered
havens to those fleeing oppression and slavery. He has done

nothing to disgrace your Church, nor to bring any others to act against it; he has upheld the Church wherever it has flourished, and has given to its causes readily and generously; those acts are recorded and known. If you will review the records of Don Ezequias Pannefrio y Modestez, Corregidor, Audiencia de Lima of his time in Cuzco, as well as the Presidencia de Acapulco, for his time in the Audiencia de Mexico, you will see this supported in all his official obligations: he has long maintained cordial and respectful dealings with your Church.

For many months I have tried to find out what became of my employer after he called upon Obispos Trineo y Alfia and Apuesta y Fogon in Portobello in the Audiencia of Panama, shortly before he was scheduled to sail back to Spain. That day was April 16th, in 1649, one day before his ship, *El Testigo da Fe*, was to leave for Cuba and Cadiz, with ports of call in Bilbao and Calais. The ship departed four days later, but my master was not on it, and indeed, no one can tell me where he is since that hour when he called upon the obispos.

Surely, good Frey, you understand why I must find my master. I am obliged to serve him, and I cannot do this if I cannot reach him. I have undertaken to maintain his business ventures in his absence, but I cannot do so without his guidance. For that reason I implore you, tell me what you know, that I may do my duty to him, see that he is not, through some oversight or misplaced zeal, mistreated or held for crimes he did not commit. I know pursuing this matter takes you away from the work you do for the Glory of God, so I am inducing a payment to your monastery in the sum of twenty-five gold reales, not to pay for your time, which would disgrace your vocation, but to help your Order continue your Christian enterprises in the New World, even as my master himself would do were I missing and he searching for me.

For your assistance on my master's behalf, and with my gratitude for any information you are able to provide me, I am most humbly at your service, and thankful to God for your willingness to hear me,

Rogerio, manservant

At Portobello, Audiencia de Panama, the Feast of the Holy Trinity, June 22nd, in the Year of Grace 1652

To the most respected, devoted Passionist monk, Frey Andres del Cruzado, of the Monasterio de Nuestra Senora, la Reina del Cielo at Antioquia in the Audiencia de Santa Fe, the grateful salutation from the manservant of el Conde de San Germanno, Rogerio.

How very gracious of you to answer my letter of the last Feast of the Holy Trinity, and I am thankful for your information, which is most welcome, for it finally tells me that my master is yet alive, and that you, of the Church, know it.

But I fear I must impose on your charity again, and ask you where the Convento dell' Agonia is located. I understand that your Order supervises the convento, and the inmates living there. If I knew the location of the convento, I might be able to arrange something with the prior that would allow some communication with my master regarding his financial dealings, particularly his shipping ventures which are extensive and in need of close supervision. If he cannot give me his orders, then at least he can provide me with the authority to act on his behalf, which, in turn, will enable me to do all that might be done to keep his ships sailing.

Those who are imprisoned may sometimes receive visits from such members of their households as the Church deems appropriate to their welfare, and I would like to put such a petition before you at this time. I do not seek this to subvert the purposes of the Church: I believe it would be useful for me to do all that I can to carry out my master's instructions, not only because his ships carry cargo for Spain, but because he has long given certain preferential attention to goods commanded by the Church, and thus has brought about a mutually rewarding arrangement that I must suppose it is his intention to continue.

Good Passionist, I ask you to advise me. I am prepared to leave Portobello and move to a city more conveniently located to my master, but if this is not the wish of the Church, I will, of course, remain where I am, or take up residence in a place that the Church approves. Yet I do not know what course to take that will bring about the resolution to my perplexity. How am I to present these requests that they may be heard with compassion and an appreciation of mutual benefit? I thank you for any recommendations you may offer in this regard. And I am sending you fifty gold reales for your Order, as a demonstration of my sincerity and thanks for your attention in regard to my request. I am also hoping that this will help to defray any expenses my master may incur while residing at the convento, and ask, that if I have reckoned insufficiently, I may know the appropriate sum in your next letter.

I have sent this letter with the messenger Dalcut de Cartagena, who has long been employed in this capacity and was recommended to me by Frey Pascual of San Tomasso, a member of your Order, and a most worthy cleric in his own right, and who has often employed Dalcut as his personal courier. Dalcut has been paid to carry this to you and to bring your message back with all due haste so that we may exchange letters in a more timely manner. I shall expect your answer within six weeks of your receipt of this, which, you will agree, will be beneficial to both of us.

With my evening prayers of gratitude and my morning prayers of industry, I thank you for your efforts, and I beseech Heaven to reward you for all your kindness to me in helping me to better serve my master, for as the servant of man must model himself on the servants of God, so I am thankful for your excellent example. With devotion and Grace, I may approach your excellence.

Rogerio, manservant
At Portobello, Audiencia de Panama, January 24th, the 1653rd Year of Grace

To the most reverend Frey Cirilo de San Ysidro, Passionist, Prior of the Convento dell' Agonia, Passionist, near Popayan, Audiencia de Quito, the respectful greetings of Rogerio, manservant of el Conde de San Germanno, and upon whose behalf

I now address you.

Your name was provided to me by a member of your Order and I have, of my own decision, made up my mind to approach you in the hope that you will be good enough to alleviate the many apprehensions that have come upon me since my master disappeared into the hands of the Church. I have spoken personally to all those religious in Portobello who might be able to advise me, and without exception, they recommended I address you, stating my concerns.

Since the unfortunate incarceration of my noble employer, I have sought to have his charges made clear and his case brought before proper authorities, all to no avail. I have been given many names with the assurance that such persoris can and will assist me, but thus far, all have been fruitless, but for the most generous information provided by your good Passionist Brother, Frey Andres del Cruzado of the Monasterio de Nuestfa Senora la Reina del Cielo, who has informed me that you, at the Convento dell' Agonia have my master in residence there; since I have been given your name and direction, I have taken the advice I have been given. This letter is the result. I pray that you will be the one to decide to uphold the law of the Viceroyalty and your Order, and address the great wrong that has been done to my master.

To be specific, my employer was detained by Church authorities and imprisoned at Portobello in the Audiencia de Panama on April 16th, 1649, and was covertly carried from there on a day I cannot yet name. He has been held incognito in what I have reason to hope now is your Convento dell' Angonia. If you will confirm this, I may, in my duty to my master, do my utmost to bring about his release and exoneration from all charges made against him. I plead with you to send me an answer quickly by the messenger Dalcut de Cartagena, who carries this to you. He has been most reliable and discreet in these matters, and you will find him spoken of most favorably by all manner of men in your Church. I ask you to entrust all communication to him, and to permit him to travel as soon as you have penned your answer to me.

Much time has passed, and although I do not doubt that my master's soul has benefited from your good examples, I fear his businesses have need of him. If he cannot come himself, pray ask him to send authorization to me to continue on his behalf his ongoing work.

I am sending eighty gold reales to you as a donation to your convento, and with the hope that they will mitigate the cost of keeping my master among you;

with these reales for his support, he need be no charge on you and at the same time need not live in a style unlike the one to which he has long been accustomed. I pray that if you need more for your work or for the benefit of my master you will inform me so that I may attend to providing the amounts you deem necessary.

In addition to providing funds for his keep, I would ask you to permit me to correspond with my master, so that I can act with the benefit of his experience and knowledge of his wishes in the matters of businesses he had undertaken in many parts of the New World. If correspondence isn't possible, then I ask that you permit me to inform him of what I have done, so that he may be kept abreast of the activities of his ships and shipping businesses. For example, I would like him to know that La Luna Negra has put into Maracaibo, Audiencia de Santo Domingo, for repairs, and that Los Lobos del Yermo has had to have new masts fitted on her, and now lies in the harbor of Veracruz, Audiencia de Mexico, awaiting orders for her next voyage, as she is no longer on the schedule that she once kept, and Santa Clara de Assisi has taken her routes for the time being, and is presently bound for Cadiz, Bilbao, Calais, and Bruges before returning to Havana and Portobello.

These, and many other matters, are in need of his attention. If I proceed blindly, I fear I will make decisions counter to those my master would make, and I seek his council, or, barring that, his declaration that I may act on his behalf according to my own thoughts.

For any information you can provide me, I will be most grateful. I may have to travel on my master's behalf, and if that is necessary, the servants of this household will know how to find me, if I must be found. Of course, if my master has need of me, I am prepared to journey to him at any time, and to put myself at his disposal for as long as he has need of me. I pray this will persuade you of my earnest desire to aid my master, who is blameless of all accusations against him. I swear this on the bones of my family and of the saints who guard and protect all who come to them.

Rogerio de Cadiz, manservant
to el Conde de San Germanno
At Portobello, Audiencia de Panama, on the 30th day of August in the Year of Grace, 1653

To Atta Olivia Clemens, widow, resident at Senza Pari, vicina di Roma.

Respected Widow, I am making bold to tell you that my master, el Conde de San Germanno, your blood relative, may have at last been found, at the Convento dell' Agonia in the Audiencia de Quito in the Viceroyalty of Peru.

As you may know, that part of the Audiencia is very mountainous, and the convento seems to be partiularly remote.

The Church has been paying very close attention to my master's affairs, reviewing all his business dealings and inspecting his records and correspondence, as the King of Spain and the Pope require them to do. You must know that this has been a most difficult time for those of us who serve him, for we must often weigh the demands and considerations of the Church against the instructions of our master, all the while aware that we, as well as el Conde, are under constant scrutiny. Try as we will, we cannot always achieve accommodation, and for that, we are often given to distress at our inability to do as we must to honorably serve both the Church and our employer. The reason I have approached you, good widow, is that I know as my master's blood relative you are in a position to be of some use to him during this ordeal. For one thing, you may be able to ask those you know within the Church to confirm or deny whether or not el Conde is actually at the Passionist Convento dell' Agonia, and for what purpose he has been sent there. I am willing to deal with the Church and the Passionists as long as they require, but I would like to know that my efforts are actually relieving my master and aiding in obtaining his release than simply adding to the Church's coffers. I have found the lack of response I have encountered most thwarting, and so I am trying to find the means to get around this bulwark of muteness; to that end I appeal to you for any help you may provide, for I am beginning to worry that I am spending my master's money to no avail.

Not that I would deny the Church any sums she may demand of me on my master's behalf, but I am obliged to put my exertions to his service as well as that of the Church, which I am certain you can understand, having such a manservant as Niklos Aulirios to serve you. It is fitting that I do this, for it benefits my master and the Church, but I want to be able to account for what I have done in a manner that will satisfy el Conde as well as the Church.

Everything we do here is examined most meticulously, and we must be prepared to submit to such inspection often, without hesitation or any appearance of such. I know it is for the benefit of the Church and the King of Spain, but for me, in this instance, it has become a difficulty, and I ask you to secure what dispensations you can to enable me to continue to search for and defend my master without the constant supervision and arbitrary inspections that now dog all I do. I know that these inquiries are for the protection of our souls, but they tend to interfere with business, as any trader will vouch. Even now, I fear my master may be taken to another place, and my hunt for him may begin all over again because my actions have been so hampered and the information I have managed to garner is not current.

What is most perplexing, I do not know of what he is suspected, for I can find no record of formal accusation. No one has been able, or willing, to tell me more than that he may be at the. convento, in what condition or capacity I cannot find out. You, being near the Pope and his court, may be able to learn

more than I have been. I know you are a devoted daughter of
the Church, and for that reason as much as any, I come to you
with my request. I anticipate your reply with eagerness, and
will instruct el Conde's ship that brings this, *El Zefiro* to wait
at Ostia for two weeks to be able to carry your message back
as quickly as possible. I have ordered the capitan to bring you
the letter himself. His name is Diego Signo y Almejada, and he
will tell you who has seen this, other than you, me, and himself.
The capitan is reliable, and he will bring your response to me
with all haste.

I am grateful to you, estimable Widow Clemens, for reading my petition, and for your kindness on my master's behalf.
I ask you to recommend other avenues I might explore, for I
am growing short of possible lines of inquiry in regard to my
master. You have always been a stalwart supporter of those
of your blood, from your days assisting Cardinal Mazarin in
France to your cordial dealings with the staff of the Vatican.
Surely your name is among the blessed for all you have done. I
pray you will have the success that has thus far eluded me, and
I am certain that my master is glad of your assistance.

Rogerio, manservant
to el Conde de San Germanno
At Portobello, Audiencia de Panama, September 1st, 1653rd
Year of Grace

To the Capitan Diego Signo y Almejada of *El Zefiro*, at Portobello, Audiencia de Panama, bound for Santo Domingo and
San Juan, Audiencia de Santo Domingo; then Cadiz; Barcelona
of Spain; Napoli, for Roma; Genova; Cadiz; then Caracas,
AudienCla de Santo Domingo, and Portobello, Audiencia de
Panama, the greetings and full confirmation from Rogerio,
manservant to el Conde de San Germanno.

In the continuing absence of el Conde, I authorize this
voyage, and provide you with four letters of introduction and
credit for your use in purchasing cargo. You have sailed on el
Conde's ships long enough to know what markets el Conde
strives to serve. I am also providing you with eight hundred

gold reales for any purchases that may exceed your letters of introduction; the sum shall also provide pay and bonuses to the crew and any such repairs as may be demanded. The ship's carpenter shall have the authority to order the ship into port if he considers this to be necessary. I have also taken the liberty of arming you with three cannon and a half-dozen musquets to use in case of attack by pirates or Turkish corsairs. Do not waste the weapons or the ammunition, for they are given in case of need, not for a vain show of strength. In addition, I am entrusting into your hands a letter which you yourself will deliver to the widow Atta Olivia Clemens who lives at Senza Pari, to the north of Roma. Only you are to carry it. You are to inform her who has read it: and under what circumstances, and you are to await her reply. You may stay up to two weeks to secure her answer, so long as you are then ready to depart. When you reach Cadiz the second time, you are to find out as much as you can about the weather ahead before attempting a crossing. I would rather you wait in port until spring than lose you and the ship to winter storms. It is fitting for you to be prudent.

I remind you that el Conde will not permit any of his ships to carry slaves, and *El Zefiro* is no exception to his rule. Although el Conde may be detained, we must abide by his rule as long as we live by his coin.

Remind all your men of the same, and be strict about your maintaining order in this, and all, regards.

Because the Church requires it, Frey Heberto, Dominican, will sail with you to Ostia, where another monk, or monks, will be assigned to you for your return trip. You are to show him all the respect and high regard he is due, and you are to provide him with full access to all you carry, in the name of el Conde de San Germanno.

May God give you safe passage and a swift return,

Rogerio, manservant
to el Conde de San Germanno

At Portobello, Audiencia de Panama, September 1st, 1653rd Year of Grace

◆ ◆ ◆

To the most sublime Obispo Hector Enrique Ventarron y Cuenco, of San Simeon, Bogota, Audiencia de Santa Fe, the Nativity greetings of the manservant Rogerio, major domo to el Conde de San Germanno, along with his most sincere inquiry in regard to the appropriate manner in which to proceed in what has become an urgent yet delicate conundrum, to wit: the present location of and conditions of detention of my master, and what means are open to me to secure his freedom and restore his reputation once again.

As a faithful servant, I must, as you are aware, seek to alleviate my master's current situation, or, barring that, secure his instructions regarding his affairs in his absence. It would not be fitting for me to undertake to manage his fortune or his business without his specific instructions, particularly since he has no blood relatives in the New World to whom such ventures may be entrusted. So it falls to me to pursue a resolution for him, and to seek to resolve all issues that may have led to his seizure by Church authorities. To do these things, I must be allowed some contact with him, and, having gained that, I will follow his instructions to the letter.

At this time of the year, when our hearts turn to the promise of mercy, I implore you to consider my master's case, and to mitigate his plight, as a show of honor to the birth of Christ, which brought forgiveness into the world.

I ask you to review the law for such cases: it is my understanding that you cannot refuse me this access, according to the edicts of the Pope, for when no blood relatives are available to act on a man's behalf, His Holiness has determined that senior servants or duly appointed deputies may take up the obligations of family members; with that as my guide, I must act to determine his will, for there are many decisions to be made, and it would be improper for me to make them without first consulting with my employer, or I may do his interests more harm than good. It is difficult to presume I know my master's intentions, and therefore I find myself in these straits; I have been unable to secure any help from anyone that would help me to carry out the duties I must undertake if I am to be worthy of my employer's trust.

Most worthy Obispo, I beg you in the name of mercy, to allow me to write to my employer, to know where he has been taken, and to discover his wishes in regard to his case. I have asked for such contact before, and explained my purpose, but my entreaty has been ignored, and thus far all my petitions have met with denials or silence. Yet this leaves me in a most precarious position, for without any exchange with my master, I am in the dark, and may, all unknowing, act against my master's wishes rather than for them. Surely you, who guide the padres and freyes who serve the Church with you, must recognize the need for instruction from those authorized to give it. You have defended the Church and undertaken the teaching of the Gospels to the pagan savages of this land, and your padres and freyes have followed your dictates for the good of their souls as well as the good of those they have brought to the True Faith. So, in the worldly sense, would I do, in order that I may serve my master more fully and in accordance with his wishes. With your release of the knowledge I search for, I may begin to carry out the behests of el Conde, and once again be sure that my dedication is to the same goals that my master holds uppermost in his plans. I ask you to consider my plight and to find it in your heart to grant my request. With my assurances of my gratitude and my most sincere expressions of appreciation in this trying time, I sign myself

Rogerio, major domo
to el Conde de San Germanno

At Portobello, Audiencia de Panama, on December 23rd, the 1653rd Year of Grace

To the most reverend Prior, Frey Vicente Puentes, Passionist, Convento dell' Agonia, near Popayan, Audiencia de Quito, the greetings of Rogerio de Cadiz, manservant to el Conde de San Germanno, and the consolation of your faith to you and your freyes on the death of Frey Cirillo de San Ysidro; may God comfort you in your sorrow. I thank you for your prompt response to my letter, addressed to Frey Cirillo and carried by Dalcut de Cartagena. Many another cleric would have returned the letter unopened, and that would not have been useful to the Church or el Conde. I thank you again for your prudence in this regard, for I know it is within your discretion to receive or return all letters to your predecessor. You were most kind to read my missive, and to consider my request. I understand that without the proper dispensation you are powerless to do anything on behalf of my employer. I have been attempting to obtain the needed releases and specific descriptions of what I may be permitted to do for el Conde, and to what extent I may act. I would have pursued such material sooner had someone in the Church been willing to explain what I needed. But such is the way of faith, and I do not question the ways of Heaven. Although you do not confirm my employer is in your care, you do not deny it either, which has given me reason to hope that you may have some contact with him. If you do, I beg you, in the name of the God all men revere, to tell him that I am doing all that I may to deal with his current state. If he is ailing, I ask you to inform me, that I may send his own medicaments to treat his ills. If he is allowed books, I would be pleased to send him books, so that he may use his time to better his soul with contemplative texts. If he is lacking anything you will permit him to have, be good enough to tell me, so that I may do what I can to supply his wants. Whatever he may endure, if there is something to succor him in his travail, let me know of it, so that I may discharge my obligation to him, and attend to his needs.

As soon as I have the required signatures and seals on the appropriate testaments, I will bring them myself to you, so that you may proceed in the certainty that the Church gives her permission to me to continue my work for my employer. I look forward to the hour when I may express my gratitude to you face-to-face. In the meantime, Dalcut of Cartagena carries a donation of ninety gold reales for your monastery, given in el Conde's name. I pray God will keep you and guide you in your faith and bring you the peace of the soul.

With many expressions of gratitude and with humble expressions of esteem,

Rogerio de Cadiz, manservant
to el Conde de San Germanno
At Portobello, Audiencia de Panama, February 10th, 1654th Year of Grace

To the most esteemed hidalgo, Don Calvino Eneas Alba Jorje Yunque y Cabolucha, Presidencia de Popayan, Audiencia de Quito, Viceroyalty of Peru, the greetings of Rogerio, manservant to el Conde de San Germanno, on behalf of his missing master.

Good Hidalgo, I must approach you in regard to a most perplexing matter. More than three years ago the Church detained my master, el Conde de San Germanno, and have given no reason for what they have done. They need not answer any questions in regard to those held in their custody, I know, but I am a man of honor, and I am required by that honor to locate and defend my master against all false accusations. So far I have not been able to confirm his present location, nor do I know anything of his condition, and so I am unable to seek the appropriate legal or clerical processes to end his most unjust sequestration.

For these reasons I come to you in this difficult time to ask you to ascertain where the Passionists have taken el Conde. I appeal to you as a man of law, and as one who knows the burdens imposed upon faithful servants, which I am bound to uphold. I have reason to believe that he is at the Convento dell' Agonia, near your city of Popayan, and so I have come to you to ask you whether or not my master is being detained there, on what charge, and in what state. Surely the freyes will tell you what they will not vouchsafe to me, out of regard for your birth and your position in the world. It is unusual, I know, to come to a civil authority with such a request, but I have found the Church is very slow to answer, and in the meantime, I have many matters of business that need a decision from my master, or I need a transfer of authority from him in order to keep his various ventures proceeding as he would like.

What is the most vexing part of this puzzle is that my master has done nothing against the Church, and has, in fact, regularly given generously to the Church and supported her good works. There are many who can vouch for him, but thus far there has been no change in the posture of the Church in his regard. I will provide a messenger to carry letters between us, the same man who has brought you this. His name is Linno van Meer, a mestizo from Caracas. He is discreet and dependable, and you may entrust your answer to him without fear. I have paid his wages and will provide him a handsome bonus on his return, so he will not be a charge upon you. He knows and approves this arrangement, and will abide by its terms. In gratitude for any assistance you can give me, I sign myself,

Rogerio, major domo
to el Conde de San Germanno
At Portobello, Audiencia de Panama, April 22nd, 1654th Year of Grace

To Atta Olivia Clemens at Senza Pari near Roma, If you are reading this, my ruse has succeeded and John Towerman has actually been able to reach you without hindrance, and in spite of the many obstacles the Church has imposed upon those traveling from the Viceroyalty of Peru and Nueva España. He has been sailing on Dutch ships and has disembarked at Genova, with instructions to make his way to you at Roma overland, and I hope has avoided the most stringent inspections given to travelers from the New World. With this in your hands, I must conclude he has succeeded. He has my instruction to deliver this, completely unread, or to destroy it and to give you a spoken account of how I have tried to locate San Germanno. He is a staunch Protestant, and has proven reliable.

My appeal to the Presidencia of Popayan went unanswered, and thus far I have heard nothing more from the Passionists, either to confirm or deny having him in their care-whatever that may be. No other official of the Church or the king, has been willing to provide me anything but polite, meaningless letters that acknowledge my inquiry and nothing more, leaving me at a loss to guess in what condition San Germanno now survives. You would know, through your blood bond, if he had died the True Death, but as you have sent no word to me, I must suppose that you assume he is still alive. This gives me as much vexation as hope, but I am glad to have it. These calculated delays and snubs, while infuriating, have steeled my determination to bring Sanct' Germain out of his durance vile.

I have paid out many handsome donations—or, more accurately, bribes; and will continue to do so as long as I must—to try to get enough information to know where my master is being held, all to no avail. I am running out of persons to approach, and I do not know how to continue the search, for no matter what I have attempted to do, I have achieved nothing. I do not lack for monies, and I can continue to make excessive payments for some time to come, but I know that the Church need not part with one iota of news if she decides not to do, in spite of gold and flattery.

Again, I ask you if you can gain some help from the various Vatican and Lateran authorities you know, for I fear I have reached the limit of my various avenues. Without some intervention from high within the Church, I feel I have nowhere left to turn, and that unless I take to the road as a vagabond to search for him, my master will languish somewhere in prison for years to come; without the intervention of a cardinal or the Pope himself, I begin to think that I am stymied. I have a few travelers in my pay to tell me what they hear on their journeys, particularly when they sojourn at monasteries. But the Convento dell' Agonia, where, as I've told you, I have reason to believe San Germanno is being held, does not open its doors to travelers, only to those seriously ill or afflicated in mind.

It is more than five years since he vanished, and I fear that another five could pass before his whereabouts are known. Given his nature, that time could be as intolerable an agony as his days on the cross for dona Azul were. I do not like to think of the measures to which he may have had to resort to keep himself from thirst and hunger. If I could locate him, I could see he need not survive on the blood of rats or other vermin. The more I try to find him, the harder the task becomes. So, much as I do not want to impose upon you, Olivia, I will do so, and thank you profusely for all the aid you can give me—and that is neither gold nor flattery, but the simple acknowledgement of the blood you and my master share.

If you want to entrust a letter to John Towerman, assume it will be read when he returns to Portobello—everything coming in and out of San Germanno's household is, and picked over for the slightest hints of heresy and intruigue. It is an unexpected pleasure to write you in such candor, even though it is on so desperate an occasion.

You know how grateful I am, so I will say only thank you for anything you may be able to do on San Germanno's behalf. It is my sincerest hope that through our combined efforts we may secure his release and bring him safe to Europe once again.

Rogerian

At Portobello, Audiencia de Panama, July 12th, 1654

To the most reverend Obispo Alejo Ignacio Ventisceste y Aisaldo of San Eulogio de Cordova, Augostino, at Antioquia, Audiencia de Santa Fe, the most respectful greetings of Rogerio, major domo to el Conde de San Germanno, currently at La Casa de Eclipse, Maracaibo, Audiencia de Santo Domingo.

I pray that this letter reaches you through the good offices of my messenger, Dalcut de Cartagena, and that you will consider what is asked of you with charity and goodwill in your heart. You Augostinos are known for your compassion, and that is why I have made bold to address you in my travail.

It is nearly six years since my employer was taken by the Passionists to an unknown location for unspecified reasons, and have apparently kept him ever since. I say apparently because no one will confirm or deny that he is in their custody, making further action on my part fruitless. This official silence is most perplexing, for it has left me in the difficult position of having little or no recourse to pursue el Conde's release. The obstinacy of the Passionists astonishes me; there has been no notification of San Germanno's condition given, or any confirmation that he is detained, or even alive, which is why I have come to you for the aid I have been unable to gain from others.

My efforts to gain any information about him have been for naught, and I come to you in the hope that perhaps you might be willing to make inquiries in regard to my master, and then be willing to impart to me all you deem appropriate that I should know. I will bow to your discretion in this, of course, and I will be thankful for any information, no matter how small or inconsequential, you, decide to provide, for it would be more than anything I have gained since the day el Conde vanished.

My master commands an extensive trading and shipping business, and without him to make decisions about his ventures, it falls to me to act in his stead, discharging his orders in accordance with the laws of the Viceroyalties of Peru and Nueva Espāna. I have done this to the limits of my abilities and I have made an effort to do all I suppose he would want, but I am still compelled to act without the authority of his mandate, which is one of the things I seek in my desire to find him.

This letter is accompanied by a donation of one hundred gold reales, to be used for the Glory of God and the Triumph of the Faith. I send it on behalf of my master, who has long paid generously to the Church, and would, were he able to do so, provide such a sum himself, as the records throughout the Viceroyalties show.

If you are unable to assist me in my search, I would be most grateful if you would propose some other means I might employ to gain the information I seek. I have few options available to me since the Passionists have decided to reveal nothing in regard to el Conde.

I am going to remain here in Maracaibo for another six months, for I must supervise repairs to three of el Conde's ships that were damaged in the terrible storms of September and are not presently seaworthy, and I have to make sure they are restored to San Germanno's standards. When the ships are once again in service, I will return to Portobello, Audiencia de Panama, probably next autumn if God will but favor our endeavors, and I will hope that Dalcut will find me there with a merciful answer from you.

I am, in all things, a devoted son of the Church and a loyal servant to el Conde de San Germanno,

Rogerio, major domo

May 16th, 1655th Year of Grace

To the most respected and honored jurist, Jose Luis Remo Septimavictoria y Trigobien, Principal of the Magistratura of the Audiencia de Quito, at Quito, the salutation of Rogerio, major domo to el Conde de San Germanno, missing now for seven years, and upon whose behalf I take pen in hand to write to you.

Most worthy Principal, I ask you to read the enclosed copies of letters I have sent these many years in my efforts to locate and secure the release of my master who has been held by the Passionists, but who refuse to acknowledge his situation among them. I know it is their right to do this, but I implore you to urge them to allow me to exchange at least one set of letters with him, so that I can carry out his commands in regard to his businesses. You will see, in my many previous efforts, I have attempted to elucidate my reasons for such contact, but I have not gained one response beyond the fobbing off of my petitions to others who are in no position to grant what I request.

You are my last hope, for I have been unable to secure any information, and I begin to think it may be that my master has turned away from the world and taken Holy Orders. If this is the case, I must have his surety of it, and his official disposal of his titles and property before I can discharge my duties to him. You know that as well as any man in the New World, and that is why I am importuning you in this way, so that I may proceed to carry out el Conde's commands, if he has any to issue.

The death of Innocent X and the election of Alexander VII to the Papacy may bring about a softening on the position of the Church in such matters, a development I would hope the law would echo, which should make dealing with such a case at this time important to a man advancing in the world.

You have given sound judgment in the past and many have praised your fairness. Let me join their chorus, in gratitude for your help. My plight is not so dire that I fear destitution, but it is severe enough to put me into a most difficult situation if, in my efforts to serve my master, I have, in fact, compromised all he has sought to achieve. He has been a most worthy patron, and I count myself fortunate to act for him, yet I must strive to do his will or I will not be eligible to number myself among those deserving of his favor.

I have done all that I think is sensible, and in accord with what he has done in the past, but after so long, the decisions I have made may now be turned from his goals. I have, for example, commissioned the building of two new ships for his fleet, one to replace the *Nubes de Marzo* that was damaged when it ran aground near San Juan, and one to accommodate the increase in business that has marked the last two years; it should be ready to put to sea in fourteen months, if all goes well. I have also maintained his schedule of ships' routine maintenance, for that is well-established and all the capitans know it, and regard it as part of their duties, for which I need only authorize payment, but to go beyond such obvious things is more than I believe it is appropriate for me to do without consulting el Conde; I trust you will understand my apprehension and do what you can to remedy my problem.

It is most alarming to have such long periods of silence, as a man in your position must know. The demands of the world impose upon us always, and we seek guidance to discharge our duties. Even orders from Madrid come twice a year. Surely you can comprehend my doubts, and if you do that, you will see why I have continued to pursue this matter for so long. To speak frankly, I am losing hope that I will be able to comply with the expectations my master has had of me, which distresses me profoundly.

If you can do nothing, I ask you to suggest someone who

may be able to help me. My messenger, Dalcut of Cartagena, will bring your answer back to me as quickly as he can, along with the copies of previous letters for your perusal. You will see that all the copies are notarized, showing that they are full and accurate copies of the letters I sent, and the dates upon which I sent them. Dalcut is a most reliable man whose mission will cost you nothing, for I have paid him for his journey to Quito and back to Portobello already. Your response will make no charge upon you, and it will earn you my gratitude.

I pray you, consider all I have done to find my master, and help me to bring him to his own again.

Rogerio, major domo
to el Conde de San Germanno
At Portobello, Audiencia de Panama, June 2nd, 1656th Year of Grace

To the most highly regarded advocate, Gualtiero Onofrio Garcia Hieloisla y Torpescalon of Buenaventura, Audiencia de Panama, the greetings of the manservant Rogerio of Cadiz on behalf of his master, el Conde de San Germanno.

You have a most distinguished reputation, and for that reason I have decided to lay this problem before you in the remote hope you might for once abandon your posture of taking no case against the Church, and make an exception for my master.

I will admit from the first that I have had no encouragement from the Church to undertake this inquiry into my master's whereabouts, and have been given no information that would lead me to him.

Every attempt I have made to find him has been ultimately unsuccessful. I wish you to grasp the extent of the difficulty I have encountered in this regard, so that you will be able to estimate the opposition that you may encounter. I cannot make light of this, nor would I expect that of you. I am including a calendar of events and letters in this case, so you may be apprized of how long I have attempted to gain information and how little success I have had. I would provide you with true copies of all the letters, but those I sent to the Principal of the Magistratura de Quito were never returned, and I am loath to part with my remaining copies if you are not in a position to accept this case. I have myself twice been questioned by the Passionist Freyes of San Cristobal here in Portobello, and twice I have been released, with no hint of wrongdoing clinging to my name. I have ascertained that you need not fear reprisals from the Church should you be willing to act on el Conde's behalf. I ask that you ponder this case before you decide what you are to do, for I am at a standstill and without some support on my master's behalf, I must give up my search for him, which appalls me.

My courier, Linno van Meer, brings you this message and will wait in Buenaventura for two weeks to carry back your answer. He has been paid and so you will not be out of pocket for sending answer to me. I hope you will not refuse me out of hand, but at least give my predicament the favor of scrutiny before making your final decision.

I sign myself with gratitude,

Rogerio of Cadiz, major domo
to el Conde de San Germanno

At Portobello, Audiencia de Panama, September 17th, 1657th-Near of Grace

To Atta Olivia Clemens at Senza Pari, near Roma Most honored Olivia, I trust my courier Linno van Meer has got this to you with no interference from the Church; he is a clever fellow and has been most energetic in carrying messages for me, all of which—until now—came to nothing. Until your letter arrived on *La Estrella dell' Aurora*, I had reached an impasse, and was unable to decide how to continue. To order Linno van Meer aboard her for her return voyage was a delight indeed. Your letter brings me joy, for it is the first break in what has been a wall of granite. My efforts have been frustrated at every turn, my petitions denied or ignored, and no matter what I have done, I have, in the end, gained nothing but indifference or enmity. Now I dare to hope that within the year I will know where San Germanno is and in what state he is being kept.

My other messenger, Dalcut de Cartagena, is presently carrying yet another petition to the Presidencia de Quito, although I have little reason to believe it will be read, or if it is, that it will produce anything more than the same courteous nothings that have been the hallmark of all my labors on Sanct' Germain's behalf. When Dalcut returns, I will put him on alert, so that as soon as the Encyclical arrives from the Pope, I can send him out again, this time for something other than disappointment.

I cannot imagine how you have managed to convince Alessandro VII to do this, but however you managed, I thank you from the bottom of my heart, and I know Sanct' Germain will be deeply in your debt, and small wonder: you have spared him from more suffering than he has already endured, and for that alone, I am grateful. I also know that you, as one of his blood, must feel for him; that you have been moved to help him will evoke all his cognizance of the debt he owes you. I look forward to the badgering you will provide him upon his return. How good you are, and how kind. I cannot say enough how deeply obliged I am to you for all you have done, for me and for Sanct' Germain.

Rogerian

Post scriptum: Burn this.

Post post scriptum: If you are having trouble with the work being done on the villa, why remain in Roma? You have other places to go, and you need not supervise all the reconstruction being done. Even if mischief is part of your problem, appoint a deputy and get away for a while. For once, Olivia, step back from difficulties. Only let me know where my letters may find you.

At Portobello, Audiencia de Panama, January 20th, 1658

To the most revered, sublime Obispo Reynaldo Martin Maria Rodriguez y Espinadoble, Trinitarian, of Sagrada Corazon, in Cartagena, Audiencia de Santa Fe, Viceroyalty of Peru, the most humble greetings of Rogerio de Cadiz, major domo to el

Conde de San Germanno, on whose behalf I now address you, pursuant to the particulars of the Papal Encyci cal Misericordia et Justus, issued by Pope Alejandro VII for all New World Bishoprics, which provides for the security of all prisoners held by the Church in the New World.

His Holiness states that anyone held by the Church is entitled to the succor of his relations and servants, and the prompt knowledge of what crimes or heresies he is accused. My employer, el Conde de San Germanno, seems to be in the hands of the Passionists and has been for nine years. I say seems to be because there has been no communication between el Conde and me, and the Passionists have consistently refused to confirm or deny that they have el Conde in their care, although I have reason to believe he is at the Convento dell' Agonia near Popayan in the Audiencia de Quito. With Pope Alejandro's Encyclical, it becomes necessary for the Church to inform me where my master is and of what he stands accused.

I appeal to you to begin the inquiries that will result in discovering where el Conde is presently incarcerated—for I can use no other word for his detention for so long a period—and I will express my thankfulness with this donation, in el Conde's name, of one hundred fifty gold reales, to help in the good work of the new Papal Encyclical. You must have many uses to which to put this money; I pray you will find it to your benefit. As a Trinitarian, you are not part of the long dispute among the Passionists and the Franciscans and Carmelites, and therefore you are more fortunately placed to carry out the Pope's wishes with dispatch.

The donation and this letter is being carried to you by my personal messenger, Oalcut of Cartagena, who travels under escort of six armed men, all of whom will be at your disposal in regard to el Conde. Oalcut will bring any missive from you to me as quickly as the roads will allow, and I will put myself at your disposal at any time you may ask it.

I am fully aware of how diligently you have followed the instruction of Innocent, and therefore I repose all my faith in you. I trust that before the year is quite over, I will have the felicity to behold my employer once again, and that he and I will both praise your justice and fairness. The vindication of el Conde. has been my goal for almost a decade, and I thank the Pope and God for this Encyclical. I cannot help but hope that he will shortly be released when it is demonstrated that he has done nothing against the Crown or the Church.

With every assurance of high regard and continuing gratitude, I sign myself,

Rogerio of Cadiz, major domo
to el Conde de San Germanno
At Portobello, Audiencia de Panama, July 19th, 1658th Year of Grace

To the very reverend Passionist, Frey Vicente Puentes, Prior, Convento dell' Agonia, near Popayan, Audiencia de Quito, the very humble petition from the manservant Rogerio de Cadiz on behalf of my master, Francisco Ragoczy, el Conde de San Germanno, and through the authorization of the Papal Encyclical *Misericordia et Justus*, for the release of el Conde de San Germanno who is said to be in your care.

Good Prior, I ask you now to confirm or deny the presence of el Conde at the Convento dell' Agonia, and to specify what charges are laid against him, and any judgments you may have reached in regard to those charges.

To help you in your good works, I am sending with this petition the sum of two hundred gold reales, my courier Linno van Meer, and an escort of eight armed men to insure the safe arrival of this letter and the reales. This is not intended to influence you on my master's behalf; the Church has many obligations, and this gold should help in meeting them. I have included—the letter from the Trinitarian Obispo Reynaldo Martin Maria Rodriguez y Espinadoble, of Sagrada Corazon in Cartagena, Audiencia de Santa Fe, one of the first of the New World obispos to receive the Encyclical from Roma, which reiterates the Pope's wishes, confirms the Encyclical, and makes it mandatory for you to reveal all information you have on el Conde de San Germanno, for which I will be profoundly thankful beyond words to express. This compassion of His Holiness is an example to all of the faithful.

Upon receipt of the information requested, I will attend upon my master to escort him back to Portobello and return him to his rights and honors, which have not been accorded him in more than ten years.

I am prepared to leave on two days' notice, with appropriate companions for such a journey.

I thank you for all you do to assist my master in this time, and I pray that we will bring this to a conclusion suitable for the Church and el Conde.

Rogerio, major domo
to el Conde de San Germanno
Portobello, Audiencia de Panama, January 9th, 1659th Year of Grace

To Atta Olivia Clemens Linno van Meer has brought this to you by his usual clandestine ways, and I am confident that he has not encountered any interference from Church authorities. He has many ways to deal with the Church, and thus far, all have been successful.

I write to you with mixed emotions, for although your most wonderful efforts brought about the *Misericordia et Justus* Encyclical, the only information the Passionists provided was that he had been there, but had been sent to the Monasterio del San Fructuoso of the Dominicans at Piura, Audiencia de Lima, and so I must pursue him there. I will need to go to that place if I am to bring about a hasty resolution of this long ordeal. This is to insure that you will know where I am, and where Sanct' Germain has gone.

Your concern for Sanct' Germain is well-taken; I, too, hope that long confinement has not wrought too harshly upon him, for creatures such as you and he do not easily tolerate long imprisonment, particularly if there is restriction of movement as well as isolation from others, for it reduces your sustenance to rats and similar unwholesome provender. When those of your blood are subjected to prolonged periods of such fare, as I need not tell you, there is a price to pay. You and I have seen what such privation can do to Sanct' Germain, and therefore I am attempting to anticipate any demands that he will need to have met promptly. As you can see, I have considered the problem already, and you may be sure that I will arrange what I can to alleviate his most pressing need as quickly as possible, which may not be easy, for I expect to continue under Church scrutiny for some little time to come. Still, no one is wholly subject to his appetites, and vampires are no exception; Sanct' Germain will bear whatever impositions he must, and I am confident that he will find restoration without exposing himself to any additional danger than what he has already endured.

There have been severe storms this winter, and so news from Europe and England has been slow to arrive, and the spring has continued tempestuous, so this will not come to you as quickly as I could like. Sanct' Germain's ships' capitans are under orders not to put to sea until the winter storms are past. Still, a minor delay will seem all of a piece with everything that has happened through the last several years, and I know you will not begrudge Linno van Meer a safe passage to bring this to you, and your response to me.

I look forward to your next letter, which will have to pursue me to the Audiencia de Lima, for I plan to leave in two weeks' time. You can send your letter directly to Piura in the Audiencia de Lima, and I will retrieve it from the magistratura. I know you will understand my decision, and applaud it, for, armed with the Encyclical, I cannot conceive that the Church would refuse to obey the will of the Pope.

This is hardly the first time I have set out to locate Sanct' Germain, but I have not often met with such obduracy as I have encountered in the last ten years.

Not even the years he was a slave in Spain, or the time he sent me to you for the duration of the Plague were as troublesome as this decade has been. You have comforted me in my complaints, and kept up my courage when my fears were bleakest. I do not say this for sympathy, but to express my continuing frustration arising from the endless delays. You have endured many of the same foilings at various times, and you know how onerous they can be. I ask you to remember those periods, and to share in my relief that this tribulation is finally ending.

Niklos Aulirios has sometimes had to search for you as I have for Sanct' Germain, and I imagine he has known the despair I have felt; I have occasionally comforted myself when I have been the most despondent with the knowledge that he, too, has been visited by hopelessness. To have it finally come to an end is a delight that Niklos can explain far better I, and doubtless more eloquently.

I will put this aboard the *Duquessa de Alba*, which scheduled to leave two days after I depart myself, weather permitting. Linno van Meer will carry your answer to me, and I will send him back to you as as he reaches Piura, with whatever news I will have to impart. Let us both hope that it is all to good.

You have brought about Sanct' Germain's liberation. May you always thrive and enjoy the favor of privilege to which you are so richly entitled.

Rogerian

At Portobello, Audiencia de Panama, January 11th, 1659

To the most admired, exalted Dominican Prior, Frey Leonardo Felipe Oviedo Cubierta y Sabiogolpe of the Monasterio de San Fructuoso at Piura, Audiencia de Lima, Viceroyalty of Peru, the respectful greetings of the manservant Rogerio de Cadiz, and in that capacity, I address you on behalf of my employer, el Conde de San Germanno.

I am informed by the Passionist Prior, Frey Vicente Puentes of the Convento dell' Agonia near Popayan in the Audiencia de Quito, that el Conde has been turned over by his freyes to you and yours. If this is true—and I have good reason to think that it is—I ask you to provide me with a full account of his detention upon my arrival in Piura, in accordance with the reforms of Alejandro VI1 expressed in his Encyclical, *Misericordia et Justus*. I will introduce myself to you after I present my bona fides at the Magistratura de Piura, and at that time will provide a donation in my master's name of two hundred gold reales for the work of your Order. This is only to show my devotion, and the devotion of my master, to the cause of the True Faith, not to influence you, but to show appreciation for all the Church has done in the New World. Once I have made a formal introduction to you, I will avail myself of the grants expressed by His Holiness in his Encyclical, and ask for the prompt release of el Conde. Certainly, as a Dominican, you must be concerned with rooting out heresy wherever you find it, but I implore you not to assume that because the Passionists held el Conde for so long it must indicate that he is heretical in his views, but rather to acknowledge that had the Passionists encountered heresy in el Conde, they would have put an end to him; his long survival points to his innocence, not to his guilt, good Prior. If you would be willing to examine all claims against him bearing my remarks in mind, I know God will guide you aright, for in my many years serving el Conde I have never known him to betray his faith in word or deed. Should you desire my testimony, I will give it to the full extent of my capacity, and under the terms of the Pope's Encyclical, which inspired document guarantees that no family or staff may be held as a means to achieve a confession from a suspected heretic or apostate prisoner.

I will travel as quickly as is possible, and my messenger, Dalcut of Cartagena, will present this to you as soon as he reaches Piura. He will be at least ten days ahead of me, giving you ample time to gather the records and make the report I have requested, for he will leave before the heavy storm brewing at sea blows in to Portobello. I, perforce, must attend to el Conde's ships, then I will depart to the south. I pray that when I arrive you will allow me to speak with my master; for as much as I need a report on his last decade, so I must present him a full account of mine. I have attempted to conduct his business affairs in such a way as I believe would serve his interests, but as I have not been permitted to correspond with him, I am aware that it is imperative that I inform him of all that has transpired in his absence.

To that end, I ask for an interview with him at as early a time as you can arrange.

In all the time my master was detained by the Passionists I exhausted every possible means of aiding him, and all to no avail, for until the Encyclical commanded it, the Passionists refused to furnish any and all information in his regard; it was as if el Conde had vanished from the earth entirely. Now that he is given into your care, I trust that such difficulties are at an end. I will bring with me authorizations from Trinitarian Obispo Reynaldo Martin Maria Rodriguez y Espinadoble, of Sagrada Corazon in Cartagena, Audiencia de Santa Fe to facilitate the liberation of my master, and to provide you with the necessary material to satisfy the Pope's officers, should any lingering questions remain. I do not ask anything more than what His Holiness Alejandro has provided, nor would I. I have proceeded upon this course with the advice and council of Obispo Rodriguez y Espinadoble, and I repose complete reliance in his wisdom. I pray you will give close attention to his most reverent expostulation.

I am filled with gratitude for the guidance and patronage that has made it possible for me to fulfill my obligations to el Conde, and to be able, at long last, to bring about the resolution I have sought.

Rogerio, manservant
to el Conde de San Germanno
At Portobello, Audiencia de Panama, January 14th, 1659th Year of Grace

To the most dependable, upright, and correct advocate, Bartolome Baltezar Bernal Hogaza y Hoja of Portobello, Audiencia de Panama, the salutation of Rogerio de Cadiz, manservant to el Conde de San Germanno.

Most worthy Advocate: in my absence from Portobello, you are charged with continuing my duties in regard to my employer's business. I have included a schedule of voyages, repairs, trading agreements, and policies which are to be upheld while I am gone, along with a history of trading for each one of el Conde's thirty-seven ships, the better to assist you in arranging new cargo. I am supplying you with five hundred gold reales to carry out these necessary duties, which should exceed your needs by almost double. I provide you so much in case there are unexpected expenses—a shipwreck, a storm that damages warehouses or my employer's villa—that must be met without delay. I am certain your judgment will be responsible in such matters.

I will send regular reports back to you as I travel, and I will expect the same from you, which is why I am leaving Dalcut de Cartagena with you to carry our messages back and forth. Dalcut knows the road I will travel, and he will find me if it is necessary for you to reach me at some unplanned point in my journey. When Linno van Meer returns from Europe, I ask you to give any messages he carries to Dalcut to bring to me at once. The six men I have hired to serve as escort have received half their pay and will be given the balance upon our return, which I hope will be swift, and with el Conde once again among us.

It is my intention to travel from Portobello to Buenaventura, then to Quito, to Guayaquil, and from there along the coast road to Piura, using the main roads established by the Crown, not only for the safety they provide, but in order to secure safe lodgings and provender along the way. Too many travelers have met with mishaps on lesser roads, even those that may offer swifter passage, for me to risk so much by departing from the Camino Real. I have decided against traveling by sea, due to the reports of pirates plying the waters from Buenaventura to Callao. My escort should be able to hold off robbers on the roads better than they can defeat pirates on the seas. If the weather is good and we encounter no serious delays, we should be in Piura in six or seven weeks, for we will use our own horses—two for each man—for the entire journey, and not depend on remounts along the way.

It may be a bit slower, but it will get us there in safety.

We will rest at Quito for three days, and have the horses

reshod. I will carry replacement shoes with us, in case one should be cast on the road.

If it should be necessary for us to remain at Quito longer, I will, of course, notify you from our inn, and I will expect to prepare you a report in that place which Dalcut may retrieve from the magistratura there, if he does not arrive before we leave.

Pray for our success, good Advocate, and el Conde till his return, his name restored and his innocence established. While I am on this mission, I will repose confidence in your integrity, and I thank you now for your most diligent attention to all the responsibilities delineated in the enclosed material.

With thanks I sign myself

Rogerio de Cadiz, manservant
to el Conde de San Germanno
Portobello, Audiencia de Panama, January 19th, 659th Year of Grace

To Niklos Aurliros, manservant to Atta Olivia Clemens at Senza Pari near Roma, the most profound condolences of Rogerian.

Your letter did not reach me until I arrived at Quito, which will account for my tardiness in answering your letter of December 21st, 1668. I cannot yet grasp your tragic news, though I have read your letter twice and am unable to comprehend what you impart there; my reason slides away like light from a shadow as I attempt to understand your account. I cannot imagine how you must feel, and I am transfixed by emotions too recondite to set down here. How incomprehensible, to know she is dead. I cannot conceive of Olivia being gone from this world! The True Death! After more than a millennium and a half of life! How this must pain Sanct' Germain, for he must have sensed her loss through the Blood Bond.

An explosion, a collapsing building, her spine broken—how could it happen? She had said she had had problems with the restorations she had begun, but who could have thought it would lead to this? It is useless to speculate how she might have survived had she gone to one of her other holdings, or abandoned the project for a time.

I am going to save your letter so that I may give it to Sanct' Germain when I finally see him, since he has already perceived the loss of her; your account of the event may help him in some way by easing what his imagination may be telling him.

My messenger will carry this letter to the port of Maracaibo and put it into the hands of the capitan for delivery to you as soon as the ship reaches Ostia.

I fear you may not see this before May, but I assure you it will reach you as quickly as possible; my concern for you and for your tribulation is ongoing no matter when you read this, for Olivia was a true linchpin in my life, and in Sanct' Germain's. I am shaken to the bone at this dreadful news. I can think nothing to say that could offer you relief for your anguish, for so enormous a loss is beyond words—no matter how heartfelt—or sympathy to alleviate.

Still, know that I share your grief, although mine is a faint echo compared to yours.

I can write no more; I am too deeply grieved. In the most genuine commiseration,

Rogerian

At Quito, Audiencia de Quito, March 8th, 1659

To the most respected, highly-regarded Dominican Prior Frey Leonardo Felipe Oviedo Cubierta y Sabiogolpe of the Monasterio de San Fructuoso at Piura, Audiencia de Lima, the greetings of the manservant Rogerio de Cadiz who is newly arrived in Piura.

I have presented my bona fides to the magistratura and my escort and I are staying at the Posada de Mil Flores on the Plaza de Santa Ynez. I will present myself to you after noonday devotions tomorrow, and I ask you to be willing to receive me. I bring you another one hundred gold reales to help you in the good work you do.

It is also my hope that I will be permitted to speak with el Conde, and to determine what he requires of me; after so many years, I feel it incumbent upon me to apprise him of all the decisions I have made on his behalf, so that he may assess for himself how well I have upheld my mission. This may not be possible, I do understand, but I am eager to assure myself that he is well. There is some news I must impart to him concerning the death of one of his blood, and I know that it would be more appropriate to tell him face-to-face than to pass a letter to him.

I am prepared to remain here as long as it is necessary to bring about el Conde's unconditional release. To that end, I will make it a point to secure the services of an advocate in order to speed the process that must be undertaken. I am fully aware that el Conde will not be vindicated in a matter of days, nor in a week. However long it takes, I will pursue el Conde's complete exoneration of all hint of wrongdoing, as I must as his manservant. I have been in his service half his life, and I cannot abandon him.

No doubt you will appreciate my position and my devotion, for the dedication of monks has long been an example to me.

You are reputed to be a most sapient, diligent monk, and that inspires me with hope, for I know that you will review el Conde's case with wisdom and tranquil evaluation, and will undertake to decide the matter fairly, which is no more than either my master or I would want, for any fair assessment of the case will readily make his innocence apparent. I will stand ready to assist my master in any way you may require. It is fitting that I should do so, as you are certainly aware. I have great faith in your sagacity, as I am sure my master does.

Anticipating our dealings together, I sign myself,

> Rogerio of Cadiz, major domo
> to el Conde de San Germanno

At Piura, Audiencia de Lima, March 9th, 1659th Year of Grace

To the most worthy advocate, Bartolome Baltezar Bernal Hogaza y Hoja of Portobello, Audiencia de Panama, the greetings of Rogerio of Cadiz, from the Posada de Mil Flores at Piura, Audiencia de Lima.

I have had my first interview with Frey Leonardo Felipe Oviedo Cubierta y Sabiogolpe, Prior at the Monasterio de San Fructuoso; I had hoped for a more congenial first meeting, but as it came about, I was asked many questions and given precious little information. The Papal Encyclical was some help, but it has not yet brought about the direct contact the Pope has endorsed, nor have any churchmen been moved to follow the dictates the Pope has outlined in *Misericordia et Justus*. This has caused me some apprehension, for I had thought that the Papal Encyclical might bring about a higher degree of accessibility to el Conde at once. I am disinclined to abide in patience, but it appears that I must.

Because I am waiting for another invitation to come to the monasterio, I feel I must inform you that I am likely to be here longer than first anticipated; I am reluctant to speculate on how long that could be, and to that end I have decided to obtain the advice of an advocate, so that I might have the benefit of council in regard to the law. I had assumed I would need this at the time of el Conde's trial—if there is to be one—but I think it would be wisest to retain legal assistance now. I have inquired about advocates in this city, but I must tell you that the few here are disinclined to accept a client not wholly in favor of the Church. There is good reason to view this turn with alarm, for it bodes ill for el Conde, in that it appears that many have already turned their backs on him and will not pursue justice on his behalf. I am afraid I may have to proceed on my own for the time being, which makes me uneasy, but not nearly so uneasy as retaining reluctant council, for I cannot believe that a hesitant advocate would achieve much use.

I have received your letter along with the sad news from Roma. I am grateful to you for dispatching Dalcut so promptly, for it was most important that I have that notification before I spoke to el Conde. I have also reviewed your report about storm damage to *Los Lobos del Yermo*, and I concur-it is impractical to try to repair her at San Juan. It will be some time before shipwrights can be sent to her, and she is safe enough to sail to Maracaibo, where she can be taken care of properly by el Conde's own men, who should be dispatched promptly, with enough money to pay for their labor, their lodging, and any lumber and other supplies to complete the work. You may authorize any and all to be paid as they are incurred, and if there is any difficulty in arranging this, send word to me promptly.

As I have remarked, it may be some time before el Conde is freed. I will continue to inform you of all developments as they occur, as I trust you will inform me. Dalcut will continue to carry messages back and forth, but if you think Linno van Meer should replace him from time to time, that would suit me very well.

I appreciate your continuing efforts on el Conde's behalf, as I know he will when he is once again at liberty.

> Rogerio of Cadiz, manservant
> to el Conde de San Germanno

At Piura, Audiencia de Lima, March 12th, 1659th Year of Grace

To the newly appointed, most excellent Obispo Joaquin Ramon Jesus Antonio Altomarea y Timonmano, Augustino, of Santa Isabel of Portugal, at Cajamarca, Audiencia de Lima, the greetings of the manservant Rogerio of Cadiz, presently at Piura. Most reverend Obispo, I appeal to you on behalf of my master, el Conde de San Germanno, who has been held by the Church for more than a decade,and in spite of the exhortations of His Holiness Alejandro VII in *Misericordia et Justus*, still remains imprisoned, currently by the Dominicans here in San Fructuoso at Piura. I have made repeated attempts the last several months to gain access to el Conde, in accordance with the terms set down by His Holiness, and I have thus far been met with excuses and delays. Now I am told that plans are being made to transfer el Conde to the charge of the Franciscans in city, at the Monasterio de 108 Angeles del Navidad If this is indeed going to occur, I ask you: indeed, I beseech you—to permit me to speak with him before he is once again held in isolation.

For more than ten years I have looked after his affairs, and during that time I have done many things which I have hoped were in his interests, but which have not, in fact, discussed with him. I am concerned, for if I have not acquitted my charge as he would wish, it behooves me to set right any errors I may have made. So far I have not been permitted to so much as pass a letter to el Conde, and so there are matters he and I have been unable to discuss even so remotely as an exchange of notes would allow. Also, for the sake of his blood relations, I would like to be able to report on his present condition in order to reassure his noble relatives that he taken no injury from his long isolation. Recently, one of those to whom he is bound by blood died, it is my task to inform him of this most lamentable event. I know that others would be much relieved if I am able to inform them that el Conde has suffered no lasting harm during his long incarceration.

With the Papal Encyclical to guide you, I appeal you, Obispo Altomarea y Timonmano, to allow me to accompany my master during his transfer. I have been unable to secure such an assurance from Frey Leonardo Felipe Oviedo Ctibierta y Sabiogolpe, the Prior of San Fructuoso where el Conde is now being held, which has resulted in my appeal to you.

This comes by the good offices of my messenger, Dalcut of Cartagena, who will wait upon you until you have a response to send back to me; he will not impose upon you, for I have paid him for his work and his accommodations during his journey. I am authorizing him to bring you one hundred gold reales to show the sincerity of my plea and to help you Augustinos in your work about the world. If you cannot bring yourself to allow me so much access to el Conde, perhaps you will permit. me to have at least an interview or two with him before the Franciscans take him in. Surely the Pope would countenance that degree of contact, and you would not be subject to any review for allowing what the Papal Encyclical requires.

To reiterate: I ask you to consider my position as well as that of my master, and to be willing to address both his situation and mine. I am sworn to serve el Conde; to do so, I must know what he requires of me. After so many years, I am troubled that I may have failed in my duty. Only a discussion with el Conde will provide me with the information I must have. It is not beyond your power to grant this, and so I ask it of you as I prepare to travel to Cajamarca in the hope of gaining audience with el Conde.

With my thanks for your consideration, I sign myself
Rogerio de Cadiz, manservant
to el Conde de San Germanno
At Piura, Audiencia de Lima, September 21st, 1659th Year of Grace

To the Franciscan Prior, Frey Camilo Beltran Horatio Bolsa y Salvaje of the Monastario de los Angeles Navidad, Cajamarca, Audiencia de Lima, the greetings of the manservant Rogerio de Cadiz, whose master, el Conde de San Germanno, has recently been transferred to your care.

I am newly arrived in Cajamarca and have presented myself at the magistratura, and to the Augustino Obispo Joaquin Ramon Jesus Antonio Altomarea y Timonmano of Santa Isabel of Portugal. It is now my intention to come to your monastery, good Prior, in hope that you will honor the mandate of the Papal Encyclical Misericordia et Justus, and permit me have words with my employer. I am fully aware that your Order is more inclined to be aware of the needs imposed by the world; as your Founder exemplified.

There are many reasons I would appreciate an interview with el Conde, not the least of which is to inform him of what has transpired among his various concerns in the last decade, that he may have an opportunity to prepare himself for the changes that confront him when he returns to the world, his innocence vindicated and his reputation restored.

Certainly, you will have to make your investigation of him and his activities, and therefore I ask you be thorough in your inquiries. Sadly, many of who might have given useful testimony in regard to my master can no longer do so. The Coregidor of the Audiencia de Lima, Don Ezequias Pannefrio y Modestez, who was familiar with el Conde's works, died last year, and his successor never met my master, so he cannot offer you anything that might throw light upon all el Conde did while in the Audiencia de Lima, some years since.

For however long you require for your process, I will remain here in Cajamara, and I will follow your acts as closely as one in my position may, for to do less would not be honorable. I have an obligation to el Conde, and I will not seek to avoid it. If there is anything you will permit me to do in service to my master, you have only to tell me of it and it is done.

I say this to you so you will comprehend my intentions, good Prior. I have never abandoned my master before, and I will not do so now. I will devote my time to his interests and his freedom until both are achieved. Your answers and summons may find me at la Posada del Potro in the Calle de las Cinco Lunas; I plan to remain here as long as necessary.

With abiding faith in your compassion and sagacity, I sign myself

Rogerio de Cadiz, manservant
to el Conde de San Germanno

At Cajamarca, Audiencia de Lima, Viceroyalty of Peru, April 2nd, l660th Year of Grace

To the most patient, persevering advocate Bartolome Baltezar Bernal Hogaza y Boja of Portobello, Audiencia de Panama, the joyous greetings of Rogerio, manservant to Francisco Ragoczy, el Conde de San Germanno, who today, at very long last, is a free man with a restored name.

After more than fifteen years, it is finally done. It has cost a fortune in time and donations, but all of it was worth the price now that el Conde is finally released, all charges against him—whatever they were—dismissed, and his possessions returned to him without any liens against them by Church or Crown. It is truly a triumph.

El Conde himself has endured much; at least the Franciscans permitted him access to their gardens and cloisters at night so that he could prepare medicaments for their infirmary, unlike the Passionists and Dominicans, who kept him in a cell for as long as they had him. You will not be astonished to learn that el Conde no longer wishes to place himself in the danger he feels the New World has for him, and for that reason, he has decided to return to Europe.

He has ordered us to hire an escort and travel in easy stages to Maracaibo, Audiencia de Santo Domingo, Viceroyalty of Nueva Espana, and take ship there, whichever of his may be eastward bound when we arrive. I ask you to send your reports to his factor there, Eugenio Joao Sao Reinaldo at el Conde's warehouses at the harbor.

I am deeply appreciative for all you have done, particularly in arranging for Dalcut de Cartagena's proper burial when the fever killed him last year, and for maintaining all el Conde's records so well.

Because of your good work, I know it will be much easier for him to reestablish himself in the world again. To express his thanks, San Germanno is sending an authorization for you to remain in his villa until the end of your life. He has also granted you a pension of sixty gold reales a year for as long as you live, and a memorial to your heirs of three hundred gold reales upon your death. He forgives you the monies you have so artfully purloined from his coffers through your subtle manipulations of figures, not only because you have done your work well, but because, compared to what has been paid to the Church, your theft was insignificant.

As you can see, this comes with many letters to be sent on, which task I leave to you, for I know that you may tend to the work far more efficiently in Portobello than I am able to here in Cajamarca, and many of the letters are distinctly to your advantage.

I estimate we will depart from Maracaibo in August or September, after the most severe summer storms are over, and before the winter storms can blow in. Before we sail, el Conde will prepare schedules and give you instructions for reaching him, and arrange for your successor upon your retirement or death, which will spare you having to find someone to take on your various responsibilities when you can no longer fulfill them.

In utmost gratitude for your faithful service, I sign myself,

Rogerio de Cadiz, manservant
to el Conde de San Germanno

At Cajamarca, Audiencia de Lima, Viceroyalty of Peru, July 22nd, 1666th Year of Grace.

A GENTLEMAN
OF THE
OLD SCHOOL

"**B**UT SURELY THE COUNT is willing to talk to the press? He's been very generous, and I would have thought he'd want to make sure people know about it." The reporter was a crisply attractive woman in her mid-twenties, bristling with high fashion and ambition; she was hot on the scent of a story. She lingered in the door of the somewhat secluded house in an elegant section of Vancouver, a tape recorder in one hand, a small digital camera in the other. "And there is the problem of the murder, isn't there? The VPMNC audience wants to know."

The houseman—a lean, middle-aged man with sandy hair and faded-blue eyes, roughly the same height as the reporter: about five-foot seven—remained unfailingly polite. "I am sorry, but my employer has a pronounced dislike of all public attention, even if the intention is benign." He nodded to the young woman once. "I am sure there are many on the hospital board who will be delighted to give you all the information you seek. As to the murder, you should speak to the police—they will know about it."

"Everyone's talked to them, and there's nothing new to get out of them," the reporter complained. "Everyone's looking for a new angle on the case, and the Center was a good place to start. That led me to the Count, and I only found out about the Count through the Donations Administrator's secretary, and that was over a very expensive lunch." She frowned. "I was told that the Count only visited the facilities twice: shortly after construction began and just before it was opened: The Vancouver Center for the Diagnosis and Treatment of Blood Disorders. Ms Saunders said the Count's donation covered more than seventy percent of the cost of building and equipping the facility, and that he provides an annual grant for on-going research. That's got to be a lot of money. I was wondering if the Count would care to confirm the amount? Or discuss the body found on the roof of the Center two days ago?"

"Neither is the sort of matter my employer likes to talk about. He is not inclined to have his fortune bruited about, and the investigation of crime is not his area of expertise. He leaves such things to the police and their investigators." The houseman stepped back, preparing to close the door.

"Then he's talked to them?" the reporter pursued.

"A crime scene technician named Fisk has asked for various samples from the Count, and he has provided them." The houseman started to swing the door shut.

"Fisk—the new tech?"

"That was his name. I have no idea if he is new or old to his position. If you will excuse me—" There was less than three inches of opening left.

"I'll just return, tonight or tomorrow, and I may have some of my colleagues with me: I am not the only one with questions." This last was a bluff: she was relishing the chance for an exclusive and was not about to give up her advantage to any competition.

"You will receive the same answer whenever you call, Ms . . . is it Barradis? If you want useful information, I would consult the police, Ms Barradis." The houseman lost none of his civility, but he made it clear that he would not change his mind.

"Barendis," she corrected. "Solange Barendis."

"Barendis," the houseman repeated, and firmly closed the door, setting the door-crossing bolt into its locked position before withdrawing from the large entry-hall, bound for the parlor on the west side of the house that gave out on a deck that was added to the house some fifty years before. It had recently been enlarged to make the most of the glorious view afforded down the hill, colored now with the approaching fires of sunset.

The house had been built in 1924 in the Arts and Crafts style, with cedar wainscoting in most of the rooms, and stained glass in the upper panes of many of the windows, all in all, a glorious example of the style, for although it did not appear to be large from the outside, it had three stories, and thirteen rooms, all of generous proportions. The parlor, with its extensive bow and the deck beyond provided the appearance of an extension of the room through two wide French doors into the outside, making it one of Roger's favorite places in all the house. Here he lingered until a beautiful Victorian clock chimed five; then he started toward the stairs that led to the upper floors, to the room on the south side of the second floor, a good-sized chamber that once held a pool table but was now devoted to books. He went along to the library and tapped on the door, opening it as soon as the occupant of the room called out, "Do come in, Roger."

Roger opened the door and paused on the threshold, watching his employer, who was dressed in black woolen slacks and black cashmere turtleneck, up a rolling ladder where he busied himself shelving books at the tops of the cases. "The reporter was back." The French he spoke was a in a dialect that had not been heard for more than two centuries.

"Ms Barendis?" the Count asked. "I'm not surprised to hear it. I'm a little puzzled that she hasn't brought more press with her, considering."

"She has threatened to do so. She said she was asking about the Center, but it—"

The Count sighed. "She had another topic in mind, I suspect."

"You mean the body they found?" Roger knew what the response would be.

"That, and her reporter's inclination to uncover information that appears to be hidden."

"Such as the size of your donation to the Blood Center; a legitimate story as well as a workable excuse to talk to you to find out about the murder victim," said Roger, a bit disgusted. "She asked about the money as well as about the body."

"I doubt she will pursue the money: it isn't scandalous enough. The murder is more intriguing than money, since it appears to be one of a series," said the Count drily. "Even the Canadians are fascinated by human predators, it would seem."

"And this young woman is stoking the furnace," said Roger.

"All the more reason for her to find more combustible fuel to consume—money hasn't the engrossing power of serial murders, especially such messy ones as this man commits—he is seeking as much gore as he can create," said the Count. "The murder is scary and exciting—large donations only spur a moment of greed, which is insufficient to hold the audience's attention."

"Whatever the public may find interesting, this reporter is proving as persistent as a burr." Roger came a few steps into the room and flipped on the light-switch, banishing the thickening shadows with the gentle glow of wall-sconces. "She says she'll be back tomorrow."

"I would not doubt it," said the Count, coming down the ladder. "So long as she confines her pursuit to the daytime, she will be nothing more than inconvenient. We have dealt with far worse than she." As he said the last, he put his foot on the floor.

"She may expand her inquiries," said Roger, sitting on an upholstered rosewood bench and giving his attention to the end-table beside it; he picked up a small ivory carving of Ganesh riding his Rat and moved it to a less vulnerable place on the end-table. "I recommended she speak to the police."

"If they lead her away from me, so much the better," said the Count, sitting down in a leather recliner. "You know, when we first came here in—was it '38?—well, after we left California, near the start of the war—I didn't appreciate what a handy place this would be, or how pleasant. Who could have foreseen the expansion of the Pacific Rim, especially then, as the war was getting under way? This has been a much better investment than the house in Winnipeg." He reached over and turned on a floor-lamp with a frosted tulip motif, banishing the last of the gloom; the shining paneling, along with the array of spines, gave the place a cozy elegance.

"Winter is easier here than in Winnipeg," Roger observed.

"You have the right of it," said the Count.

Roger brushed his hand over the embossed leather cover of a book printed in Amsterdam almost five hundred years ago. "Do you think you will want to remain here much longer?"

"Perhaps a year or two, until the Center is fully established. It will depend somewhat on the state of the world then; I am not in any particular hurry to return to my homeland, not as things are going now. The government has already seized half the money I left for the university I endowed on the pretext of using it for cultural projects: I would just as soon not provide them more occasions for another raid." He shoved the recliner back, sighing luxuriously as he did so. "These are wonderful inventions."

"So they are," Roger agreed, knowing it was prudent not to press the Count about his plans. "And it is not difficult to conceal your native earth inside them."

"Another advantage," said the Count, and closed his eyes.

◆ ◆ ◆

"A fifth body," Solange exclaimed as she stared at her computer screen some twelve days after her second fruitless visit to the Count's house. "Near the University, this time." She shoved back from her workstation and stood so she could see over the top of her cubicle. "Hey, Baxter! You seen this?"

The Night City Editor came over to her, his silk regimental tie loosened and his well-cut hair slightly mussed. "Seen what?"

She pointed to the computer screen. "Another one with a cut throat, blood everywhere, and mutilations. Fair-haired, cut short, above average height, on the plumpish side, between twenty-five and thirty-five years of age—a cookie-cutter victim for this guy." She stamped her foot. "And Hudderston isn't doing anything! Crime Desk—yeah, right!"

"How do you mean?" Baxter asked. "I have his column on the daily report from the police—they say they've doubled patrols, and the crimes are getting top priority, the crime scene tech is preparing a new report."

"Fisk also says the forensics are inconclusive, even though there are pools of blood around the victims, the same thing you can get off the Internet, or on the hourly news spots," said Solange. "You saw the report on the confusing DNA results—animal blood mixed with human and both contaminated with chemical additives. Any identification they may make from the analysis of the blood, even though it's accurate, won't hold up under rigorous cross-examination."

"But five women with cut throats, multiple stab wounds in the upper bodies, and perforated uteruses! The public won't stand for much more of this, and arrest—let alone a trial—is a long way off." Baxter sighed. "McKenna has the story on days; if you want to take it on for nights, I won't stop you. I'll clear it with Sung." Louie Sung worked the night crime desk, and was known to be territorial about his fiefdom.

Solange tried to contain her excitement. "Sung could say no."

"Not to me," Baxter told her.

"Okay, then. You clear it." Eyes glistening with excitement, Solange picked up her recorder, her camera, and her tote, then reached for her coat. "I'm on it, boss," she vowed, and tapped in her code to block access to her terminal. "I'll call in before one, and I'll report before six."

"Sounds good," said Baxter, and stood aside as Solange swept out of the city room of the Vancouver Print and Media News Corporation, bound for the parking lot and her hybrid hatchback.

◆ ◆ ◆

At police headquarters, Solange avoided the press office and the front desk where the usual assortment of denizens of the night were gathered with arresting officers; she made straight for the squad room and the desk of Neal Conroy, who shook his head as soon as he caught sight of her. "Barendis, get out of here," he said cordially. "You know I can't talk to you." He was slightly stooped, slightly scruffy: pushing forty, and forty was pushing back.

"Sure you can: here or at your house, Uncle-in-law—you know Aunt Melanie won't keep me out. If you don't tell me what I want to know, she will. And don't tell me you don't talk to her about your cases, because you do," she said, sitting down in the old, straight-backed chair that was intended for visitors and victims of crimes. "The murders. What's happening? And why is the DNA inconclusive? It is identifiable or it isn't."

"You're too nosy for your own good, Barendis," said Conroy.

"That's how I earn my living," she countered, undeterred by the frown he offered.

"Well, use a little good sense for once in your life and keep clear of this one. For your own protection. Melanie would agree with me, if you bother to ask her," Conroy advised her seriously. "This murderer targets women alone, in their late-twenties to early-thirties, cuts their throats and then chops at the bodies, and adds cows' blood to mess up the crime scene. You know the basics already."

"Chops—with a knife?" Solange asked, pulling out her pen and notebook, saying nothing about her recorder in her tote's outer pocket, already in the *on* position.

"Stop it, Barendis," said Conroy, sounding tired. "I hate it when you fish."

She shook her head, undeterred. "Not a knife, but it cuts throats? For all five women?"

"What can I say—the guy likes blood, lots and lots of it," Conroy told her, deliberately harsh. "Don't put that in your story."

Eyes sparkling, Solange shrugged. "I can't promise anything, but I'll try not to get you into trouble."

"It's not getting *you* into trouble that concerns me," Conroy riposted. "I mean it, Solange. Don't try to make your mark on this one—it won't do you any good, and you could become a target."

"Not a knife, but something that slices, that's for sure," said Solange, paying no attention to Conroy's last statement. "A dagger—I do know the difference between a knife and a dagger—or a poignard . . . no."

Conroy took a long, slow breath. "If you will give me your word you won't go after Melanie about any of this, I'll tell you what the medical examiner thinks made the wounds, but you have to keep this out of your story, or you compromise the whole investigation."

Solange sat upright in the chair, and managed to say, "I promise," all the while staring at Conroy.

"It's some kind of curved sword—a saber, a scimitar, a katana— or something like a Medieval battle-hammer, with a long, pointed claw at the back of the head—we can't say for sure. There's too much damage." He had lowered his voice and now was more pale than he had been.

"That's really . . . " She stopped before she said something she would regret.

"Appalling," said Conroy.

"God, what grisly stuff," said Solange. "I wish I could use it."

"You try and I'll have your press-badge pulled until the perpetrator is caught."

"You know you won't do that. Aunt Melanie would never permit it." She showed him a smug smile.

Conroy sat back. "You're probably right, but that doesn't change anything. Let Fisk and the M. E. do their jobs, and keep your two cents out of it. You can screw this investigation royally if you don't play by the rules, and that would mean more people getting killed."

"You mean more *women* getting killed," Solange corrected

as she got out of the uncomfortable chair. "I'll go along for now, but you had better give me a first call on the story when it breaks."

"Certainly," said Conroy. "You know I'll do that."

"Yes. Or Aunt Melanie won't—"

"—let me hear the end of it," he finished for her.

◆ ◆ ◆

The restaurant was elegant, the lights low and golden instead of brilliant and white, the upholstery heavy tapestry to match the draperies, the silverware was sterling, the napery linen, the china Spode, the glassware Reidel. Solange, in her second-best cocktail dress—a designer-label, bias-cut, cobalt-blue, bat-sleeved sheath—was trying to conceal how impressed she was while reading from the six-page menu. Finally she looked up at her host and asked, "Why did you change your mind, Count?"

"About the interview?" he countered, his demeanor urbane and genial; he was in a tailor-made black-silk suit, a very white silk shirt, a burgundy-red damask tie, with tie-tack and cufflinks in white-gold with discreet black sapphires for ornamentation.

"Yes," she said, glancing at the approaching waiter. "What are you having?"

"The pleasure of your company, but do not let that deter you in ordering anything you want." He waited for her to ask something more, and when she did not, he went on, "I fear I have a number of . . . allergies, I suppose you could call them. I must constrain my dining, and so, to avoid any unpleasantness, I take my nourishment in private. I am used to having others eat when I do not." He signaled the waiter to take down her order. "And if you have a wine-list I would like to see it."

Solange's eyes lit up. "Then you *drink*–" she began.

"The wine will be for you," he said, adding, "I do not drink wine."

She laughed aloud. "You know who says that, don't you?"

With a swift, ironic smile, he answered, "Vampires."

Her laughter increased, and she had to choke back her amusement in order to tell the waiter, "I'd like the cream of wild mushrooms soup to start, then the broiled scallops in terrine; for an entrée, the duck with cherries and pearl onions in port, next the endive salad, and I'll think about dessert when I've finished dinner."

"Very good, Ma'am," said the waiter. "I will bring the wine list, Count."

"Thank you, Franco."

"So they know you here," said Solange, her curiosity engaged again.

"I have a minor investment in this restaurant, and the hotel across the courtyard." He held out his hand for the wine-list as the waiter approached, bringing that and a basket of fresh-baked small loaves of bread and a ramekin of sweet butter.

"You are a man of surprises, Count," said Solange, idly wondering if his investments might be a story worth pursuing at another time.

"Am I," he said, and opened the wine-list, settling on a Cotes Sauvage. "It may not go well with the scallops, but it will compliment the soup and the duck."

"For a man who doesn't drink wine, you have a discriminating pallette."

He turned his dark eyes on her. "I hope so, Ms Barendis."

To her astonishment, she felt herself blushing, and she tried to stop the color rising in her face. "I . . . Well, thank you for ordering such an unusual wine." This sounded lame, even to her own ears, so she made another attempt. "I'm very flattered that you're willing to talk to me." That was a little better.

"You're a very persistent young woman, Ms Barendis; I decided we might as well arrange a discussion, and if we are to discuss difficult questions, we may also be comfortable."

"I wish all my subjects were so reasonable," said Solange archly. She broke one of the small loaves of bread in half and set it down on the bread-plate. "It smells wonderful, doesn't it?"

"Yes, it does," he said, rather distantly.

She paused in the act of cutting butter. "Will my eating

bother you, considering we will be talking about murder during the meal?"

"No; it is not my appetite that could be compromised," he said wryly, and went on, "I realize you are on assignment tonight."

"Yes," she said, as if she had forgotten it. "This is an assignment, and an important one."

"That is why I agreed to the meeting," he said.

"Then I'll thank you for the very civilized way you have of conducting it, even to this public setting, so my reputation wouldn't be damaged. As if gossip can damage a reporter." She took a bite of the bread, feeling somewhat embarrassed for being hungry.

"It may be an unnecessary precaution," he said, "but you are not the only one who could be endangered by the appearance of collusive arrangements."

Her smile was at once worldly-wise and relieved. "You mean that you don't want it said that you are influencing or being influenced by me—it's not worry about people speculating what our relationship might be."

Before he could speak, the waiter brought her soup, promising to return at once with the wine; for the moment all aspects of her story were set aside in favor of the meal.

◆ ◆ ◆

Mid-way through the duck, Solange was able to return to the matter that had brought them there; she began to ask the Count questions about the bodies and their ties—if any—to the Blood Center. "Some so-called experts have speculated that the man is close to the investigation, and that is making the police nervous. My aunt's husband is a cop, and he said he feels as if he's under suspicion."

"Do you find your aunt's husband reliable?" the Count inquired. "Some policemen are more so than others.

"Conroy is a model of rectitude," said Solange, and decided the wine was going to her head—she would rarely use the word *rectitude*, especially to describe Neal Conroy; she did her best to soften her meaning. "Dependable, honorable, hard-working, responsible."

"Commendable qualities in any man," the Count approved.

"Yes. He let me know he has questions about the state of the investigation, including similar ones to the reservations expressed by the expert. He's a bit worried about the kind of questions being raised in the press, as well. He wants everything in the case to be above doubt." She was delighted with the meal, in part because it allowed her to spar with the Count while she had this excellent repast.

"Do you recall which expert said the things that bother your aunt's husband—about the killer being close to the investigation?" the Count asked, unperturbed. He studied her face. "Did your aunt's husband have any opinions on the current uncertainty?"

She pondered for several seconds. "Not about the investigation, not directly, no. The expert isn't a cop: I think it was Fisk; the crime scene tech: he's been talking to the media recently."

"No doubt he has," said the Count, a suggestion of a frown forming between his brows.

Now Solange was alert. "What do you mean?" She had the uneasy suspicion that the Count, not she, was guiding their conversation, and so she prepared a number of lines of inquiry to pursue.

The Count shrugged. "Unlike Fisk, I am no expert, but I find it strange that a man who is so responsible for the quality and preservation of the evidence in this case should call so much of it into question. He has an obligation to keep an open mind, but from what I have read, Fisk is doing more than that." He took the bottle of wine and poured her a third glass.

Much struck, Solange gave this her consideration. "He is only living up to his function, and gathering evidence impartially—evidence is just that: evidence. It has no opinions, only existence."

"That may be, but Doctor Fisk certainly has opinions," said

the Count. "He impugns his own work at almost every turn. Had an arrest been made, I would have thought Fisk was a member of the defense,"

To give herself a little time to think, Solange took a long sip of the wine, then remarked, "When you put it that way, I see what you mean."

"Is there anything in his past to account for his behavior? Did he give testimony in a trial that was found to be–"

"That could be it!," Solange exclaimed. "He used to work in Moose Jaw, or so he says. I'll check with the cops there."

The Count held up his hand. "I can understand wanting not to appear too much a part of the prosecution instead of an investigator, but this man Fisk has–"

"I know," she interrupted. "Thanks for the observation. You have a point. I'll look into it." Drinking more wine, she had to resist the urge to call Baxter at once; instead she asked one of her mental lists of queries, "Do you think the murder has taken away any of the community benefits the Blood Center promises?"

"For some, no doubt it has," said the Count. "But once the murders are solved and the guilty party brought to book, then the Center will quickly show its value."

"Aren't you being a bit too optimistic?" She cut a little more duck. "This is very good. I'm sorry you can't enjoy it."

"That's kind of you," said the Count. "No, I don't think my optimism is unrealistic. But time will tell, and time is often the test in these cases."

"Then you're thinking in the long run?" Solange asked.

"For a man in my position, it is the only perspective that makes sense," he told her as she went on with her dinner.

◆ ◆ ◆

Applause burst out in the city room as Solange sauntered in, twenty-six days after her first dinner with the Count. She went to her cubicle, but stood outside it to curtsy three times, smiling proudly. "Thank you, thank you. You're all too kind."

Baxter, who had hung back, now came up to her. "Don't

be modest, Barendis," he advised. "Conroy says you were the litchpin in their investigation."

"I'm not being modest," she said. "I know how much luck had to do with catching the guy."

"You put them on the scent, and you kept at the story," Sung said from his office doorway. "You could have followed the rest, hassling the cops for not getting the guy, but you went after Fisk, asking about his reluctance to do anything to break the case. The thing about saying animal blood and human blood could not be separated enough for a valid DNA profile. Very good."

"Thanks," she repeated. "It seemed a good place to begin."

"Did you think it was Fisk?" Hill, who covered building and expansion, made his question sharp.

"I didn't know who it was," said Solange, delighted she had accomplished so much. "I just thought it was odd that Fisk kept running down the evidence he himself was collecting. A crime scene tech needs to be skeptical, but what Fisk was doing was well beyond skepticism and leaning toward subversion."

"Well, you helped bring him to justice, and you're a credit to the paper," Baxter approved, then went on, "Everyone back to work. You don't want to have to chase the paper tonight."

The celebratory mood vanished at once, and the night staff of the Vancouver Print and Media News Corporation returned to their tasks.

"Management is preparing a bonus for you, Solange," said Baxter, lingering in the opening of her cubicle.

"Thanks," she said.

After a short silence, Baxter said, "So what are you looking at now?"

"I got a lead on a smuggling operation. Not drugs, but high-quality antiques," she told him, unfamiliar hesitation in her response.

"What about the Count—the exile?" Baxter prompted. "The one with so much money in the Blood Center."

Her smile was slow and had a sensuality to it that Baxter

had never seen before. "He's a gentleman of the old school—no real story there, except that he still exists."

Baxter pounced on her remark. "Something going on there that I should know about?"

She shook her head. "Only dreams."

"*Those* kind of dreams?" Baxter asked her.

"None of your business, boss," said Solange.

Baxter chuckled. "So long as it doesn't get in the way of your work, dream away."

She contemplated his profile. "It was something the Count said that got me thinking about the smuggling scheme."

"He fed you information?" Baxter seemed surprised.

"No; not even enough to qualify as an unnamed source—he mentioned something a week ago, about trouble his shipping business was having. I decided to ask around, to see if his problems were isolated."

"And I gather they're not," said Baxter and slapped the side of her cubicle. "Well, keep me up-to-date on your project." He started away from her cubicle.

"You can depend on me, boss," she responded, and began to work on her new story, all the while anticipating the late-night supper she would have with the Count, three hours from now. Grinning inwardly, she promised herself she would have particularly delicious dreams tonight, as a reward for her tenacity, and the result of her rendevous with the Count.

AFTERWORD

I F ANYONE HAD TOLD me when I began my work on *Hotel Transylvania* back in 1971, that I would still be writing about Saint-Germain more than thirty-five years later, I would have laughed out loud with incredulity. Originally I conceived of the series as having five books—the first five: *Hotel Transylvania, The Palace* (not my title), *Blood Games, Path of the Eclipse,* and *Tempting Fate.* I had trouble convincing my then-editor that there were five books—she thought three at most until I turned in *Blood Games,* then saw the wisdom of my plan. She left Signet before *Tempting Fate* was turned in, and the new editor was glad to let the series end, and so, as it seemed, was St. Martin's Press, which had acquired hardcover rights to the books from Signet—an unusual arrangement back in the 70s. So that, I thought, was that.

But vampires, as folklore the world over tells us, have a talent for rising from the grave.

The five novels weren't the only tales I had written about Saint-Germain. During the time I worked on the first five novels, I also did five shorter works about him, from which came the collection of those five shorter works I had done in the 70s and 80s, *The Saint-Germain Chronicles.* I had no other stories in mind at the time, and went on to many other things. Years went by, and the four book clubs carrying Saint-Germain books continued to get sales. From those book club sales developed a small but steady source of royalties and a continuing interest in the character.

When Tor took on a reprint of my alternate-world fantasy *Ariosto* they inquired if I could do more Saint-Germain. At the time I said probably not, but I could do some Olivia books. I did three of them: *A Flame in Byzantium, Crusaders' Torch* (Tor changed the apostrophe), and *Candles for d'Artagnan* (Tor made the candles singular), and Madelaine's *Out of the House of Life*. By the end of those four novels, Saint-Germain was back in action, talking to me and gearing up for another go at the many precarious points in history.

Let me explain that last a little more: I'm one of those writers who has to have characters come alive before I can write about them. Largely because of this emphasis on the autonomy of characters most of my work is first draft; the vision of the story is never so clear to me as it is the first time through. At the inception of a work, I immerse myself in the environment of the story, the history, the circumstances, and as much actual information we have regarding how people of the time saw themselves and their world. I watch the characters develop as my grasp of the time and its people reaches a kind of critical mass, and finally I set to work. Until I can see and hear the characters in full round, I can't write about them beyond an occasional note scribbled to myself. This process makes revisions difficult, since the story tends to set up quickly—like cement. Once it is set, my hands are mixed-metaphorically tied. I can make minor alterations, but the form of the work, its story-line, its timbre and style, and particularly the characters whose story it is, are established; if I try too much to diverge from what I have done, the whole thing is apt to unravel on me and lose all coherence. Generally speaking, this makes Saint-Germain stories more appropriate as novels, but there are exceptions, and those events end up in shorter forms.

The difference between the nature of short stories and the nature of novels plays a part in the kind of perspective possible within the confines of the event or events in the story—in short stories, one thing happens and when it is resolved, the story is over; the narrative focus is confined to one or two characters. There are two short stories in this collection, the first and the last. The novelettes (about

10,000 words each), the second and fourth tales, have one thing happen and then the ramifications of that event shape the story, needing more developments in order to resolve its argument. Novelettes take in a slightly wider focus than short stories do to include a bit more development of secondary characters, although nowhere near the inclusion possible in novels. The novella at the center of this collection is 42,000 words long, or roughly one third the length of *The Palace*, and has two focuses in its characters—Orazia and the students. This means that the two levels of events can happen and be resolved by the end, with a bit broader view of the social environment of the time incorporated into the vision of the story. Novels, by their very nature, cast much broader nets and reveal a great deal more about the secondary characters, so that the focus is more layered and complex, needing more comprehensive conclusions than it can be achieved in shorter works.

In the last few years some critics have posited that the Saint-Germain stories have rehabilitated the image of the vampire, which, while flattering, was not my intention; my original intention was to see how far the Dracular image of the vampire found in Stoker could be moved to the positive and still have a recognizable vampire. I have never been interested in the self-indulgence of Byronic posturing that marks many modern literary vampires, but I am deeply intrigued by how someone might survive after losing all contemporaries, family, territory, culture, language, social cohesion, and a place in the world.

That means putting emphasis on two things: the problems of extreme longevity, and the metaphor of vampirism itself. Fortunately these two crucial elements dovetail nicely—the difficulty in keeping a human context during an unnaturally long life fits in well with making the vampiric experience one requiring genuine intimacy. It also does another thing that has fueled these stories for three decades: it puts the emphasis of the stories on Saint-Germain's partners. These stories are for the most part stories about the lives of women, and when women are not the focal factors, survival is. Even vampires have vulnerabilities, and they make for some serious trouble for Saint-Germain.

To answer a few questions about the on-going characters: Saint-Germain is from the Carpathians, is proto-Etruscan royalty, and, because he was born at the dark of the year, entered the vampiric priesthood of his people's gods when he was thirteen. His family was destroyed when an army from a client-region of the Hittites conquered them. Saint-Germain—then thirty-three—was captured and sent into battle with his own soldiers against foes of the Hittites, a battle he was supposed to lose, but won. For that he was condemned as a dangerous rebel and was disemboweled, which isn't an effective way to kill a vampire, as the Bronze Age leader found out.

Roger/Rogerian became Saint-Germain's bondsman upon Saint-Germain's restoring him to life in *Blood Games,* in the first century in Rome. Before that Saint-Germain had had a restored bondsman named Aumtehoutep. Both of these manservants were ghouls. In accordance with folkloric traditions, the ghouls live on raw meat, do not share vampiric strength but sleep almost as little as vampires do. None of the ghouls have lovers of any kind, and their devotion to Saint-Germain, or in the case of Niklos Aulirios, Olivia's ghoul-manservant, his devotion to her, is as much a matter of convenience as any other factor. Also, the ghoul-servants are the closest thing to a contemporary the vampires have, and visa versa.

In her introduction, Sharon Russell touches on a number of factors that resonate with how I have come to see the Saint-Germain stories of any length, and I find that reassuring. To find that the perceptions of readers are not far removed from how the tales appear to me makes dealing with those whose perspectives differ significantly from my own less disquieting although I do agree with those critics who say that readers get out of a work what they want to find, not necessarily what the writer put there. Saying that, I should add that it usually takes me a decade to be able to look at any of my work with objectivity, and even then, I suspect that because the series is a continuing one, that I am never going to be able to do the kind of cumulative assessment that Sharon Russell has achieved.

Like their namesake, the Saint-Germain novels travel fairly successfully. They have been doing well in Russia and Italy, which I find encouraging, since both countries have readers who prefer their history accurate, and who know when it isn't. In fact, the Russian editions have footnotes, identifying historical characters and specific events referred to in the stories. So far neither country has secured rights to the short stories, but I am fairly confident this one will appear in Italy.

In the meantime, I should begin work on the twenty-second Saint-Germain book—this is the twenty-first—in February, 2007, so by the time this is out, that book should be done. With the help of you readers, the schedule will continue for some time to come.

—Chelsea Quinn Yarbro
Berkeley, California
24 December, 2006
Saint-Germain's birthday

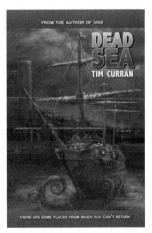

EXPLORE TERRIFYING LANDSCAPES
OF SCIENCE UNBOUND

EDITOR: WILLIAM JONES
COVER BY DAVE CARSON
336 PAGES

LIMITED, SIGNED NUMBERED
HARDCOVER :$45.00
ISBN: 0-9779876-2-0
TRADE PAPERBACK: $15.95
ISBN:0-9779876-3-9

Uncanny contraptions, weird devices, technologies beyond the control of humanity abound in the universe. Sometimes there are things that resist discovery. When science pushes the boundaries of understanding, terrible things push back. Often knowledge comes at a great cost. 21 unsettling tales of dark fiction are gathered in this volume, exploring the horrors beyond our reality.

Featuring Lovecraftian horror, dark fiction and science fiction by William C. Dietz, Richard A. Lupoff, A. A. Attanasio, Jay Caselberg, Robert Weinberg, John Shirley, Stephen Mark Rainey, Paul S. Kemp, Gene O'Neill, David Niall Wilson, Lucien Soulban, C.J. Henderson, Paul Melniczek, Greg Beatty, Ekaterina Sedia, Michail Velichansky, Tim Curran, Ron Shiflet, Alexis Glynn Latner, John Sunseri, and William Jones.

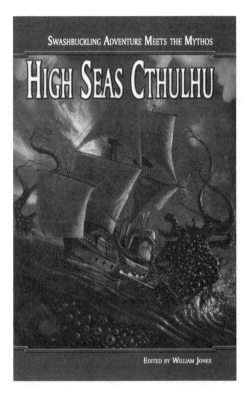